Through the Glass

by

Lisa J. Hobman

This is a fictional work. The names, characters, incidents, places, and locations are solely the concepts and products of the author's imagination or are used to create a fictitious story and should not be construed as real.

5 PRINCE PUBLISHING AND BOOKS, LLC

PO Box 16507
Denver, CO 80216
www.5PrinceBooks.com

ISBN 13:978-1-939217-51-6 ISBN 10: 1-939217-51-2
Through the Glass
Lisa J. Hobman
Copyright Lisa J. Hobman 2013
Published by 5 Prince Publishing

Front Cover Viola Estrella
Author Photo: Craig@craigphotographystudio.com

First Edition/First Printing August 2013Printed U.S.A.

5 PRINCE PUBLISHING AND BOOKS, LLC.

Dedication

For Mum, Dad, Rich & Grace
The stars in my sky
I love you more than words

Acknowledgements

Gosh, I honestly have so many people to thank right now that I'm sure to miss some...so please forgive me if I do...Here goes...

Thank you first of all to my husband and daughter for their continued support and encouragement. You are my world and I love you both to the moon and back. The fact that you allow me the time to stare at my laptop for hours on end with minimal complaint tells me that this means as much to you both as it does to me and that feels wonderful.

To Mum and Dad. Regardless of what has been going on around you, you have always been there for me when I've had my mini meltdowns. There aren't enough words to express how much you both mean to me. But know that I love you both a million bags of sugar. Yet again you have been encouraging and have helped me to believe in myself that little bit more.

To Claire. I am pretty sure I have driven you mad with talk of rankings and reviews but you have listened and enthused nonetheless and for this I am eternally grateful. Love you sis.

To my fab beta readers Ali, Claire, Liz and Claire – thank for once again giving me honest feedback and for being willing to let me thrust huge piles of paper in your face when you already have such busy lives. Your eagerness to read my manuscripts just bowls me over and I love you all for that.

To Ali. Thank you for continuing to shout at me and talk sense when I have my wobbles. You're my Scottish voice of wisdom and not only do I adore your accent I think *you* are pretty fab too ;-)

To Craig. I've known you since I was tiny and you travelled all the way up from *Yorkshire* to *Scotland* to take my photo. What a wonderful friend and talented photographer you are. Thank you from the bottom of the dog bowl ;-)

To all the 'Happy Hobman Dancers' the wonderful supporters on my Facebook page. You guys are the best encouragement an author could wish for. Many of you have been with me from the start and I think the world of you all! You guys are what make this whole thing so bloomin' exciting!

A huge shout out to I Heart Books, First Class Books, Totally Booked Blog, Globug & Hootie Need a Book, Island Lovelies Book Club, Booked on Romance and A Book Whores Obsession pages on Facebook. Along with many others. Your support has been immense! Thank you sooo much!

To Borderline Tattoo Collective. I took a crazy step to commemorate my first book and you helped me to do it. You are amazing artists and made my time with you so special. Thank you!

To all the bloggers who have allowed me to take over their precious space from time to time – thank you, thank you, thank you!

To the amazing authors I have met during this journey – Bernadette Marie, Kate Roth, Lila Munro, Carmen DeSousa, Christine Steendam, Denise Moncrief, Y H Forward, Jon Rance, Allan Bott, Jan Romes to name only a few and there are so many more – your advice and chats mean so much – thank you.

5 Prince Publishing – you took a chance on an unknown author and I continue to be a proud member of your team. Thanks to Linda for your support and advice – I'm looking forward to working with you in the future!

Last but certainly not least a special thank you to my editor and friend, best-selling author Bernadette Marie. It's been a rollercoaster and I know I've driven you crazy but you've stuck with me through my continuing neuroses and I'm so grateful that you put up with me. You are teaching me so much and I'm enjoying every bit of it.

Dear Reader

First of all I want to say a huge thank you to you! Seeing as you are reading this it means you have already purchased Through the Glass or that you are considering doing so. I can't tell you how much I appreciate that...okay I think maybe I just did.

Ahem...anyway, moving on... If you follow me on Facebook you will know that I'm a little bit bonkers and that I'm totally obsessed with writing. Through the Glass is my second novel and I have other projects in the pipeline so keep a look out!

I discovered this passion for writing almost by accident and I have to admit that I'm now completely consumed by it. I love creating characters that, I hope, are believable and that you, the reader, can relate to. My story lines are about ordinary people dealing with relationship issues that any one of us could have experienced.

I don't profess to try and change the world but I live in hope that my stories have a positive effect on people and leave them feeling a little warm and fuzzy at the end. You maybe won't get the ending you were anticipating every time but I aim to leave you happy and wanting to read more. I hope that this happens. If it does then this has all been worthwhile.

As you take this journey with Felicity and Jim I hope you are drawn into their lives as they try to discover which path to take and whether to take it together or separately. And once again I would like to say thank you for embarking upon this journey with them...and with me.

Best wishes

Lisa J Hobman

Through the Glass

Chapter 1

February 2009 - The Break-up

"So, that's it then, Flick?" Jim raised his arms in exasperation. "You're leaving? You've completely given up?" He was past trying to convince Flick that they could make a go of it, work things out, get through this and come out the other side stronger. The past few months had been one argument after another and Flick had spent less and less time at home.

"It's for the best, James. And please don't call me *Flick*." She sighed. "It's not my name. Not anymore. I *grew up*. It's good in the adult world you should visit sometime, you might like it." She snorted derisively.

Jim shook his head, sadness oozing from every pore. "Aye, well you'll always be *Flick* to me. And I'll always be Jim. What's with all this *Felicity and James* bollocks anyway?" His accent always became stronger when he was angry. This was one of those occasions when the true Scotsman came out fighting. His chest heaved as he tried to calm the storm raging beneath his skin.

He almost didn't recognise the woman standing before him in their bedroom, her fitted designer clothes complete with pearls and a shoulder length smooth sleek hairstyle. Such a contrast to the girl he fell in love with. Back then it was all flowing blonde waves and long, floating skirts. She was softer then, in every way.

"Well, as I said James, *Felicity* is my name… Flick was left behind at university. She was doe-eyed, foolish, and rash… Look, there's no point us going over old ground." She pulled the handle up on her wheeled suitcase. "I'll be staying with Polly and Matt for a while whilst I figure out my next move."

Matt had once been Jim's closest friend but that friendship had somehow fizzled as his relationship with Polly had intensified. That saddened Jim.

Felicity went on. "Nilsson-Perkins have offered to help find me a new place near the city centre so I can be closer to the main gallery." She wandered over to him and placed her hand on his arm. "It's for the best, James. I think you know that deep down."

He looked, pleadingly, into her eyes, his chest still rising and falling at a rapid rate. "For whom? For me? I don't think so." His voice cracked as he shook his head. He stared intently and for several moments she seemed caught in his eyes. He thought he saw her shield begin to melt but she shook her head and looked away.

Turning back to him she shrugged her shoulders. "It was inevitable when you think about it. We're from two different worlds... We want *completely* different things, James." Her voice softened as she squeezed his arm. Her blue eyes, that were once full of love were ice cold.

She wheeled her case toward the bedroom door and turned back to face him one last time. Her eyes were glassy with unshed tears now and Jim was relieved to see *some*, albeit small, expression of human emotion from the woman he had witnessed slowly becoming some kind of hard, Siberian robot.

"For what's it's worth...James...I *do* love you. You were my first love and so I probably always will. I just feel like..." She paused. Clenching her eyes closed as if to find the strength to carry on speaking, a tear escaped. "Like maybe we're not *good* for each other. We've grown apart. I'm ambitious and you...you want *babies* and the white picket fence thing... I'm just not ready... I'm not sure I ever will be. In a way I'm doing you a favour." A sob escaped her throat as she spoke. "This way at least you get to meet someone new and have children and do all the family things that I'm just not capable of." She sounded to Jim as though she was trying to convince herself.

Jim's lower lip began to tremble. "I don't want anyone else…it's you. It's always been you." He clenched his jaw. "What I don't get, *Felicity*, is that *you* wanted those things too. We were both on the same page. I don't understand how we changed."

"*We* didn't change. *I* did. Like I said, I *grew up*." She shook her head. "I know that *you* haven't changed." She snorted. "Sorry, Jim but it's true. In all these years you've kept the same hairstyle, the same clothing, and the same laid back attitude. You *still* work in the same second hand bookstore, you *still* drive that ancient Land Rover, and you *still* take that bloody dog everywhere you go! You're not a student anymore, James. Maybe I want more, huh? Maybe I want someone who makes an effort!" Her voice gained an octave as her emotions began to get the better of her.

Jim widened his eyes in horror. "Whoa! Now just hang on there, lassie!" He held up his hands and his stomach knotted at her stabbing words as they sliced his heart.

He stepped toward her. "You can't say that I don't make an effort. Just because I'm in no way materialistic doesn't mean I don't care. I *love* you. I always have. *You* are my world! I don't need *things*, Felicity. I need *you*!" His heart ached as it bombarded the inside of his chest. "I've done everything in my power to make you happy. I don't know what else I could have done. And for the record, I'm not the one who's given up here!" He raised his voice too, finally giving in to the pent up frustration he'd been harbouring.

"James, we want different things. Accept it. Move on...please!" She opened the door and he made a grab for her. She swung around and crashed into his arms. Without thinking he took her face in his hands and kissed her with all the passion he could muster. To his amazement she didn't slap him; she kissed him back. Dropping her suitcase she seemed overwhelmed by desire, anger, passion, lust, whatever the hell it was. She grabbed at his dark, shaggy hair as he ran his hands through hers, desperate to express his love for her, desperate to make her change her mind.

He moved from her mouth to her neck, his kisses urgent. Her head rolled backward and she moaned, grabbing at his T-shirt and pulling it over his head in one swift aggressive move. Before either could realise what they were doing or how they got there, they staggered backward and tumbled, wrapped around each other, onto the bed. Their lips locked as their tongues danced and probed each other's mouths.

~~~~~

Jim tugged at the hem of her skirt until it was up around her hips. She ground herself into him, needing to feel him. She gasped as he slid his hand up her inner thigh to her panties. Grabbing them, he dragged them down her legs and then returned his hand to massage her where she needed his contact the most. She whimpered and moved her hand down his toned torso, skin on skin, until it rubbed against the hardness, evident through his jeans. He reached for her breast and, releasing it from her bra, he took her erect nipple into his mouth, teasing with his tongue. She gasped again as pleasure and desire rocketed throughout her body, desperate for him.

Fumbling with one hand Felicity unfastened his jeans and slid her hand inside, releasing him. A low growl escaped from his throat. Felicity pulled at him and urged him on until he slid inside her, worshipping her breast with his mouth as he moved. Before wrapping her legs around him, she clawed at his buttocks willing him deeper. He rested his forehead on hers and looked deep into her eyes where tears had begun to escape and cascade, relentlessly, down her face, soaking through her hair.

"I love you, Flick. I love you so, so much…don't leave…please don't leave," Jim breathed. His eyes sparkling as the dampness in them threatened to spill over.

It didn't take long before their breathing became shallow and erratic; their movements faster, more and more urgent. Their eyes stayed locked. Suddenly they were climaxing together, sharing a delicious, overpowering orgasm that left them both spent and gasping for breath.

~~~~~

As his breathing calmed, Jim kissed her and smiled, stroking her face tenderly. He caught her tears with his thumb. "I knew you still loved me. I knew it couldn't be the end of us. I just *knew* it, Flick." He smiled lovingly, his lip trembling again with overwhelming emotions fighting for release.

He manoeuvred to lay by her side and held her to him. "We'll work this out. You and me, Flick. We can get through anything. It's always been you and me." He whispered as he stroked her cheek and kissed her again, deeply, passionately.

She pushed him away, releasing herself from his arms, touching her swollen lips where his had just been. She stood, adjusted her skirt and blouse, and looked down where he still lay.

"I'm so sorry, Jim… Nothing has changed. I'm still leaving." Her wavering voice broke as she whispered the stabbing words that he did not want to hear.

He pulled his brow into a frown and sat upright. "What? I…I don't understand." He rose to his feet adjusting his clothing. So many emotions battled and stirred inside of him. So many questions. He shook his head and asked again, his heart pounding so hard he thought it would burst from his chest. "What do you mean *nothing's changed*?" He pointed to the now crumpled bed. "We…we just made love. Flick…I…I don't understand. Why would you do that if nothing had changed? It has to have meant *something*?"

With regret visible on her face and a look of deep, deep sadness in her eyes, she touched his face, tears leaving trails down her own cheeks. "Oh James…it was just…such a beautiful way for us to end things…it was goodbye." Gently, she stroked his cheek and left.

Jim stood for a moment, stunned, trying to figure out what the hell had just happened. An uncomfortable silence fell over the house and he was momentarily paralysed as if time had stood still. Hurt and angry, he wondered how the hell she could be so damn cruel.

Eventually, after what felt like an age, he recovered the use of his legs and walked over to the window. He looked down to the street and observed her throwing her case into the back of the silly little convertible she was so very proud of. She was all designer suits, first class flights, champagne dinner meetings, and sports cars. Well, at least she fit in well with her new crowd, if not with him.

She looked up to the bedroom window and their eyes met. He saw her begin to raise her hand to wave but she stopped as if deciding the gesture was somewhat inappropriate, given the circumstances. She gave a sad half smile, climbed into the driver's seat and drove away.

Jasper silently came into the room, walked over and nuzzled Jim's hand. It was as if he knew his master's heart was breaking. Jim scratched the Labrador's head and crouched down so that his face was level with the affectionate animal. He sunk his head into Jasper's fur. It was then that he was overcome with emotion. It was then that he began to sob.

~~~~~

On Saturday and Sunday there were a few comings and goings from the house. Jim made the effort to be absent when Flick's friends came to collect more and more of her personal belongings. They didn't speak much to Jim when he *was* there. They hardly made eye contact. The actuality of Flick's belongings gradually dwindling saddened him. The more items she removed the less chance there was of reconciliation. Jim had gradually lost contact with his friends from university as they had gone off around the world to begin various careers and they had made new friends as a couple—Art world friends. These people didn't even have to choose sides. They were already on one.

Felicity's.

If Jim was honest, however, the fact didn't concern him too much. He had always found her friends a little too *arty farty* for his liking. He preferred straightforward and down to earth people.

Flick and her friends were always discussing topics he couldn't really care less about. They'd sit for hours making comparisons between the work of modern artists such as Tracy Emin and Damien Hirst and the more traditional but prolific artists such as Claude Monet, Gustave Courbet, and Salvador Dali. James often sat staring into space thinking that one day he would write a book about how pretentious some people could be. In his opinion, it was all an expression of the inner workings of someone's mind and was all subjective anyway, so what did it matter? If you liked it, you liked it, enough said. He was an intelligent man but he never volunteered any content to the lengthy and rather tiresome debates.

One particularly nice friend of Flick's from university did show concern for Jim. Polly Goodfellow. She had the name of a story character and was actually rather sweet. She was the only one who had ever made the effort to include Jim, even though he'd rather she hadn't. She was a short, flame haired woman with a very smiley face and a lovely demeanour. She had been upset when she'd heard of the couple's separation and had sent Jim a lovely card telling him that she still considered him a friend and that he could call on her any time. Of course he wouldn't and she probably knew that but the gesture was kind.

Monday morning, after the terrible, heart-breaking weekend, hadn't come around soon enough. Jim loved his job. He had worked at The Book Depository for what felt like an eternity. Before working there, it had been his favourite place to visit. He would sit in the tired old wing backed armchair with a dust covered, tattered old book and a cup of coffee from the machine. He had spent hours in there and had gotten to know the owner, Charles, quite well. When he had discovered Charles' surname was Oswald he had laughed out loud and complimented Charles on his choice of names for the shop. Charles had appreciated that Jim really *got* him.

Jim had looked after the shop on many occasions when Charles had nipped for lunch or to the bank, and so one day Charles simply decided to make it an official arrangement. The pay wasn't immense but it wasn't minimum wage either, so Jim couldn't complain and wouldn't have wanted to.

The tube ride to work was short and he was surrounded by the delightfully fusty smell of old books and coffee all day long. Two of his favourite things—coffee and old books.

When he arrived at work Charles was already there. He was a very well-spoken and dapper man in his early fifties. He always wore a colourful bow tie and a tweed jacket with elbow patches, much like an old English professor. It suited him and the shop down to the ground.

On seeing Jim today, Charles's face scrunched as if he had encountered something rather unpleasant. "Bloody hell, Jim, are you alright? You look bloody terrible, old chap." Charles used the word *bloody* in almost every sentence. At first it amused Jim, then it irritated him, and now, years on, he was completely immune to it.

"Not great, if I'm honest, Charles, no. Err… Flick left me on Friday." His lip began to quiver again as it had on so many occasions over the weekend, and so he bit down on it, slumping into the wingback chair and fighting for composure.

Charles gasped. "Oh, bloody hell, my dear chap, are you sure you should be here? I can manage today if you'd rather be at home."

"No, no, it's fine. I'm better off being busy I think. No point wallowing in self-pity all alone, eh?" Jim tried to snap himself out of the drop in mood.

Charles fidgeted as if wanting to make some kind of physical gesture but struggling to know quite what to do. "No…quite…quite. Well if you need anything…" He paused as he seemed to be calculating his next words. "And in my opinion, old chap, it's her bloody loss."

"Thanks, Charles, I appreciate it." Jim forced a smile. "I'd love a coffee if you're making one, eh? I'll go splash my face with some cold water and dump my bag in the back." He stood and headed for the rear of the shop.

"Certainly. Bloody good idea. I'll get onto it."

The day passed without real incidence and James was happy to be thumbing through the latest batch of antique finds that Charles had procured during his recent trip to a Parisian book fair. Amongst the finds had been a rare first edition of *Wuthering Heights* by Emily Bronte. He had enquired as to how much the book had cost, but Charles had winced and shook his head. *Obviously quite a lot then!* The book was one of a select few which were locked in a cabinet not to be touched by just *anyone*. One had to prove the funds were available to purchase such a rare and delicate piece prior to being granted permission to handle it, and even then white cotton gloves were insisted upon.

Jim arrived home to a message on his answering machine. He pressed play and immediately regretted it when he heard Felicity's voice.

"James, it's Felicity…listen… I've been talking to my friend Rory and…well…he's a lawyer, as you know… He says we can get a relatively smooth divorce… We can claim irreconcilable differences… That way we can both move on…you know, permanently… I know this is hard, James…it's hard for me too." She paused and Jim thought he heard her crying. *"Anyway, I'll leave that thought with you. Take care, James…. I hope you're okay."* Her voice broke and the line went dead.

It felt too sudden and was not the news he wanted. It cut him to his core and he felt physical pain at her words. *Divorce.* That was that then. It really was over. Jim leaned forward and rested his head in his hands, his elbows on his knees. *Divorce.*

~~~~~

Felicity, on the surface of it all was handling things remarkably well, *only* on the surface. She still couldn't help wondering how much of this was her own doing and how much was the influence of her mother. Penelope had never really liked James. She didn't *dislike* him per se. She just didn't like him for *her Felicity*. Felicity had potential. She had goals. She had ambition. Since university Felicity had shone in her field of Art History and everyone said that she would go far.

Jim knew that after graduation Penelope had hoped that this *silly fling* with him and Felicity would just fizzle out. Much to Penelope's chagrin, it grew and grew. Jim was a very intelligent man, an erudite scholar in fact, just like Felicity, but whereas he had been admitted to Oxford via a Scholarship, Felicity came from a long line of Oxford fellows, her father included. It was the expectation that she would simply follow in their footsteps.

On hearing the news of the break up, Penelope had insisted that Felicity come home to stay with her and her father. She wouldn't hear of her newly single daughter staying with friends. She needed to be around family. Penelope was *very* persistent.

"Good morning, darling." It was Monday morning after *the* weekend and Penelope was in rather high spirits. Felicity, on the other hand, was not.

"Good morning, Mum." Felicity yawned and stretched. Her eyes were red and puffy, her face drawn and pale.

"Are you feeling better, dear? I heard you crying quite late into the night." Penelope knew that her daughter was far from feeling better. She was broken hearted from the events of the weekend. Penelope had assured her that it was sure that this was for the best. After all, James just didn't fit in with her lifestyle. He hated her friends, knew nothing about art, apart from the knowledge she had imparted, and he had no ambition. None. Not a jot. He was just happy to write stories and read old dusty books. He had graduated with a First from Oxford. The world was his oyster, but it was almost as if he had done it all just to prove to himself that he could. After that he was done trying, done achieving.

He had always said that when they had children he would be more than happy to be a stay-home dad so that Flick could continue on in her career. Initially, she had thought it very supportive and sweet, but then the more she thought about it—and the more her mother went on about it—the more she decided that it was just laziness. Penelope had talked about nannies and the fact that they would *obviously* have one. What would be the point of him staying home? Just so he could watch TV or tippy tap on his wretched old typewriter?

"I'm not great, Mum, to be honest. I feel drained. Completely drained." She rested her chin on her hand as her mother poured her some fresh coffee.

"There's no wonder, darling. You should maybe call in sick today, dear. Catch up on rest?" her Mother suggested.

"No, I can't. We're meeting with the Tate this morning. It's a really big deal, Mum. They want me to go out to New York to see some potential pieces for the gallery. Nilsson-Perkins recommended me as the best dealer to go. If I call in sick, I'll look like a flake."

"Perhaps Rory will take you out tonight to cheer you up?" Penelope adored Felicity's lawyer friend, deeming him a much more suitable mate for her daughter. Felicity rolled her eyes and didn't answer. Her dad walked into the large kitchen where the two women were sitting, and Felicity was grateful that the discussion was over before it started.

"Good morning, Poppet." He kissed his daughter's head affectionately. "How are you bearing up?" He gave her a knowing look. She burst into tears. "Oh, Poppet, don't cry. You can always go back to him. You know he would take you back in a flash. Tell him you've made a terrible mistake." Her Father took her hand and stroked her hair.

"Oh, don't be so ridiculous, Edgar!" Penelope chimed in. "What on *earth* would she do a silly thing like that for?" She stood to leave the room. The two were clearly at loggerheads over the situation.

"Because she clearly still loves him, Penny, that's why!" His frustration with his wife's cold demeanour was evident. "Can't you see what you've done?" he continued. "You've put all these silly ideas in her head and she's started to believe you! She adores Jim." He squeezed his daughter's hand as she sobbed. She sat upright and pulled herself together.

"No, no, Daddy, Mummy is right. James is just not the right man for me. I need to get over him. I need to focus on work. In fact, I am going in today." Her father opened his mouth to protest but she held her hand up to stop him. "It's over two hours away and so I need to go get ready. I'll let them know I'll be late. I'm sure they'll understand given the circumstances." She sighed. "I think perhaps staying with Polly will be better for me too if I'm honest." She smiled sadly. "Not that I don't appreciate you having me home…it's just…not as far to travel…and I need to work." She looked to her father and then to her mother. Neither spoke. Their conflicting opinions on the matter momentarily silenced. She rubbed her hands over her face to rid herself of the tears, donned a fake smile, stood, and left the room. As she walked down the hallway she paused as she heard her father speaking.

"I hope you're satisfied with the mess you have caused, Penny. You've meddled once too often in their relationship. I honestly don't understand why you couldn't just let her be happy and be in love. I can't support you in this. Frankly, I think it's unforgiveable." Penelope gasped at her husband's harsh words and stormed out of the kitchen, leaving Edgar to sit in silent torment over his daughter's heartbreak.

Felicity felt awash with emotion. She hated the thought of her parents fighting over this and turned to walk back toward them. Hearing footsteps, however, she decided she couldn't face the confrontation and dashed toward the stairs.

Chapter 2

January 2010 – Eleven Months After the Break-up

"I just don't get it, Jim. It's breaking my heart to see this happening to the two of you." Edgar rubbed his forehead and shook his head. The decision his daughter had made to leave the love of her life eleven months ago still dumbfounded him.

Jim had managed to visit his old friend and father-in-law one last time prior to making his journey north. Edgar was saddened that this may be the last time in a long while.

"I know, Ed, but we've tried to work through it. Comes a point you can't try any more. You just have to admit defeat." Jim tried his best to smile but struggled under the weight of emotion in the air.

"She's a silly, *silly* girl. She'll regret this. I know her, Jim. She will. One day when you've moved on and met someone new, she will realise what she had." Edgar patted Jim's arm affectionately.

He looked down at his hands, unable to respond. How could he? What could he possibly say? After a long, thoughtful pause he spoke. "I didn't want any of this, Ed. I honestly don't know what I did wrong. I supported her. I was there for her. We were saving for a house, you know. I reckon we could have afforded one. I was willing to put all my inheritance into one. She just wouldn't commit. I really thought we both wanted the same things. I think we did at first."

"I know, son. I remember how excited she was when you got engaged. She lit up when she looked at you. I wish she could think for herself and not listen to…" Edgar's words trailed off as if he felt he had said too much.

"Listen to whom, Ed?"

"Oh, nothing. Don't take notice of me... I was looking forward to grand kiddies." Ed's lips quivered as he spoke. Jim squeezed his arm.

"Aye...I know...I know. We had a pregnancy scare once, a couple of years back."

"What do you mean?" Ed sat upright as this news.

Jim began to explain the events of July 2008. It was after Felicity had recovered from a throat infection. She had been taking antibiotics, which had affected her contraceptive pill...

~~~~~

July 2008 – Seven Months Before the Break-up

"So what does it say?" Jim was almost boiling over with excitement. Felicity remained taciturn as she stared at the little white stick, her hand shaking. After a while she blinked as if coming out of a trance.

"Erm...it has a cross... I think that means it's...positive." Her eyes welled up with what Jim presumed were happy tears. He grabbed her in a bear hug and showered her with kisses.

"Oh, Flick! We're going to be Mummy and Daddy!" He spun her around.

"Put me down!" she shouted at him. He immediately placed her back on her feet. He was a little surprised at her tone but put it down to the shock of the news. She'd come around.

She just stared at the stick in her hand.

"Flick, staring at it won't change it, sweetheart." His voice was tinged with sadness at her reaction.

"It can't be right...it can't be... I *can't* be pregnant, Jim. Not now. There's too much going on. We've not bought a house... My career is going well... You're still at The Book Depository, which pays next to nothing... We're not ready." She sat on the side of the bath, her eyes staring into space once again.

"How can you not be happy, Flick? We're married. I adore you. This wee bairn will get spoiled by its grandparents. I'll be the best dad—"

"Stop it, Jim. *Please*. I can't think straight. I can't do this. Not now!" She stormed out of the bathroom pushing past him and slammed the door to their bedroom.

~~~~~

Jim didn't sleep well and neither did Felicity. She went downstairs very early and after a while he heard her talking on the phone. He pulled on his shorts and walked down to the lounge where she sat, phone in hand.

"Yes, yes, I have a urine sample ready from this morning. Yes...okay...uhuh...okay...okay, see you at nine. Thank you...bye." She hung up.

Jim sat beside her, "What was all that about?" He rubbed her back gently.

"I've made an appointment at the doctors. I need to get this confirmed officially, Jim. Then I can decide what to do."

"Decide what to do? What do you mean *decide what to do*? We'd prepare to have a baby, surely there's no other decision involved?"

"Jim, this is *my* body. And *my* career. *I* have to make sure that *I* am ready for this." She was calm as she spoke. Her voice was low and quiet.

Jim tried to smile. "Hang on...there are a lot of *I's* in there... What about me? And what, exactly, are you saying? Are you saying that there's a chance you'll get rid of our baby?" He stood and ran his hand through his messed up, morning hair.

Felicity didn't look up. "I'm saying I'll have some decisions to make." She wrung her hands in her lap.

Jim began to pace the floor, "Oh…oh *you'll* have some decisions to make, eh? *YOU* not *US*?! Oh right…right…I get it. I get no say in this? *My* child, *our* child, and I get no say?" His voice became louder.

"Don't raise your voice at me, Jim. This is hard enough as it is."

"What's hard? We wanted kids. This is a no-fucking-brainer!" He flung his arms in the air in exasperation. What was she thinking?

"I will *not* speak to you whilst you are acting like this. I'm going to get ready." She stormed back upstairs into the bathroom and locked the door. He followed her and shouted through the barrier she had put between them. Again.

He leaned his head against the door. "Well, I'm coming too! I *need* to be a part of this, Flick. You can't shut me out!"

"Whatever, Jim," she mumbled.

~~~~~

The doctor's surgery was overflowing with people coughing and sneezing. Felicity sat silently staring at her hands. Jim watched as myriad emotions made their mark upon her face. *She should be excited. I just don't get this.* He was about to take her hand in his when the doctor called her through. Placing his hand at the small of her back, desperately needing contact, Jim accompanied Flick through into the room to see the doctor.

"Good morning, Felicity. What can I do for you today?" The female doctor beamed at them both but didn't address Jim.

"I took a pregnancy test yesterday which came out positive. I...I thought I ought to get checked properly to make sure."

"Oh yes, wise to do so. Did you bring an early morning urine sample?" The doctor's smile remained in situ.

Felicity handed over a small bag with a little container in it. The doctor opened a long, white plastic package, about the size of a biro and dipped the end in the sample.

"It doesn't take long. I'll give you a quick once over whilst we wait." The doctor proceeded to check Flick's blood pressure and pulse. "You seem fit and well, which is good news."

After a few more minutes of Jim scrunching his hands anxiously, feeling somewhat invisible, the doctor checked the test.

"I'm very sorry...the test is actually negative." The doctor's smile finally gone, Jim sat upright, confused.

Flick let out a huge puff of air as if she'd been holding her lungs full. "Right, well that's that then." Felicity's voice was back to its normal breezy self.

"Hang on...that can't be right? The one yesterday was positive," Jim barked

"I know, Mr Johnston-Hart. And it is very rare to get a false positive. More likely to get a false negative but in this instance it *is* a false positive. Your wife is not pregnant."

"It's MacDuff...Mr. MacDuff...and you said yourself false negatives are more frequent...so what if yours is wrong?" He was clinging onto the last shred of hope, although he had no clue why, considering Flick's reaction.

"I'm very sorry Mr. MacDuff, but you can always try again." She spoke in a very patronising tone which made Jim angry. He stood and stormed out of the surgery, not stopping until he reached the Land Rover.

~~~~~

Flick followed him, trotting along on her stilettos. She opened the car door and climbed in awkwardly, muttering under her breath how she hated this car.

"Don't you think you were a bit harsh on Dr. Jacobs in there?" she spat as he sat there, white knuckled, holding on to the steering wheel and staring straight ahead.

"No." He growled back through gritted teeth.

"Jim, it can't be helped. We have plenty of time. No need to get so stressed." Now *she* was patronising him, making him bristle.

After a long silent interlude, Jim found the words he wanted to say, however hurtful. "The fact that it was negative after I got my hopes up was painful...but what's even more painful is that you thought the prospect of carrying *my* baby so abhorrent that you would have had *decisions* to make." His eyes stung and he bit the inside of his lip, determined not to let her see him cry over this.

"Jim, it just isn't the right time. My career is going so well—"

"Your fucking career? Is that what's more important to you than us creating a new life?" His eyes were ablaze with hurt and anger as he turned to face her.

"Please don't swear at me, Jim. Clearly you're more ready for this type of thing than I am." She snorted out a half laugh, fuelling Jim's pain.

"*More ready for this type of thing?*" he repeated, his voice cracking as an angry tear escaped, much to his chagrin.

Flick softened. "Oh, Jim… I don't know what to say. I love you so much, but I'm not ready to be a mother yet. And yes…I was relieved to find the test was negative… I'm so sorry. Please don't be upset with me." She leaned over to him and kissed him, wiping away the errant tear with her thumb. He breathed in sharply.

"Well, at least I know where we stand on the issue now." He didn't look her in the eyes.

"We have plenty of time, sweetheart. You need to find a better job and we need to save up for a house. It's just not the right time." She squeezed his thigh.

"Maybe not. But it scares me to think about what you would've done if the test had been positive, Flick." He swallowed hard. Flick turned to face front. She didn't make any attempts to answer, which in effect gave him the answer he was afraid of hearing from her. He started the car and they drove home in silence…

~~~~~

January 2010 – Eleven Months After the Break-up

Edgar shook his head in frustration over what he had just heard. He was clearly as confused as Jim over Felicity's reaction to a possible pregnancy.

"I had no idea about any of that. She kept it very quiet," he whispered croakily. "You will make a wonderful father one day, Jim. I'm just so sad that it won't be *my* grandkiddies you're fathering." The emotional old man squeezed Jim's arm. He couldn't bear to see Edgar cry over this ridiculous situation.

"I'd better be off, anyway. I have a long drive and I really should get on." Jim paused and then threw his arms around his father-in-law—soon to be ex. Edgar reciprocated the strong embrace and patted Jim's back.

"Keep in touch, eh? Maybe not straight away, I know you'll be busy getting set up. But drop us a line every so often and let us know how you're getting on, eh? You're still family as far as I'm concerned." Edgar fought the tears that were threatening as he placed a firm hand on his son-in-law's shoulder.

Jim headed for his Land Rover and opened the door. He called to his black Labrador, who also seemed reluctant to tear himself away. "C'mon Jasper! C'mon boy!" The dog somewhat hesitantly jumped into the vehicle and James slammed the door. He looked back to Edgar who was now wiping tears from his haggard face with the back of his hand. In his chest, Jim's heart squeezed as he watched the old man he had known for many years and had been very fond of trying to deal with the fact that his daughter's marriage had collapsed and he'd been helpless to stop it.

"You know, Ed, I just want her to be happy. I hoped that I could be the one to do that for her, but perhaps she's just from a higher plane than me?" He smiled, doing his best to make it easier for the old man.

"Gah! Pish tosh!" Edgar was having none of it. "She is so hell bent on succeeding in that damned career of hers she can't seem to realise that she could have had both!" The man was clearly angry about his daughter's most recent life choices.

"You take care, Ed. I'll write when I get sorted. I'll send some photos. Perhaps you could come and visit?" He knew there was little chance of Edgar making the journey hundreds of miles from his country pile in East Boldre, Hampshire, to the Scottish Highlands, but he at least wanted to make the gesture.

"Yes, yes, dear boy. That would be marvellous." Edgar nodded but Jim was unclear as to which part he was agreeing to and didn't want to ask.

"Say goodbye to Penny for me. I'm sorry I missed her." He wasn't sorry in the slightest. His mother-in-law—soon to be ex—thankfully—was not his biggest fan and he wasn't allowed to call her Penny. She preferred Penelope and made a point of saying so whenever Jim tried to be a little more familiar. He had no doubt where *Felicity* got it from.

"I will, Son. I will. You drive carefully. Make sure you have plenty of breaks. And don't drive if you feel tired!" *Bless him. Such concern. A kindred spirit. Unlike Penelope.* Jim had simply never been good enough, rich enough, or posh enough for her liking. "And get writing, Son. You've plenty of books in you just waiting to spring forth. Make this fresh start the new beginning of your new career as an author." Jim had always loved that they had writing in common. Edgar had always told Jim that he believed Jim was a potential best-selling author and that Jim just needed the right setting and the right encouragement. He now hoped that Scotland would give him that.

Jim climbed into the driver's seat and gave a final wave before setting off down the long driveway. When he was nearing the gates, he saw a little convertible coming toward him. He slowed when he realised it had pulled over. He, too, then stopped. The driver of the car climbed out, long lean legs first, followed by slender body and pretty face complete with stern, serious expression. Felicity made her way to the driver's side of Jim's car.

"I didn't expect to see you here… You're going then?" Jim took the question as rhetorical. He mused at how, in that moment, she looked harder and more severe than he had ever imagined possible. Her blonde, blunt cut hair resting at chin level, unlike when they had first met. Her designer sunglasses were perched atop her head and she squinted in the sunlight of the cold winter morning. She had an air of superiority about her now that belied her true self. They both knew it.

"Aye, I'm all packed up and ready for the off." He forced a smile but did not let it reach his eyes.

"The Decree Nisi papers came this morning," she stated matter-of-factly. "That's it now…things are finally done," she said breezily. Jim shook his head, the curve of his mouth taking a downturn.

"Aye well, I guess mine will be forwarded with the rest of my mail." He felt sadly resigned now. After a pause, he looked back at her and said, "Flick, we've been apart for ages now, and yet you *still* manage to make it sound like you're escaping some horrible, despicable fiend of a man."

She seemed to squirm under his gaze. "It's *Felicity*, James. I don't think you're despicable at all." She snorted. "You and I both know that we didn't work. It's over. We can happily get on with our respective lives, just the way we want now." She pulled invisible lint from the sleeves of her smart winter jacket, avoiding eye contact. Jim realised he was flogging the proverbial dead horse yet again.

"Aye, well it's *Jim*, thank you, *Felicity*. And there are those of us who disagree with your opinions on our marriage. I, contrary to what you may think and feel, will remember our time together with fondness and will sign those papers with a stab of regret and sadness in my heart." He put the car into gear and drove away without giving her the opportunity to have the last word.

"How did we end up here, eh, Jasper? I really wish I knew." Jim leaned over and scratched the top of the dog's head as he began his journey northwards, the sound of

Beautiful Day by Three Colours Red resonating around his beloved car.

Chapter 3

January 2010 - Eleven Months After the Break Up

Although he was raised in Scotland, Jim was by no means heading home. Dumbarton, place of his upbringing, held no pull for him now with his parents gone. They had put every penny they could aside for their sons. The brothers discovered after their parents' deaths that this was the reason for their frugal existence. The modest town house they inherited on top of the savings had meant that Jim could buy himself a place, albeit small and a little run down. Although the money had always been intended to set him up in a home with Felicity, he'd sat on the money for years not daring to dip into it lest it be swallowed up on minor frivolities. But *that* home—*their* home—clearly was never meant to be.

The choice of his new location, Shieldaig in the West Highlands, was more of an escape. He had visited as a child with his family when they were on holiday, but he didn't remember too much about it. His memories were all in the family photos he'd kept. He just knew that it was a peaceful, almost undiscovered place, certainly more his pace of life than London. Because he had no memories of Flick here, he knew he could start afresh.

Wipe the slate clean.

There would be nothing around each corner to remind him of what a mess he had made of things. He could reinvent himself if he so wished. Not that he would do that. He wasn't pretentious. That had kind of been the problem really. He couldn't pretend to be anyone but himself and this hadn't been good enough. He'd come to realise, in recent years, that Flick was out of his league. But he also knew that he wasn't a bad person. Other than a failed marriage he had nothing to be ashamed of. He had loved his wife more than life itself. He'd tried so damned hard to fit in with her life and all its glamour. But he simply wasn't that good an actor.

His brother, Euan, had escaped too. He had emigrated to Australia to be with the woman of his dreams whom he had met two years ago whilst travelling through Europe.

Jim was slightly envious of Euan's relationship with Tara. She was very easy going and fun to be around. Every bit the beach babe, she had a petite frame, sun bleached curly hair, and eyes as green as the brightest emeralds. Euan had always been into sports and had excelled in football at school. He had been travelling around Europe with some of his football team mates when he was introduced to Tara in a bar in Germany by one of his friends.

Euan was due a visit to the UK. He had promised Jim, during their phone call a few days ago that he would be back at some point this year and would be bringing Tara back with him.

"It'll be great to see you, bro! I can't wait! I'm looking forward to seeing where you end up living now that you're rid of Cruella De Ville!" Euan chuckled. He had actually always seemed to like Felicity but in recent years that clearly had changed.

"Euan, please don't call her that," Jim said flatly.

"Hey, why the fuck are you defending her? After what she did to you, I think you could be forgiven for calling her a lot fucking worse!"

"Aye…well, it won't change anything, so what's the point?" Jim's voice was a low resigned rumble.

"Look, bro, I'm a fair distance away, I know that, but I'm only at the end of the phone, okay? You call me if you need to talk."

"Aye, I know. Thanks… Love you, bro."

"Aye and I love you too, you ugly fucker!" Euan chuckled and hung up.

~~~~~

Jasper slept as Jim drove through the towns and cities of middle England and on up through the industrial landscape in the north of the country. He breathed a sigh of relief when he finally drove across the border into Scotland. It was early evening and the Borders were aglow with the low winter sun. The snow-capped Cheviot Hills dazzled on the horizon as the sun glinted on the bright, glistening canvas, spread over them like a crisp white blanket. It was a truly stunning sight.

Thankfully the weather had been rather kind and the snow had not yet arrived in earnest. Jim was sure that this would most likely change once he had arrived at his new home. This was the worst time of year for getting snowed in after all.

As night fell the journey was drawing to its conclusion. There had been several stops for Jim to stretch his legs and for Jasper to do his necessary doggy business. Service station coffee had most definitely improved, Jim had mused, as he had drank his third of the journey. At least these days the well-known coffee chains had lodged themselves nicely in there, meaning that at least what he drank actually *tasted* like coffee.

The moonlit Highlands in winter—what a sight to behold. The rugged, stony outcrops sparkled with a light dusting of snow, like icing sugar on a slice of rocky road cake. The temperature had dropped and the sun had given way to the bright white full moon. Myriad stars were visible like diamonds strewn across black velvet. It really was beautiful. He could clearly make out *The Big Dipper* and

Orion as he drove. He had to keep reminding himself to look ahead at the road so he could drive straight; the sky was such a glorious distraction. The road, however, was empty apart from Jim's Land Rover and the odd motorbike or car. Other road users were certainly few and far between, giving Jim's surroundings a particularly eerie atmosphere.

Jim was beginning to feel exhausted. He was thankful that tonight would not be his official moving in. He had managed to get a removal firm that would hold his furniture overnight, meaning he could at least get a decent night's sleep at a bed and breakfast prior to the gruelling day to come. He had located a *dog friendly* bed and breakfast where Jasper was allowed to sleep on the floor beside his bed. This was a relief as he didn't fancy having to make his best friend sleep in the car on a clear night like tonight when there was certain to be a frost.

It was late when Jim arrived in the Highlands. He checked into the bed and breakfast on the outskirts of Dingwall and snuggled up for the night, exhausted after his long, lonely drive. Sleep came quickly, but Jim was plagued by dreams of his ex and their failed marriage. The fitful night's sleep ended at six o'clock when he gave up the fight and climbed into the shower.

~~~~~

After a rather delicious and much needed full Scottish breakfast of succulent sausage, salty bacon, haggis, fried egg with a runny yolk, just how he liked it, and a tattie scone, he made his way to collect the keys for his new place. The estate agent congratulated him on his new purchase and handed over a small bunch of keys. He made a comment that stuck in Jim's mind.

"So, Mr. MacDuff, it's the end of one chapter and the beginning of a whole new book, eh?"

Jim had smiled and nodded. He was right. This *was* a fresh start, albeit thrust upon him in many ways. He had to grasp the opportunity with both hands, otherwise he would fail at this too, and he couldn't let that happen. And talking of books...well...maybe he would give that a go too.

Jim pulled up the Land Rover outside the little whitewashed cottage on Main Street facing Loch Shieldaig. The double fronted building was very pretty, if a little on the small side. It had everything he needed—two bedrooms, in case Charles or his brother came to visit, a dining kitchen, a cosy lounge, and outside stood a small adjacent building that he would convert to a little coffee hut so that he could make a little money when tourists came by. The small campsite behind the house was something he hadn't bargained for, but at least he would be kept busy.

His furniture would be arriving a little later so Jim had the opportunity to check that the place was clean. He carried a box of cleaning products into the little house, Jasper following close behind sniffing at everything in a bid to familiarise himself with his new surroundings. The house smelled of damp due to the fact that it had been standing empty for quite a while. It had been several months since he had first seen and offered on it. It was a low offer but luckily for him the owners had been desperate to sell.

The lounge had a lovely open fire, which would get plenty of use. It quickly became apparent that the owners had cleaned everything prior to Jim moving in. That saved him a major job, however he decided to clean the kitchen himself, and besides, it would keep him busy until the removals firm came to reunite him with his belongings.

The day whizzed by and was a blur of comings and goings. Piles of boxes appeared in every room and Jim set about opening each clearly labelled box and setting his personal effects in their new and rightful place. By six in the evening the place was beginning to resemble a home. Jasper lay out on the rug in front of the roaring fire that Jim had made a priority. Most of the boxes were now broken down and had been placed outside the back door. He had resolved to burn them the following day, wind permitting.

Whilst putting his clothes away in the built-in cupboard in his low ceilinged bedroom, Jim came across a box of photographs. He was already feeling melancholy and so figured it wouldn't hurt to look through them. He sat on his bed and took out a packet. Jasper appeared and lay at his feet as Jim travelled back in time to the fancy dress party they had attended a few years earlier at Polly and Matty's house.

They had gone as Sid and Nancy. Both had worn wigs and Felicity had worn far more makeup than usual. She looked totally different, but then again, so did he. Jim had pulled off the sneer perfectly and had scared a couple of elderly ladies as they walked down the Kings Road. Felicity had nearly peed herself laughing as the two old ladies scarpered as quickly as their stockinged legs and shopping trolleys would carry them. They had almost fallen into a heap through the door when they arrived at the party and Felicity had made a mad dash for the loo.

The next packet contained photos of a holiday to Majorca. Felicity looked amazing in her bikini and Jim had struggled to keep his hands off her. Instead of lazing by the pool or lounging at the beach they had spent a large chunk of the holiday inside making love. It had been one of the best holidays of Jim's life. He reminisced about making love in the sea for the first time on that holiday...

~~~~~

Majorca 2006 – Three Years Before the Break-up

"Are you coming in? The sea's quite warm once you get used to it!" Jim shouted to his gorgeous girl as she lay in her white bikini on a sun lounger reading a book. She removed her sunglasses and placed her book on the sand. Slowly and sexily she stood and slinked toward the water's edge. He was transfixed. The inward, sweeping curve of her waist got him every time, and when she walked and her hips swayed he almost lost control. The teeny, tiny bikini top only just covered her rosy, protruding nipples. Her breasts looked superb.

He felt the familiar sudden rush of blood south of his waistline and a grin spread across his face. "God you look good enough to eat." He growled as she made her way toward him.

"It could be arranged," she replied suggestively.

Jim threw his head back and groaned. "Oh, you'll be the death of me." He smiled.

"Hmmm, I can think of worse ways to die," she said as she slipped into the water. Her breath appeared to catch at the sudden chill and she made her way over to Jim. She slid her arms around his neck and took his mouth with a deep, passionate kiss.

He pulled away. "I want you…right here…right now," he whispered as he looked at her through his half-closed eyes.

"Well, you know what to do." She nibbled his earlobe. Jim looked to the shore. It was almost four o'clock and most people were either engrossed in novels or were packing up to leave the beach for the day. Jim swam out a little farther, pulling Flick along with him to a rock, which was protruding from the sea. Feeling safe that they were far enough out for no one to be aware of what they were doing, and feeling rather impressed at Flick's newfound confidence and daredevil nature, he slid his hands down her body until he found the strings holding her bikini briefs in place. The strings untied easily. Flick lowered his swim shorts just low enough for...

"Wrap your legs around me," he instructed in a low voice filled with heat. She immediately did as he said. Clinging onto the bikini briefs, which he held at her back, he slid into her. She gasped as she welcomed him in.

She nuzzled and nibbled his neck. The water held them in perfect balance as he moved himself back and forth, creating a delicious rhythm until their breathing became ragged. They grasped onto each other tightly.

"Ahhh, Flick, you feel amazing." Jim moaned as he stared intently into her eyes, his jaw clenched.

"Unh...Jim, I love you so much... I can't get enough of this feeling." Flick sounded breathy as she began to clench around him. Her head rolled back as she ascended into ecstasy. In a split second he joined her with a throaty growl, taking her mouth ruggedly with his own, claiming her once again.

~~~~~

January 2010 – Eleven Months After the Break-up

Back to his present day reality, where a stinging sensation behind his eyes broke Jim's reverie. "Oh Jasper...this is doing me no good at all, boy." He took the dogs face in both hands and looked into his chocolate brown eyes. Jasper licked his nose in response. Jim rubbed his face roughly. "C'mon lad, let's go for a wee walk, eh?" Jasper's ears pricked up at the mention of his favourite word and the pair made their way to the front door.

The view was beautiful. It was definitely something he would not tire of quickly. The two friends, man and canine, walked together taking in their new surroundings. The majestic, rocky mountain backdrop was the stuff of Sci-Fi movies yet the place was definitely grounded. The little piece of garden across the road that belonged to his cottage was in great need of a tidy up. There was a shingle beach beyond it that led to the loch's edge. As they walked Jim took in the vista of the small tree covered, uninhabited island just off the coast.

The cottages lining the loch were all built in a similar way, single or one and a half stories low and hunkered down against potentially inclement weather threats. All had whitewashed exteriors, but each one had its owner's little personal touch, from wind chimes hanging by the door to the colour of the window frames. It had the feel of a seaside fishing village. The sky was a bright cornflower blue but there was a distinct January chill to the air. He found the pub and a little shop with an exterior that had seen better days. Jim called in and picked up some bread, milk, biscuits, and a bottle of red wine. The shopkeeper was an elderly gentleman who introduced himself as Malcolm McLeary after Jim said he was the one who had bought Sunrise Cottage.

"Have you a wife and family with you, Jim?" the old man had asked.

"Sadly no, Malcolm. Maybe one day though, eh?"

"Aye, wonderful place to bring up wee bairns, Jim, this place."

After chatting briefly to the old guy, Jim and Jasper made their way back to the cosy cottage to warm up their extremities. The frost-filled air had a mean bite to it and both males were feeling the effects. As they sat on the rug together staring into the flames, Jim absentmindedly stroked Jasper's smooth, glossy coat and sighed. Jasper wagged his tail.

"I really wish I could go back in time, Jasper. I would do things differently. I don't know *what* exactly, but I'm sure I'd figure it out. Then you and I wouldn't be sitting here without her, boy." Jasper's tail beat out a rhythm on Jim's leg, as if he understood every word. He licked Jim's hand as if by way of reassurance. "Aye, lad…if only time machines had been invented, eh?" He turned back to the dancing, crackling flames and reminisced about 1998, the year that changed his life. The fateful year he had met his true love, his soul mate. His Felicity.

Chapter 4

"Earth to Jim! Come in Jim! *Jim!* What on earth are you staring at?" Matthew Clinton-Jones poked his relatively new friend's arm. Jim was no longer partaking of the debate that the rest of the Fresher's were locked in.

"Sorry, what's that?" Jim didn't take his eyes off the subject of his focus.

"We've been discussing the merits of classical literature versus contemporary and all you've been doing for the last ten minutes is staring into space... Wait a minute...you're staring at that blonde girl, aren't you?!" Matthew followed James's line of sight. "She is rather gorgeous, Jim. I have to say!"

Matthew was from a very well to do family who were mainly practicing G.P.'s or surgeons, but Matthew had plumped for reading English Literature with a view to becoming an English professor. His floppy dark hair and round rimmed spectacles made him look the part, even before his time. His accent was an acquired taste, but Jim was slowly realising that you shouldn't judge a book by its accent...or something like that.

Jim didn't take his eyes off the blonde girl as he nodded. "Aye, you're not wrong. She looks a bit lost. Think I'll go over and see if she needs any assistance." He rose, and without looking back to his stunned friends, wandered across the dining hall and over to where the pretty but terrified-looking girl was crouched, shuffling a stack of papers. She looked up and blushed beetroot red as he approached. "Hi, are you okay there?" At that moment the papers that the girl was fiddling with did a somersault into the air and landed scattered like oversized snowflakes all around her.

"Oh, for goodness sake!" she exclaimed, dropping her head into her hands and looking even more flustered. Jim immediately kneeled to help her pick them up.

"I'm Jim," he informed her as they gathered up the errant items. "And you are…"

"I'm…I'm Felicity… My friends call me…erm… Felicity…not that anyone has even bothered to *make* friends with me in this hell hole!" she snapped as her bottom lip began to tremble.

Jim smiled. "It's early days yet Felicity. Fresher's week. We're only in week one of term you know." He patted her arm trying to reassure her and her face coloured again. He laughed. "Keep blushing like that and your legs will go dead through lack of blood supply."

~~~~~

She relaxed and looked up at the man who had come to her aide. Realising how melodramatic she was being she sighed. "Sorry, I just feel a bit like a fish out of water." She smiled. She sat back for a moment whilst he worked to gather the last few sheets. He was a nicely-built young man. His hair was shaggy, dark brown, with a natural looking wave but not in an untidy way, and it fell almost to his shoulders. *Mummy wouldn't approve at all.* She smiled as the errant thought crossed her mind. And he wore jeans and a scruffy looking T-shirt with *Pearl Jam* emblazoned on its front and an image of a group of men. The middle one bore a striking resemblance to Jim. His arms were quite muscular and he looked like he hadn't shaved in a while.

Not what one would normally expect from an Oxford scholar.

"Hey, don't worry about it. It *will* get easier." He seemed to be trying his best to reassure her again. "Look there's a party tonight for the Fresher's in the refectory. Should be some good craic, why don't you come with us?" He gestured toward his friends. A feeling of dread washed over her at his words, and she wondered what kind of place she'd come to. She stood and backed away slightly, wobbling from the head rush of standing too quickly.

"Oh, n-no thanks. I don't do crack…or any drug for that matter. I…should go…thanks for the offer." She felt the colour drain from her face as she reached out for her papers.

Jim burst out laughing. "No! Not *crack*! Craic! It a Scottish-ism…it means it'll be a wee laugh…lots of fun? A good night?" She had completely misunderstood his Gaelic turn of phrase.

~~~~~

Felicity's pallid features gradually increased in colour again as relief clearly swept through her and embarrassment took over. "Oh gosh I'm so sorry." She looked horrified at her mistake. "I didn't mean to insinuate…I didn't mean…"

"Hey, don't sweat it. It's fine. Look, I'm in room twenty in the old quad, overlooking the meadow. If you fancy going with me, you know, so you don't have to enter alone, just give me a knock around six thirty, okay?" He scribbled the details down on a scrap of her paper and handed it back to her. She smiled looking relieved that he hadn't taken offence at her misunderstanding and naiveté.

"That's really sweet, thank you. Thank you…Jim." She smiled nervously as he turned to head back to his friends who were once again engrossed in their debate, arms flailing and voices raised.

~~~~~

Felicity went back to her little room and sat on her bed, trying to decide what to do. She stood at her easel—one of the first things she had made space for—looking at her latest sketched-out canvas intently as if the answers would just jump out of it. It was no use; she just didn't know what to do. She was inexperienced with the opposite sex as it was and really didn't know what made them tick. If she called on this Jim fellow would she look desperate? Needy? On the other hand, he had invited her so would it be rude *not* to show up? She grabbed her wash bag and decided a shower would clear her mind. She was relieved that Daddy's connections had helped land her an en-suite room. The advantages of being the daughter of a former Oxford fellow were several-fold it seemed. It would have been horrid to have to share with total strangers. It was bad enough to be sharing cooking facilities, let alone showers.

She blow-dried her hair shaggily and pulled on a pair of jeans and a baggy sweater that fell off one shoulder. She made sure to put a vest top on underneath so as not to be too provocative. She smeared a little gloss on her lips and wrapped her Oxford scarf loosely around her neck. That was it, she was ready. Taking a huge breath and mustering up as much courage as she could, she made her way down the stairs and over to Jim's block. She located his room, checked her watch. It read six twenty-five. She knocked lightly almost hoping he didn't answer so that the decision would have been made for her. He opened the door. *Dammit!*

~~~~~

A wide grin spread across Jim's face at the sight before him. He had expected her to be late, in true female fashion, or to simply not turn up at all. His respect for her grew as she stood before him looking simply gorgeous. "Oh hi. Felicity, right?" She nodded. He smiled at how anxious she appeared. "Want to come in for a quick drink before we go? I think we'll be too early if we go now." He stood aside to let her in. She looked so nervous as she stepped into his tiny room. He handed her a bottle of Budweiser and removed the cap for her. "Sorry, I've no champers." He laughed, trying to make her feel at ease.

"Oh, that's fine. I quite like Bud." He watched as she picked at the label. An awkward silence descended and the two of them looked around his room as if grasping for conversational topics upon the blank walls.

He saw her eyeing his guitar. "Do you play at all?"

"Sadly, no. I wish I did, but I spent so much time painting at home that I never really made time to learn."

"So…you paint? *What* do you paint?" His interest in this pretty, gorgeous girl was just growing and growing.

"Whatever takes my fancy really… I like to observe scenes on train journeys, car journeys, and so on… Then I sketch what I remember seeing through the glass onto canvas…then I paint."

"So are you working on anything right now? I'd like to see sometime."

Felicity blushed and fiddled with her bottle. "I'm not that good. I don't tend to show people…apart from my parents."

"Ahem, isn't art supposed to be subjective? And shared? Shouldn't the viewer be the one who decides whether it's good or not?" he teased.

"Well...I... I suppose but—"

"So, what are you working on right now?" He was determined to knock down her defences. She was so painfully shy.

The red in her cheeks grew stronger. He felt a surge of guilt as she sat avoiding his eyes. Eventually she spoke. "Oh ...it's just a scene that I saw through the car window on the way up from Hampshire...just fields and trees with some ponies. Nothing special..."

"Aye well, I think you should let me have a look. I bet you're selling yourself short." He hoped he had encouraged her. She sat silently picking at the label on her bottle. *Idiot, now you've scared her off.*

They sat for a while and Jim felt awkward. He coughed and tapped his fingers on his bottle. "Aye...aye...well....err...ooh, hey, look we should give you a nickname!" He was full of bright ideas. This wasn't one of them. "Aye, I reckon Felicity is too...proper...you know? Too...serious." He pulled a scowl at her to mimic his meaning.

Felicity's nose scrunched and she seemed to ponder his words. "Do you think so? My mum used to hate nicknames, so I've always just been plain old *Felicity*. I hate it. It's very formal...I think you're right. I...quite like the idea of being a little rebellious."

Jim saw a glint in her eye. "Aye? Well then...let me think...ooh I've got it!" A flash of inspiration came from goodness knows where. "*Flick*! We'll introduce you to everyone as *Flick*! They'll all think you're cool and interesting and not at all posh!" He cringed as he wondered if he had overstepped the mark.

A grin spread across her face and she nodded. "Flick?...Hmmm...I quite like that." She stood up and held out her hand to Jim. "Hiya, I'm Flick...Flick Johnston-

Hart…pleased to meet ya." She made a mock introduction, in a bad cockney accent as Jim stood there grinning.

He shook her hand and blurted out, "Watcha, Flick, I'm Jim." He also failed miserably to mimic the accent, resulting in a cross between Geordie and Welsh. *Epic fail.*

Flick burst into fits of laughter. "Good grief, Jim! You're worse at that accent than I am and I usually talk like I have plums in my gob!" She was beginning to relax. It felt good. Flick was a sweet girl and insanely cute.

When they had calmed down, Jim stepped closer. "I like you in that scarf." He flicked the knitted standard issue Oxford garment up in the air playfully. Secretly he was thinking that he would quite like to see her in the scarf and nothing else. She giggled and wrapped it around her neck with a flourish.

They headed out for the party at around seven thirty, laughing as they walked. They had covered just about every subject known to man in the short time they'd been chatting. Jim had learned all about Felicity's dad, well know biographer Edgar Johnston Hart, and her middle class upbringing, whilst Flick had discovered that Jim came from Dumbarton and thanks to his many educational merits had received a scholarship to attend Oxford. Felicity was bright-eyed and enthusiastic when she spoke of her dad. He sounded like an amazing man. Her mother on the other had sounded rather like the Ice Queen from the Chronicles of Narnia.

Jim held the door open for Flick and she hesitantly walked under his arm, chewing on her lip, and into the busy refectory. The room was large with arched windows that reached almost to the beamed ceiling. The woodwork and flooring was a rich mahogany and it was evident that the room hadn't changed much over the years. There were tables and chairs arranged around the edge of the room and a band was set up at one end on the stage.

~~~~~

A delicious aroma, which smelled remarkably like lasagne wafted through the air. Flick's stomach growled. Jim waved to his friends and walked her over to introduce her to them. Matthew, Charlie, Clara, Stubbs. Jim later informed her that no one knew why he was called Stubbs because his name was actually Levi DeWinter, which made her giggle. Polly, Melodie, and Stefan. All made Felicity feel very much at ease, all came from similar backgrounds to hers. They had much in common. Unlike Jim who hadn't quite noticed he was, in some ways, an outsider.

After the introductions, Flick, as she had now become known, felt a lot more at ease and thought she could maybe fit in after all. The band began to play and included a lot of covers that Felicity knew. Jim was clearly into his music and sang along to almost every song. They jigged about chatting loudly over the noise.

She watched him as he moved in time with the music. He looked good, graceful even, for a ruggedly handsome, unsuspecting, tall, longhaired man. The band began to play a slow melodic number, announcing it to be a cover of Pearl Jam's *Black*. She had never heard it before but the fact that it sent shivers down her spine told her she definitely liked it. The words were heart-breaking but beautiful. She vowed to listen to more by the band, especially seeing as Jim obviously liked them.

She smiled as he closed his eyes and swayed, the coloured lights from the stage highlighting his almost shoulder length, dark brown hair, turning it from red to blue to green. His face was incredibly handsome and she noticed the shivers traverse her spine once again, though this time it had nothing to do with the music. His forearms were very sexy and her eyes followed the line of his tendons as they transitioned into the muscular biceps under his T-shirt sleeves. His shirt this time had the words *Soundgarden* and *Louder Than Love* on the front, and she presumed that one of these must be the name of another band she was yet to hear. Her eyes trailed down his back and rested on his tight bottom… Felicity shook her head to dislodge the thoughts.

"You okay?" Jim lowered his head so that he spoke directly in her ear, causing her to shudder. "You looked a bit like you've seen a ghost." She snapped her eyes up to his and nodded fervently.

~~~~~

He smirked. He had actually caught her looking at him. He liked the fact that she'd been watching him and looking him up and down. He found her very, *very* attractive. Her long, wavy, blonde hair was just stunning. Her exposed shoulder and neck just begged for attention, but he wouldn't be so bold. She had the curves of a goddess, too. In no way skinny, just as he liked. He wondered what it would feel like to have that luscious hair trailing over his face as she sat astride his torso…*naked*. He gulped his drink down hoping to quench the fire that had begun to blaze inside him.

The band was taking a break and No Doubt's *Don't Speak* came over the PA system. He glanced over at Flick again, plucking up the courage he needed to ask the question on the tip of his tongue. "Oh sod it," he muttered. "Flick…would you like to dance?" He gestured toward the space in the middle of the room that had become a makeshift dance floor.

"Oh...okay?" She accepted almost as a question. She took his hand and he led her to the dance floor where other couples had begun to congregate. Jim slid his arms around her waist and pulled her a little closer. Her hands started out at his elbows as he gazed into her eyes. A shot of heat ran through him as she slowly moved her hands up his arms until her hands were clasped around his neck and she took the final step to align their bodies.

~~~~~

Jim lowered his head and nuzzled her neck, sending electric shocks down her spine, right to her core. Overcome by shyness, she rested her forehead on his chest. Being this close to him felt so right, like she was meant to be in his arms. The closest she had come to this before was when she had kissed Adam St. John on the doorstep when his father had returned them home from the cinema. Her mother had caught them and been very upset.

"*You most certainly do not kiss a boy on your first date and especially not when you are sixteen-years-old, Felicity!*" her mother had chastised. "*What kind of girl are you?! Think of the reputation you will have once he goes back to boarding school and tells his friends!*"

"*Oh for goodness sake, Penny, leave the poor girl alone!*" Her father had done his best, as always to defend her.

Jim sang along with the words of the song as he held Flick tight against him. She lifted her gaze to meet his. He smiled down at her. Their noses were almost touching. Her heart was pounding so much she was sure he could feel it too. As he looked directly into her eyes, he lowered his face toward her, paused as if waiting for her to pull away. When she didn't, he gently brushed her lips with his. She inhaled sharply. His lips were soft against hers, and his stubble lightly scratched the edges of her mouth.

Despite the fact they had only just met, she had wanted him to kiss her, but there was no way she would have made the first move. Now that he had, she gained the courage to reciprocate the kiss, and he seemed encouraged by this as his hand moved up her back until he reached her hair. Her body tingled and her heart rate increased further. He held her to him and kissed her deeper, his tongue flicking out tentatively. Her insides turned to jelly and her legs felt weak. Heat rushed to parts of her body she wouldn't have expected from a simple kiss. But then again there was nothing *simple* about this kiss. She broke away from him and locked onto his gaze.

His brow furrowed, a look of guilt washed over his gaze. "I'm sorry, Flick… I-I just got carried away."

She watched his expression cloud with regret. She didn't want that at all. Keeping her hands around his neck and stroking her fingers through his hair, she shook her head. "No, Jim, please don't be sorry…I-I think I had to just check…"

"Check what?" He looked confused.

"That I wasn't dreaming." She smiled and tiptoed to meet his lips with hers once again. She felt him smile against her and she parted her lips to invite him in. His tongue danced with hers, and he scooped her up into his arms so that her feet were dangling just over his shoes. She gave a little squeal of delight as he spun her around. *Wow…literally swept off my feet,* she thought gleefully as he swayed her to the music.

At the end of the night, Felicity was aglow with the events of the evening. Jim had been by her side all night and they had kissed several more times. Jim offered to walk her back to her room and she accepted. They chatted comfortably as they walked.

Jim tentatively took her hand and laced his fingers with hers as they made their way across campus. "So did you enjoy the craic then, Flick?" He smiled remembering her reaction to this phrase when they had first met.

"Yes, the *craic's* been great." She smiled up at him, mimicking his accent and blushing as she did. He laughed at her attempts and squeezed her hand. They walked in silence for a few moments.

He suddenly stopped and pulled her to him. "Can I ask you something?"

"Yes, Jim, you can." She felt shy again and her gaze darted around, anywhere but to meet his. He held her chin gently between his thumb and finger and smiled down at her.

"Do I make you nervous?" he asked, frowning a little but still holding a half smile.

"Is that the question you wanted to ask? I…thought it would be something different." She tilted her face to one side, finally meeting his inquisitive gaze.

He laughed. "Oh…no…no. Sorry, that wasn't the question. That was a pre-amble."

Felicity liked his laugh. It seemed to come from somewhere in his boots and vibrated through his body. She pursed her lips before answering, "Well, I *am* a little nervous but not because of anything bad. I'm just…a little bit shy." She dared to hold his gaze and her breath caught. Even under the street lighting she could see he had the most amazing brown eyes, like melted caramel.

"Don't be nervous. I don't bite… Well, not on weekdays." He winked.

"So what did you *actually* want to ask?" she whispered, hoping she knew the answer.

"I wanted to ask if I could see you again?" He lowered his face until their noses were touching, and her heart relentlessly pounded at her ribcage.

"I was hoping that's what you were going to ask." She breathed. Her mouth met his for another mind-blowing kiss. When they broke apart, he held out his hand and she weaved her fingers in his once again.

"Shall I take that as a yes then?" He grinned.

"You shall." She hoped her smile said it all.

Just like a perfect gentleman he walked her right to her door and made sure she got inside. She hesitated and took a deep breath. "Do you want to come and look my latest sketch?" The words rushed out of her body as if desperate to escape.

"Hmmm, so you're inviting me in to see your etchings, eh?" He sounded like Sean Connery and it made her giggle.

"Hardly. It's just the one sketch and it's a bit rubbish really. I just—"

He placed his fingers on her lips. "I was teasing, Flick. And yes, please, I would love to. Just to see the sketch and then I'll go." He stepped inside and walked over to her easel. "Oh yes, I see what you mean. It's totally rubbish." He teased again.

She hit him playfully on the arm. "Thank you but you could have been nicer."

"Flick, this is beautiful. The attention to detail is…amazing. I can't believe you did it from memory."

"Thank you. Like I said, it's just what I see through the glass…nothing fancy." She smiled, pleased with his compliment. "I'm glad you like it though."

He walked back to the door, pulled her into him and kissed her again. "Goodnight beautiful and talented, Flick," he whispered placing one last kiss on her nose.

"Goodnight…handsome and sweet, Jim." The heat in her cheeks rose again. She closed her door after him and then collapsed on her bed with a huge sigh of contentment and a smile as wide as the Thames on her face. She had a pretty good idea what she was going to dream of that night.

~~~~~

As Jim walked, he couldn't help grinning like the Cheshire cat. Checking that no one was watching, he did a little happy dance in the middle of the road, only to be caught by a group of Fresher's walking around the corner. He covered his eyes with his hands. *Great.* They whistled and cheered as they passed him.

"Oh, fuckity shit! I'll never live that one down." He sniggered aloud to himself.

~~~~~

Work at university was harder than she had imagined, but for the next few weeks after that initial date they spent every possible minute together. Their friendship had deepened and their relationship was secure and special but not yet intimate. They were part of a large group of friends and all socialised together (mostly when they were supposed to be studying).

Matthew caught up with Flick and Jim as they walked back to halls. "You guys up for a club on Friday night? We're thinking of heading into Oxford to the tastefully named *Razzles!*" He sniggered. Jim walked along with his arm loosely draped around Flick's shoulders. He looked for her acquiescence and she nodded.

"Sounds like good craic, Matty. Aye. Reckon we could make one in!" Jim kissed the top of Flick's head.

Flick smiled at Jim's loving gesture. He had been the perfect gentleman since that first kiss. Never expecting too much of her. They spent a lot of time alone but things never progressed beyond kissing, albeit passionate. He had only touched her breast once, but she had recoiled at the sensation and he had apologised profusely for pushing her too quickly. He hadn't done it since. She regretted that incident so much. She'd never been touched in that way before and it had taken her breath away, but she *had* liked it and mentally kicked herself for her immature reaction. She was an adult now, for goodness sake, but thanks to the beady eye of her mother she had never got past *first base* with a guy. And by definition even *first base* was a little iffy. She was ready to change all that now. She just needed to find a way to convince Jim.

~~~~~

Friday night came around, and Flick and Polly were getting ready in Flick's room. Polly was Flick's best female friend at University, Jim being the obvious *male* candidate in that department. Polly was really sweet and quite shy too. Her long, fiery red curls cascaded down her back. She used them as a veil, too, hiding behind them most of the time.

"Flick, can I tell you a secret?" Polly took a swig from the bottle of wine she had been glugging for Dutch courage. Flick pulled on a long tie-dyed skirt, camisole, and lace top as she listened to her friend.

"Of course you can, Pol. I won't tell." Flick grabbed the bottle and took her own gulp of courage. She needed it for what she had planned.

"Ahem…erm…I have a *massive* crush on someone." She blushed beetroot red at the admission and slapped her hand over her mouth.

"*Really?*" Flick was intrigued now and dropped to her knees before her friend. "Who? Tellmetellmetellmeeeee!" Flick patted her leg as if trying to slap the info out of her.

"Matty," she blurted. "He is *so* gorgeous. I love the way he swipes his hair back off his face and pushes his glasses up his nose with his finger… And his hands…oh what I'd like him to do with those hands."

"*Polly!*" Flick burst out laughing at her friend's brazen wantonness. The two girls fell about in fits of almost hysterical laughter. Suddenly, there was a knock at the door and they froze. Their laughter ceased.

"Oh shit! Do you think they heard?" Polly's face drained of colour, and she slapped her hand over her mouth again, making Flick giggle uncontrollably. Matty and Jim had agreed to call for the girls at eight o'clock and it was now eight oh five. *Dammit!*

"Oh dammit! Just act *normal*, Pol. *Normal!*" Flick grasped her friend's shoulders trying not to snicker. Her friend stared back in horror.

"Normal…yes… I *can* do normal." Polly burst into hysterics again and collapsed on the bed. The girls calmed themselves down and answered the door.

"Bloody hell, Flick, what took you so long?" Jim chuckled in reaction to the girls who were trying their best not to laugh. "What's so funny?"

"Oh…just a bit of girl talk." The girls exchanged knowing looks and stifled any further giggles as best they could under the circumstances, i.e., the alcohol-induced giddiness. Matty, as Matthew had now become known, went a delightful shade of crimson at seeing Polly. His famous nervous stutter came out with a vengeance.

"H-hi, P-Polly. You l-look l-lovely." He gazed at the buxom red head, who just melted into his eyes.

"So do you, Matty…just lovely." Her giggles were gone and she turned to give Flick and Jim an enormous grin when Matty took her hand in his.

The atmosphere at the club was buzzing when they arrived. It seemed that ninety per cent of Oxford Uni was out for the *craic*. The DJ played decent music, despite the club's somewhat corny name. Jim and Flick spent most of the time on the dance floor wrapped around each other, even when the songs were fast paced.

The end of the night came around too soon. At one in the morning, the gang of friends walked back to their dorms. Some of the group had been a little too eager with the beer and were singing rather loudly, tempting the wrath of the hierarchy without seeming to care. Stubbs and Clara were the two worst culprits. They had all the musical intonation of a pack of howling banshees.

"Some of this lot won't be seeing the light of day tomorrow." Jim chuckled as he walked along with his arm around Flick. Matty and Polly had stopped and were locked in a smouldering embrace.

"Oh, bless them. They finally got together," Flick said, looking over her shoulder as Jim turned to see what she meant.

"Aye, thank goodness for that. Maybe he'll stop rambling on about her hair and her eyes and her lips." Jim mimicked Matty's posh accent and swooned, as Matty had apparently been doing.

"Really? Oh, that's so sweet." Flick smiled in their direction.

They arrived at her door and Jim kissed her deeply, exploring her mouth with his delicious tongue. "See you tomorrow then, sweetheart?" he breathed as he rested his forehead on hers.

"Would you like to...erm...come in? For...coffee?" she stumbled over her words. Her heart rate had increased and her palms were sweating.

"Oh...I'd love to. Could do with a cup really. Clear my head a bit. Oh and to see how you're doing with your painting." Jim smiled enthusiastically and followed her in. *Dammit, is he dense or just plain oblivious?*

As soon as they were inside, she grasped at him, crashing her mouth into his and thrusting her tongue into his mouth.

He pulled away from her. "Whoa, hey! Flick, what are you doing?" He gasped, grasping her shoulders, and stepped back. She stepped away too, feeling stupid and more than a little embarrassed, but somehow she summoned up a little of the courage she had felt earlier.

"I...oh sod this...courage Felicity... Jim, I want you...*naked.*" She lifted her arms up in the air, not knowing why. "There I said it. If you don't feel the same, then we have a serious problem." Her chest heaved as adrenalin coursed through her veins and her heart tried to escape through her chest.

He gaped open-mouthed, as if at a loss for words. Then suddenly as if a realisation had hit, a sweet smile spread across his gorgeous face. He stepped toward her and his expression changed again. His eyes became darker as he reached up to stroke her cheek.

"We don't have a problem, Flick," he spoke quietly and huskily. Heat rushed through her body. "I've wanted you since the first time we kissed...no, even before that. I just got the sense that you may be...ah...a virgin and didn't want to take advantage of you. Things had to be on *your* terms." He tucked her hair behind her ear and continued to stroke her face.

"Well…I'm sick of being a bloody virgin. I want to experience things. I want to experience sex…with you…now." Her hands grabbed his checked shirt. She was desperate to convey her feelings but worried it was all coming out wrong.

"There *is* a slight problem, then." His eyes stayed locked on hers but her heart sank.

She bit her lip. "Oh? Do I want to hear this?" She gulped.

"I don't want *just* sex, Flick. I want *us* to be a *permanent* thing and so I want to make love to you. However cheesy that sounds, it's the truth." His voice was soft. He took her face in his hands and lightly brushed her lips with his. She realised she was holding her breath and was feeling a little lightheaded. The air rushed from her lungs as she absorbed his words.

"That would suggest…that you, kind of…love me… Is that what you mean, or am I getting this all completely wrong?" She gulped as she placed her hands over his.

He took a deep breath and paused. "I think I've loved you since that morning you were trying to do origami with all your paperwork." He chuckled. She blushed at the memory. She had felt so stupid on that day and was a little overwhelmed to hear that he had fallen for her *then*.

"Oh…wow." She was trembling now. He kissed her again, their tongues danced as they tasted each other. She ran her hands through his hair and he pressed his body against hers. She inhaled sharply when she felt his arousal press against her stomach.

Stepping away slightly, he eased her denim jacket from her shoulders and slipped her pretty lace top over her head, followed by the camisole underneath. Her chest rose and fell rapidly as she gazed up into his eyes. He crouched and slid the skirt down her thighs. Then he stood and held her at arm's length looking at her, all of her, standing there before him in her white lace underwear.

"Wow…just as beautiful as I imagined," he breathed as his eyes scanned her body.

Stepping into him, she nervously pulled his shirt down his arms and discarded it with the other clothes. His T-shirt came off next, exposing his sculpted pectorals and defined abs, the kind she had only ever seen on posters. His low hanging jeans revealed a little trail of curls leading down under his waistband. Suddenly, she froze. Jim stroked her cheek and unfastened his belt. He slipped his jeans and boxers down his legs never moving his soft gaze from her. She gasped and shivered as he stood before her naked and in a state of arousal.

"Hey, you're cold." He pulled her into an embrace. She wondered if he could feel her heart pounding against him. "Shall we get into bed? Warm you up?"

She nodded silently, feeling in complete awe of his form. They climbed into the limited space, and he lay beside her propped up on his elbow. He trailed his finger down her cheek and placed his palm over her heart. "Hey, are you okay? If you're having second thoughts—"

"N-no…no second thoughts." She lifted her hand and pulled him toward her. The kiss was gentle to begin with. She felt his heart rate increase as he moved his hand from her heart to her breast to gently caress her through the lace. She breathed in sharply at the overwhelming sensation and he stopped. "Don't stop, Jim…I'm fine…honestly," she breathed.

Flick was certainly feeling warmer as her own arousal took over. She felt heat pooling between her thighs. Jim's fingers continued to toy with her nipple through her lace bra and it hardened under his caress as a rush of pleasure traversed her body. A moan escaped her and he smiled. Reaching around her back, he released her bra clasp,

"Is this okay?" Jim whispered.

She nodded. "Yes...please don't stop." He removed the bra and let it fall to the floor over his shoulder. After admiring and caressing her for a few seconds more he leaned toward her body and took her pink bud into his mouth. Flick gasped as her eyes rolled back and she grabbed at his hair, desire coursing through every fibre of her being. She released another husky moan and his mouth played there a little longer. His hand, however, slid down...down...down, tracing the outline of her waist and her hip...to the front of her panties. He gently stroked her over the fabric and she opened her thighs for him. His breath caught in his throat and he moved to kiss her stomach. Slowly, he slid his hand inside her panties. As he continued with the feather light kisses, his fingers found her dampness. He let out what sounded like a low appreciative growl as he explored her there, his thumb circling her sensitive place.

She writhed beneath him, her breathing became irregular, and she felt an amazing tension building inside her as his fingers moved. "Oh, Jim! Oh, Jim, don't stop." She clung to him as if he were her lifeline. Her eyes were clenched shut, her head thrown back, and her inhibitions set free. Suddenly, she cried out as searing pleasure ripped through her body like an electric current. She felt as though she were soaring above the earth and having an out of body experience simultaneously. It was better than any orgasm she had given herself (and there hadn't been that many). He moved so that their eyes were locked again.

"Are you okay?" he asked again, concern playing on his face as he watched her come back down to earth.

"Please stop worrying. I'm better than okay." She kissed him gently. "And Jim? *Please* do that to me again."

With a wide, handsome smile and needing no other encouragement, he leaned to grab his jeans, fumbled around until he found his wallet and removed a little foil packet.

He sat up to look down at her as she lay beside him. "I wasn't planning this, you have to know. But I bought a pack just in case. I wasn't going to pressure you…please believe that—"

She placed her hands over his lips. "Jim…you don't need to say anymore…just put it on…please?" He did as she asked, and his eyes remained on her as she slipped the white lace panties down her legs. He swallowed hard.

Flick watched as his Adam's apple moved in his throat. She glanced down to look at him in all his masculine glory. She had nothing to compare him to, but in her humble and inexperienced opinion he looked big and pretty damn fine. But now she was scared—scared she would make a fool of herself or that it would hurt. But she was in no doubt that she wanted this, wanted him. He manoeuvred so that he was kneeling between her thighs and bent to kiss her stomach, stroking his fingers down her body until he was touching her again. Her back arched involuntarily and she closed her eyes, moaning and sighing with pleasure.

"Are you sure about this, Flick, sweetheart? There's no pressure, I don't want to rush you—" His voice was soft, almost a whisper.

"Jim, please, I'm fine. Just take it steady okay? I'm a little scared." She gave a nervous laugh.

~~~~~

Looking down at her as she lay beneath him, he felt he had never witnessed a more beautiful sight. Her smooth skin lay before him, only for him. An overwhelming array of emotions flooded his body: love, lust, pride, admiration. She was perfect. She was *his*. He gently lay on top of her first, and they kissed and caressed each other. Eventually, when he had plucked up the necessary courage, he guided himself inside her, relishing the feeling, as he worshipped her breast with his mouth.

"Ahhh!" she yelped and he froze.

He panicked. "Oh my God, are you okay?!"

She smiled reassuringly and nodded, grasping at his buttocks to urge him on.

"Oh, Flick, you…you feel amazing." He peppered her beautiful face with kisses as he moved inside her. Finding her tender spot with his fingers again he massaged until she groaned in ecstasy once more. Hearing her sent him over the edge. His movements became faster and more urgent. "Oh, Flick…Flick, I love you!" he shouted out as he came, grasping onto her and hugging her to him.

When he had reconnected with planet Earth again, he looked down to find tears cascading down her face, and she was shuddering beneath him, the drops if saltwater trailing down and soaking her hair. He was horrified and immediately felt tears sting the back of his own eyes. He needed to comfort her. She had given herself to him, and now she was sobbing? *Oh God, what have I done?*

"Hey, hey, shhh. Flick, it's okay. Did I hurt you? I'm so sorry… I'm so sorry." He sat and pulled her up into his lap. He stroked her hair and hugged her close, wiping away her tears and biting back his own. *This was not supposed to happen.*

Suddenly, she laughed through her sobs. "No…no…don't be sorry, Jim. That was amazing. I was expecting it to be really painful and terrifying but it was wonderful. It was lovely. *You* were lovely." She placed a hand on each cheek and held his gaze. She kissed him fervently to communicate her feelings. Relief washed over him. "I think I'm just a little...overwhelmed that's all." She sniffed and laughed again. "I'm so glad you were my first." At her words, he felt that sting behind his eyes again. Apparently, it had been a pretty emotional experience for both of them.

"I do love you, Flick. I meant that." His voice quivered as he tried to rein himself in. He ran his thumb along her bottom lip and kissed it.

She sighed. "Jim...I love you too."

~~~~~

May 2002 – Seven Years Before the Break-up

"I can't believe we've done it! We've finally finished! It's all done. Goodbye education, hello big wide world!" Polly's melodramatic spinning and swooshing of her arms in her robes made everyone laugh. The gang of friends were standing around taking photos whilst their parents chatted and compared notes. Jim's parents hadn't been able to make it due to his dad's rapidly failing health. He was disappointed but totally understood.

It had been an exhausting and emotional day. Flick had sent her parents off for some R and R at their hotel and she informed him that she was going back to her dorm to pack up the last of her belongings. They had secured a little house to rent in Kentish Town and would be moving in straight after graduation, much to her mother's disappointment. Jim had secured some work as a proof reader and Felicity was starting work at a gallery in London.

"Come up in about twenty minutes, honey bun, and you can help me load the car up before we set out for dinner with my Mum and Dad." Flick winked at Jim and squeezed his bottom. He agreed to see her up there. She wandered off through the University grounds reminiscing about the wonderful times they had all shared here. It had been a difficult few years but fun all the same.

Her room was all but cleared, her painted canvases wrapped and piled up carefully with the rest of her belongings. Jim had insisted her art would be adorning the walls of their new place.

She had already helped him pack his room the day before. It had taken longer than either of them had expected because they had ended up looking through some old photos of his family holidays in the stunning Scottish Highlands. She was amazed by the beauty of the remote places he had visited with his parents and brother. They were the types of places she could sit and admire and paint for hours. Actually sitting and painting a view whilst it remained before her instead of painting from memory would be a novelty. She hoped one day he would take her there and then maybe *those* paintings could adorn their walls, too.

She had used the excuse about loading the car to get out of the way and have some time with Jim before dinner. She had a little surprise planned for him. Piling all the boxes on the floor by the door to create a temporary wall, she stripped herself of her gowns, clothes, and cap. Butterflies set about tripping the light fantastic in her tummy as she readied herself for Jim's imminent arrival.

~~~~~

Jim stood chatting to his friends, but idly wondering what Flick was doing. *She's scheming. I wonder what she's up to.* Curiosity eventually got the better of him, and he made his excuses to leave. He walked across campus to Flick's room. On arrival, he knocked on the door. "Hey sweetheart, it's me. Can I come in?"

"You certainly can," she purred from inside.

Jim nibbled on his lip, as he walked in, wondering what was about to happen. He was greeted by the wall of boxes. Flick was hidden behind them. Closing the door he peeped around the barrier and inhaled sharply at what he saw. She lay reclined on her bed, not a stitch of clothing on her delectable curves apart from her mortarboard and Oxford scarf tied loosely around her neck and draped between her breasts, the tassels just covering her special place. Jim couldn't help but grin as he slowly prowled over to her, dropping to his knees before her and diving straight in to kiss her underneath the tassels. She gasped as pleasure surged through her body. After gifting her with a delicious orgasm he discarded his clothes and climbed onto the bed, little foil packet in his hands at the ready. She snatched it from him and threw it across the room.

"Hey!" He pouted at the prospect of not having his way with her.

She grinned. "No need for those anymore." Her eyebrows wiggled suggestively. "I've been on the pill for a while now and we're safe to go commando."

A low moan erupted from him and he rolled his eyes back before climbing between her thighs, removing her mortarboard and sinking himself inside her. "Seriously, I think I've died and gone to heaven." He gasped as he moved.

Jim made love to her, slowly and languorously, enjoying the new sensations they were experiencing together, devouring each other with their mouths and exploring each other's bodies with their hands. It was an intense and powerful experience. When they had both had their fill and were completely sated, gazing lovingly at each other as their breathing calmed, Jim decided it was time to put his own surprise into action.

He leapt from the bed. "Sit up and close your eyes," he commanded. She giggled at his bossiness.

"Why?" She was clearly in a playful, stubborn mood.

"Just do it!" he demanded as he fumbled around in his jacket pocket.

Reluctantly, she perched herself on the end of the bed. The scarf was still in place around her neck.

"Keep them closed!" he demanded again. She was sniggering uncontrollably. "You cannae open your eyes 'til you've calmed down," he chastised, but he too was trying not to laugh. Pursing her lips, she finally managed to quell the giggles and sat eyes closed, back straight. "Okay, you can open them now."

She opened one eye and then both eyes wide. "What the—" she gasped.

Jim kneeled in front of her, naked, holding out a diamond ring in his shaking hand. "Now, I know this is a bit unorthodox…and I'm a tad naked…but I wanted to remember this moment for the rest of my life." He gulped and swallowed hard, but the huge grin on her face encouraged him to continue. "I only intend on doing this once and…so it had to be special."

He cleared his throat before continuing. "Felicity, I've loved you since the moment I first set eyes on you. And I'm sorry for doing this whilst you're naked too…although let me just say that you are *the* most stunningly gorgeous woman on the face of the Earth right now...I've never loved you more... S-sorry, I digress...ahem...I was going to do it later...at...at dinner but seeing you like this...beautiful...wearing my favourite outfit yet...I had to do it now...Flick...Felicity...will you marry me?" His words came out in such a rush he could have passed out when he had finished.

She gaped at him as he kneeled feeling quite vulnerable in every sense before her. He hoped she could see the sincerity in his eyes and not be too distracted by how ridiculous he must look. His heart pounded harder the longer she stared at him. He gulped and pleaded at her with his eyes, suddenly thinking he had made a mistake. He dropped his gaze momentarily along with his hand. When he lifted his head again, she had covered her mouth with her hand and tears had escaped from her glistening eyes.

Oh no, this wasn't meant to happen. "Flick?"

She shook her head. "Oh Jim, I'm so, sorry. I ruined that whole thing. I was just a bit...stunned. And I thought you were joking."

He inhaled sharply. "No...I've never meant anything more...but I think maybe I shouldn't have—"

"Ask me again." She wiped at her eyes.

"Sorry?" He was confused.

Her eyes softened. "Ask that important question again, please, Jim."

"Erm...okay..." He took a deep breath, and this time feeling a little calmer, he spoke more steadily. "Felicity, I've loved you since the day I met you. You make me so happy. I want to share my life with you. I want to be with you forever. Please will you make me the happiest man alive? Felicity, will you marry me?"

"Oh yes, Jim! Yes!" She threw her arms around him and they tumbled back on the bed to start all over again.

Chapter 5

"Oh, my darling, you look…you look…radiant!" Edgar stood dewy eyed as his only daughter descended the wide, sweeping staircase at her family home. Seeing her dad wrought with emotion only served to make tears well in her eyes too.

She had taken all of ten minutes to choose her wedding dress. It was long and fitted to accentuate her curves. The bottom kicked out and there was a long train to the back. The lace-up bodice was strapless to show off her beautiful décolleté, and the front sparkled with tiny diamantes. She had chosen white roses tied dimply with white ribbon. Her hair was smooth and sleek, in a low bun off to one side and dotted with crystals. To complete the look, she wore a silver tiara with real diamonds that her father had insisted upon for his adorable princess.

The stunning and in-demand village church had been booked for the wedding ceremony, thanks to the connections of one Edgar Johnston-Hart. The beautiful building wasn't huge but it held a special place in the hearts of the family, and Flick could think of nowhere else she would rather marry her darling Jim.

The service was booked for noon on a chilly September Saturday. Flick couldn't feel the cold. She was too excited. Thankfully, the sun made an early appearance and set a warm glow about the place, even though no one could feel the benefit of its radiating heat, just the colours made it feel warmer. The bridesmaids wore long sumptuous, burgundy gowns and carried white and burgundy roses tied with white ribbon. All four were friends of Flick's from school and University. They looked stunning.

The white Rolls Royce had already taken the bridesmaids and Flick's sobbing mother to the church, and it now returned to take her on her way to becoming a married woman.

There had been much debate about her name and whether she would take Jim's as her own. Her mother was totally against it. She did make one valid point, however, that the Johnston-Hart name carried a certain amount of weight and that *her Felicity* was already building up a reputation using her maiden name as an art dealer at Art and Soul, a small but well thought of gallery on the outskirts of London.

Jim had been hurt. He'd wanted her to be Mrs. Felicity MacDuff, but after a lot of cajoling by her mother, Flick agreed that it would be best for her to keep her own name. Jim had reluctantly acquiesced, simply because he desired her happiness above all else. "It's not as if I won't wear a ring, for goodness sake, Jim, and I will be Mrs. Johnston-Hart," she had told him. And so that was that. Mrs. Felicity Johnston-Hart she would become. She couldn't be happier. Jim could.

~~~~~

"I now pronounce you, husband and wife." The Vicar concluded the beautiful ceremony, and Jim couldn't wait to kiss his new bride. She beamed from ear to ear as he took her in his arms. The congregation applauded and cheered as the newlywed couple shared their first passionate embrace as Mr. and Mrs. They walked down the aisle hand in hand and gazing at each other, only breaking away to shake hands with well-wishing guests.

Flick's mother continued to sob.

~~~~~

The honeymoon was an exciting dual destination holiday. Florida's Disney World for the first week, where they met all the famous characters and tried every single ride on the insistence of Jim who was having a roaring time reverting back to childhood. They left with bags full of soft toys and lots of wonderful memories.

The second week was spent in a beautiful villa at Naples Beach. The villa was a one story white house with a stunning outdoor pool. The interior floors were tiled in white marble, and the furniture was plush and luxurious in shades of cream, beige, and white. It was like a little piece of heaven.

They spent the week by the pool, lounging lazily and eating fresh fruit. When they weren't by the pool they were making love in every possible place around the villa. It was magical. The large whirlpool bath had been their favourite place to make love and they had spent almost every evening in there. Jim had joked that they would wash their golden tans away if they weren't careful.

Flick looked amazing in her skimpy red bikini and huge sun hat. Her long tanned legs stretched out before her. Her curves visible for Jim's eyes only. It was the final day of their wonderful honeymoon and every moment in this private villa was precious. He had to work hard to restrain himself as he gazed at her longingly from under his shades. He closed his eyes and relaxed on his lounger, a contented smile on his face and his bare chest soaking up the sun's rays. Suddenly, something was blocking out the light, and he opened his eyes, ready to complain, but reined himself in when he snapped his head up to see his beautiful new bride gazing down at him.

She had removed her sunglasses and hat and looked down lustfully at him as she slowly removed her bikini top. Suddenly, his whole body stood to attention. His contented smile was replaced by a lascivious gawp. She threw the scanty item to one side and tugged on the ties at her hips, teasing him. He swallowed hard, his Adam's apple dancing the tango in his throat. She pulled the little triangle of fabric off and discarded it along with the top. She stood, completely naked before him. Jim's breathing became shallow, and his arousal was clearly evident in the thin fabric of his swim shorts.

Bending, she grasped the waistband of his shorts and slipped them down his hips, brushing her fingers gently over his skin, over his buttocks, and down his legs, making him spring free. She smiled and straddled the lounger, bending once again to kiss him deeply before positioning herself and taking him in, her hands stroking his pecs. His hands found her hips and he grasped her, relishing the feeling of being deep inside the woman he adored. She moved on him, groaning and throwing her head back as he fondled her breasts, raising up to take each one in his mouth and worshipping it reverently.

The excitement of being outside in the open made their movements urgent and needy. She scratched lightly down his back as she stroked him on and on with her body. The heat was rising and the pleasure building, their breathing became erratic and their touching rougher as they both soared toward ecstasy. He found her tender spot and caressed her, increasing the pressure infinitesimally until she called out his name, her orgasm taking hold and shooting her somewhere toward the stars. Hearing, feeling and seeing her climax, he ascended to join her, calling out her name as he landed amongst the clouds.

They lay huddled together, naked on the lounger for a while after, holding each other and basking in the glow of the warm Florida sunshine.

~~~~~

The return home was tinged with the sadness of leaving their little cocoon for two, but Jim was excited, too, at beginning their new life as a married couple. Once they had slept off the time difference, they began the delightful task of opening their gifts. Their wedding list had been placed between the most prestigious stores in London. Although certain people had completely ignored the list, buying the most bizarre gifts imaginable. They laughed hysterically at the matching bedside lamps adorned with shells and plastic fish.

"Charity shop!" they had said in unison.

The weird ornament of a bull was a puzzler. The book entitled *How To Let Go When Things Don't Work Out* had no gift tag but was completely inappropriate, given the reason for the gift. Surely it was a practical joke? Although Jim had his suspicions.

~~~~~

Monday came and it was back to work for Flick. She was quite excited about going back. There had been several new and exciting artists invited to show their works at Art and Soul, thanks to Flick. She was looking forward to seeing how it was all going. As the newest member of the team, she was determined to make a good impression. It seemed to be working.

She bent to kiss Jim, as he lay naked in their bed while she got ready. He grabbed her arm and pulled her onto him.

"Awww, Flick, come back to bed... I want you." He groaned.

She was wearing a sexy sharp suit, partly because she knew it would drive Jim wild. She had braided her long wavy locks in one long strand down her back.

~~~~~

Jim looked sulkily up at his wife. Stunning as ever, he wanted to untie the braid and let the hair fall onto his face as she straddled him like the time on the sun lounger.

"*Jiiiim*, I have to *go*." She tried to pull away. "We've had our fun this morning...now it's time for me to go bring home the bacon." She giggled.

Jim was supposed to be job hunting, as spending the past few years of being a freelance proofreader were not really what either of them had wanted. The money was good but it didn't feel like a secure income. He wasn't good at job hunting, however, and he had been visiting The Book Depository so often he had become like the old wing backed chair—part of the furniture of the place. Charles and he had started to have a laugh and a joke like old friends. He had even helped answer the telephone one morning whilst Charles had been busy.

"I will get a job, I promise." Jim kissed Flick's shoulder as she leaned on him.

"I know you will, when the right thing comes along. But until then, I expect you naked waiting for me when I get home." She licked his lips, her tongue dipping into his mouth. He groaned and flung himself back onto the bed.

She rushed out the door before he could convince her otherwise.

After he had showered and dressed, Jim headed for The Book Depository. He vowed with himself that he would have an hour there and then he would go to the Job Centre. Just the thought of that was enough to put him in a bad mood though. He hopped on the tube for the short journey to the shop.

It was late September following the honeymoon and there was the nip of autumn in the air. He arrived at the shop at around ten to find Charles in a flap about some book delivery that had gone completely belly up. Jim walked in as Charles was trying to sort the matter out on the phone.

"I am bloody annoyed though, Simeon! This can't keep bloody happening! I am up to my bloody eyes in it, old chap! I simply cannot keep accepting books I haven't bloody ordered!" Charles barked at the man at the other end of the line.

A customer walked in and began to browse. Jim stepped from foot to foot feeling he should do something. Suddenly, the customer approached him.

"Ermmm, excuse me. I'm looking for a first edition of *The Velveteen Rabbit*. Would you happen to have a copy? I know it's a long shot but it's my wife's favourite book and it's our tenth wedding anniversary. I want to get her something special that she'll treasure, and I would love to get her that particular book. But I would really rather have a first edition. It'd be all the more special." The man rambled at Jim who was not even an employee.

"I'm sorry mate but I don't actually work here… It's…Charles…there…that you need to speak to." Jim felt guilty as he gestured toward the now red-faced and flailing shop owner. Charles placed his hand over the mouthpiece of the phone.

"Jim, you're hired! Start now!" Charles snapped in a loud, hoarse whisper at the bewildered Scotsman. It had come up in conversation a while ago that Jim was looking for work, but this was unexpected.

"Oh...oh right...great!" A grin spread across Jim's face almost splitting it in two. "Right then, sir. First edition...Velveteen Rabbit... I think we may have just the thing." He showed the relieved customer to a cabinet where all the first editions were kept and unlocked it with the key he had grabbed from the cash desk.

The customer left with a huge grin on his face, but it was nothing compared to the one on Jim's as he realised he had just, inadvertently, acquired his dream job and made his first—very lucrative—sale.

Charles hung up the phone and let out a huge sigh. "Some bloody people should bloody well learn to do their bloody job's properly!" he shouted. Jim just stood there with his grin still fixed in place. Charles looked at Jim and burst into fits of laughter. "I have never seen anyone so bloody happy to be working in a dusty old bookshop." When he calmed down he managed to say to Jim, "Welcome a-bloody-board, Jim. And thank bloody goodness you didn't bloody say no!"

"Not a bloody chance!" Jim laughed. "Right, what you want me to do first, boss?" he asked Charles, who was dabbing tears from his eyes with a navy and red spotted handkerchief and still spitting out a chuckle every few seconds.

"Oh...I don't know... I've never had an employee before. Shall we have a coffee and discuss your terms?"

"I'll get us a coffee," Jim enthusiastically chimed, walking over to the machine, which stood on an old dark wood table in the corner of the shop.

The shop wasn't huge but consisted of two rooms filled with second hand and antique books. There was shelf upon shelf, floor to ceiling, all crammed full. The smell was a damp and fusty one, but Jim loved it. Each and every book had its own history, and Jim liked to imagine how many people had read each one; how many different owners each had had; how each person had come to own and then let go of each book; and how each book had affected each reader. It was a fascinating place.

There were two very old armchairs. One was an old beaten up wingback chair, something akin to that which one would find in a *Gentleman's* club. It was once bright gold and burgundy when its tapestry fabric had been brand new. Now, however, it was frayed and the pattern had rubbed off in lots of places. Jim loved it because it was so very comfy and had character befitting of such a treasure trove where any bibliophile would feel at home. It was as if a thousand people had all imprinted themselves on it, making it squashy and moulded perfectly to the right shape. The other chair was an old leather armchair which creaked and groaned when sat upon. It was still a comfy chair but not quite the same as *his* chair, as he now called it.

Charles had reluctantly joined the 21st century and bought a digital cash register. But it was hidden around a rack of shelving, away from view, as if Charles was ashamed of its very presence in the shop. *Admittedly, it's not quite as pretty as the old antique push button thing, but it certainly makes life easier and is quieter to use!*

Jim arrived at home before Flick, but he had called at the little supermarket near home and picked up some chicken, salad, French bread, and a bottle of wine to celebrate his good news. Flick walked in at six looking exhausted. Dinner was ready and Jim had laid the table placing candles in the middle. It all looked very romantic. Her eyes lit up when she saw what he'd done.

"Jim? What's all this?" she asked hugging her man tightly.

"I've got good news." He could hardly contain his excitement as he spun her around in the small hallway.

"What? What is it?!" She grabbed onto him, pulling at his shirt.

"Go get changed into something comfortable, before I ravish you and I forget, and come down to eat. All will be revealed!" He ushered his beautiful wife up the stairs as he spoke. Whist she was gone he sat at the little table in their lounge/dining room tapping his fingers in eager anticipation of her return. She joined him and as always took his breath away. She wore pale blue, checked pyjama bottoms and a grey off the shoulder sweater, bare feet and her long corn coloured, wavy hair scrunched up on top of her head accentuating her sensual long neck. *Wow*, he thought, *wow*.

"What? Why are you looking at me like that?" she asked, a blush spreading up her chest and into her cheeks as he stared.

"Flick…you are simply exquisite," he breathed. She gasped at his words and immediately came to straddle him on his dining chair, kissing him as she did so.

"Okay, handsome, what's your exciting news?" she asked as she stared lovingly into his eyes.

"Weeeell…. I got me a job!" He grinned.

"Really?! That's fantastic! I didn't even know you had any interviews lined up. You kept that very quiet. Is it in the city?…Wa-wa-wait…let me guess! Is it with a publishing house?…Nonononono…is it with a Literary Agency?…Oh I give up! Tellmetellmetellme!" She bounced up and down on his lap. He began to feel like he was about to disappoint her. He had graduated with a First from Oxford and had such potential after all. Everyone said so.

"Erm…no…none of those." He sighed.

"Okay, so where?" She scrunched her face in apparent confusion.

"Well, you know that I go to that little book shop…The Book Depository?"

"Yesss?" Flick looked confused still.

"Well, Charles the owner just gave me a job completely out of the blue! Isn't that great?" He was now trying to convince them both.

"Oh right. Sorry I thought you meant a *job*-job. I didn't realise you meant a stepping stone. You had me all excited then. That's great, sweetie. It'll certainly put you on for a while whilst you're looking for something permanent," she chimed, kissing him on the nose and climbing off his lap.

"Hmmm…yes…it will," he mumbled, not daring to tell her that this was all he had ever wanted.

Chapter 6

January 2007 — Twenty-five Months Before the Break-up

"It is with great pleasure, therefore, ladies and gentlemen that I introduce to you, our newest team member and exceptional art critic, buyer, and discoverer of unique talent, Felicity Johnston-Hart." Applause rumbled around the room as Felicity took the microphone from Franco Nilsson, her new employer.

"Many thanks, Franco...ahem... This year has been quite a year, to say the least." She smiled at her audience. "I was delighted when Julian Forster was awarded the Carlson Art prize as it meant that all our hard work had paid off. Julian is a most talented and prolific artist, and I was proud to be the one who discovered him and presented him to the world. Julian will now go on to display at the Tate and has been offered space at Le Louvre for a short time to see how his work is received there.

"When Franco Nilsson and Daniel Perkins made contact with me and offered me the position of International Art Dealer here at this most prestigious of companies, I jumped at the chance. I'm happy to say that the proprietors of Art and Soul gave their blessing and full support to this next chapter of my life. I'm very excited to be embarking upon such a wonderful journey here at Nilsson-Perkins and look forward to encouraging you all to buy art in the near future." A chuckle from the audience was followed by applause.

~~~~~

Jim stood at the back, observing proceedings from a safe distance. He had worn the grey suit Flick had chosen for him at some expensive designer shop. He had protested about a tie and she had relented. So there he stood, shaggy, shoulder length brown hair, neatly pulled back into a ponytail, stubble trimmed to designer level, waistcoat fully buttoned, jacket open, white shirt open at the collar. He felt trussed up like a Christmas turkey. It wasn't his favourite look. But he had done it for Flick.

He listened as she spoke eloquently about her new role and her excitement about the fact that one of her hand-picked artists had won such a prestigious award. He felt proud but detached. Flick had been spending more and more time away. Paris. New York. Milan. He was happy for her and outwardly supported her every venture. He just felt like he was becoming a square peg in the round hole of her new life.

He glanced around the gallery. Its walls were adorned with the most amazing and striking pieces of modern art. There were some more traditional pieces, too, but they seemed out of place. Just like Jim. He could quite easily liken himself to the more traditional works.

Thankfully, the music chosen for the evening's festivities was eclectic just like his own taste. Debussy's *Claire De Lune* began to play over the P.A. system as Flick walked toward him, her hips swaying. Everyone in the room could have disappeared, he wouldn't have noticed.

"Hello, handsome, look at you all sexy." She slipped her arm around his neck and kissed his cheek, whispering in his ear and making him shiver with desire.

He returned the favour. "You don't look too shabby yourself, darlin'."

She blushed. Her hair was now shoulder-length and straightened within an inch of its life with her newly purchased, ceramic hair straighteners. It looked very sleek. Her fitted black shift dress accentuated her womanly curves in all the right places and the teardrop shaped cut out showed just the right amount of cleavage to send Jim's mind racing whilst remaining classy for this, her first work function.

~~~~~

They arrived home after what had been deemed a very successful launch of Flick's career with the very highly regarded Nilsson-Perkins. Once inside the door, Jim grabbed her and pressed her against the wall, her hands found his hair releasing the band that held it back and he kissed her neck just under her ear. She groaned and ran her hands down his back to his buttocks. He pressed his now prominent arousal into her and inhaled sharply.

"God I want you…right now…in this dress." He grabbed her bottom and lifted her so that her legs wrapped around his body. He ground his pelvis into hers and it was her turn to gasp. With one hand he unzipped his fly and released himself. Then pulling aside the black lace panties, which were his only barrier to what he desired, he sank himself deep in to her.

"Flick, you feel so good… I've wanted this all night."

"Oh…me too." She gasped as his thrusts drove her wild.

He felt his emotions winning the battle to escape. "I don't want to lose you… I'm scared." He gasped as he kissed her neck.

"What? Not…going…to…happen!" She climaxed around him urging his orgasm. As always, he called her name. This time his voice was tinged with desperation.

Once he had lowered her to the floor, he stood with his face buried in her neck, one hand in her hair, holding on for dear life, and the other wrapped around her torso, cradling her to him.

"Hey…Jim, sweetie, what's wrong? Look at me, Jim," she urged. He raised his face. Her eyes mirrored the sadness he knew his must show.

"Flick…I'm…I'm so scared," he admitted.

She frowned. "Of what? I don't understand." She stroked his face and kissed him gently.

"You have this new job…. You'll be jetting off all over the world. How will I keep up? Will I still be enough for you?"

Suddenly, she looked perturbed. Not in the least bit compassionate. "What kind of question is that? I don't know where all this is coming from. When have I given you such an idea that you won't be? I thought you'd be happy for me, Jim."

He realised she hadn't answered his question.

"I *am* happy for you. I am *so* proud of you. I *really* am. I'm just worried that I won't fit into your new life anymore. That you'll get tired of me…a lowly book salesman." He smiled as he rested his forehead on hers, hoping for reassurance.

It never came.

"Jim, this is beyond ridiculous." She snorted, freeing herself from his grip. "I'm going to take a shower. Open a bottle of champers, please. There's one chilling in the fridge," she called back to him as she made her way up the stairs.

Jim's heart sank.

February 2007 — Two Years Before the Break-up

Flick had worked quite a few late nights since beginning her new job a month earlier. Jim had done his best to just ride it, not to get stressed and certainly not to lay a guilt trip on her.

He wanted her to be happy and this job seemed to go some way to fulfilling her creative side. Although he had noticed that she painted less and less, a fact that concerned him somewhat. Painting was a part of who she was. It had *always* been her passion. Her job, however, seemed to take her away from the one thing that sparked her desire to study art in the first place.

It was Jim's birthday. He didn't really care that he was getting older. Age was just a number. What he did care about was the fact that he was more than likely going to spend his birthday without his wife. It was already seven in the evening and she wasn't home. He hadn't prepared dinner just on the off chance that Flick was taking him somewhere as a surprise. It was a long shot but he could hope.

He had dozed off on the sofa when the door opened bringing a cold draft into the small lounge diner. Flick breezed in carrying a white plastic bag, Chinese food and a bottle of wine. She dumped them on the floor in the hall and shouted, "Take these to the kitchen sweetie!" to him as she ran back out to the car.

When she returned, she insisted that he sit on the sofa with his eyes closed. A grin spread across his face. There was a surprise!

He heard Flick walking in and whispering, "Shhh…shhh," as she did.

Was there going to be a surprise party? Had she brought him a surprise guest? The suspense was killing him. Flick's knees cracked as she crouched down in front of him.

"Open your eyes!" she said excitedly.

He did as instructed and before him was a large white box with large holes punched in the lid. He slowly removed the lid and gazed inside.

"Happy birthday, sweetie."

"Oooh." He gasped. "Flick, he's gorgeous. Thank you so much."

He scooped up the little black pup that wriggled and jiggled with excitement. Jim held the little bundle to his face and the pup licked him. The pup began to pee and Jim and Flick laughed as they ran to the kitchen trying to make it through to the back garden, but by the time they made it the pup had finished.

"So what are you going to call him?" she asked as he tickled the small black Labrador pup's belly.

"Jasper. It suits him, don't you think?"

"I think it's a lovely name." She squeezed his shoulder.

She began to serve out the Chinese take away she had brought home with her. It smelled divine, and he was ravenous. So was Jasper, judging by the way he sniffed the air. Flick produced a tin of dog food from the take away carrier and handed it to Jim.

"I hope that's for the dog and it's not our appetiser.'" Jim winked.

She chuckled. "Best feed him now, eh?"

"Aw, Flick this is the best gift I've ever received. He's just gorgeous. Thank you so much." he kissed his wife lovingly before feeding his new little friend.

~~~~~

February 2008 — A Year Before the Break-up

Jim was waiting by the phone on Valentine's Day, alone. Flick had been in New York on business for almost a week. She had telephoned a couple of times, but the conversations had been quick. Today, however, he was expecting a longer call. He missed her like crazy. At around nine, the phone finally rang.

"Hey, Jim. We've just had the most amazing meeting with a phenomenal artist. It's looking like we may get the UK rights to her work! Isn't that fantastic?" Flick blurted without even saying hello.

Jim's knee bobbed up and down and his jaw clenched. *Nice greeting from the wife I'm missing like crazy.*

He felt heat rise in his cheeks. "Hi, Flick... Oh hi, Jim... I miss you so much... Yes, I miss you too, Flick, and wish you were here." He snorted sarcastically.

"Sorry, sweetie. I'm just so excited. Anyway, I can't talk long. We're going sightseeing before dinner. Can you believe I've been here a week and I haven't even been to Times Square yet?" She laughed.

Jim did not.

"Flick, I was hoping we could talk...you know...properly. I miss you so much it hurts," he pleaded.

"Oh, I'll be home before you know it and then you'll be sick of the sight of me! Anyway, I really must dash. I want to shower and change, and I'm running late already. Love you, sweetie, bye."

"Oh...so you *really* meant you couldn't talk long then...okay...bye." Jim hung up without reciprocating the breezy *I love you.* He was angry and hurt. He threw the handset onto the sofa and slumped down into the seat.

Jasper came and placed his head on Jim's lap. "At least you love me, eh, lad?" He scratched Jasper's head.

To top it off, it was going to be the first birthday he had had since they got together that he would be spending without her. Flick was due home two days *after* his birthday. At least, last year she was here. Late…but here. No, this year there would be no surprise gift in a box with holes in it, and instead of spending a romantic evening with his wife, he would be spending it with Charles. They were going to the Taj Mahal restaurant and then to the cinema to see *In Bruges*, which wasn't really a film that appealed to Charles—he was into Film Noir—but it was either that or a chick flick, and Jim had to draw the line somewhere considering this birthday was already sad enough as it stood.

~~~~~

Jim's birthday arrived. He met Charles at the cinema. Charles insisted on buying the largest bucket of popcorn available along with chocolates, nachos, and jelly sweets. The majority of which were gone by the time the film started. Silly, really, considering they had a table booked at the Indian restaurant as soon as the film ended.

The film turned out to be excellent. Dark, but very funny in places. And Jim had thought that Bruges looked like a place he would love to visit someday. The architecture was remarkable, despite the armed men running around killing people.

They moved on to the Indian restaurant and once again Charles insisted on paying. "No, Jim. Put your bloody money away, old chap. My bloody treat. If a chap can't treat his best bloody friend on his birthday, when can he?"

"Best friend? Aw, Charles, mate." Jim hugged his friend, feeling quite touched at his words. After the meal they headed to the Nags Head for a few beers. A few beers turned to many beers and Charles got quite tipsy. Jim found drunken Charles hilariously funny, although he was by no means sober himself. They stumbled out of the pub after being chatted up by too rather scary looking, overly made-up older women. As they waited for a taxi at the nearest rank they could stumble to, Charles made a confession.

"My dear, Jim." He sniggered at the fact that Charles remained *posh* even when inebriated. "Jimmy, Jimmy, Jim-Jim." His snigger became a chuckle. "You are my *beshtest* friend…didjoooo know hathat?" Charles slurred.

"I did *not* know that until earlier tonight, my old pal…but I dae now!"

They swayed as they chatted in their nonsensical way, Jim's Scottish accent thickening with the alcohol.

"Ohhh yes. Beshtest friend in the whooole world. In fact…I am *so* best friends with you, I'm gonna tell you a sheecret." Charles looked around conspiratorially and leaned on Jim for support. "I don't like ladies, Jim…nononono." He wagged his finger vehemently. "I like men. I am what one would call a hhhomosexshalll." The revelation surprised Jim a little, although he had always wondered. "But don't worry…nononono, don't you worry…*you're* not my type." He patted Jim's shoulder.

Jim's mouth fell open. He felt rather affronted. "Eh? Whaddya mean I'm not your type? What's *wrong* wi me?" The brusque and rather offended Scotsman was speaking now. "I'm a good catch me you know," he informed Charles.

"Oh, yesss, yesss, I bloody *know* that old boy…don't be hoffended. I just like you asafriend…thass all. Hafriend. And besides…I would be wasting my time because I know that you're...erm...heter...hetrara...hetooosesh...you like girls. Especially on account of the fact being that you are married, as well too." He nodded, rambling on.

"Aye...that I do...that I am, my friend. Fair comment...fair comment. Well, one girl actually. But I think she's going off me, Charles, and it makes me hurt in here." Jim pointed to his chest. Hearing himself admit this openly made him suddenly feel quite sober and more than a little bit sad. The pair stood in silence after their session of openness and waited for a cab.

~~~~~

Jim arrived home at just after midnight and saw the answering machine light flashing. He pressed the play button.

"Hi Jim...it's Flick. I'm sorry I didn't ring earlier but I've been so busy. Anyway, I'm sure you've had a wonderful night out with Charles. I'm guessing you will be home around one in the morning so I will call you at one. Okay? Bye."

No 'I love you'. Great. He went into the kitchen and drank a pint of water to try and fend off the hangover that would undoubtedly hit at some point in the not too distant future. He made a pot of fresh coffee and took it back into the lounge. He would stay up and wait for her call at one.

He woke with a start and looked at the clock. Two forty five. She hadn't called. With a heavy heart and a pounding head he took himself off to bed.

Chapter 7

January 2012 - Two Years and Eleven Months After the Break-up

The sky looked heavy with snow and Jim had already lit the fire, even though it was only nine in the morning. It was Saturday which meant the coffee shack was scheduled to be open at ten. He sat by the fire with Jasper, eating his porridge and staring into the flames as they danced. Someone knocked at the door.

"Blimey, Jasper, the postie's early today. Must be getting it done before the snow comes, eh, lad?" He placed his porridge bowl on the coffee table and went to answer the door. On opening it, he pretty much got the second biggest shock of his life (the first being his wife's request for a divorce…oddly enough she was involved in *this* shock, too).

"What the hell are you doing here?" His greeting was far from cordial.

Felicity stood shivering on the doorstep. "C-can I c-come in please, Jim, it's important," she pleaded.

Reluctantly he stepped aside so the Ice Queen could enter his cosy little cottage. As she walked past him into the lounge, the cold, biting air from the outside followed her as if it emanated from her very being. He shuddered.

"I have no idea why the hell you would be here. You're miles away from home," he spoke to himself really. "Do you…do you want a coffee?" he asked, still befuddled as to why his ex-wife had driven for almost ten hours to turn up on his door step without prior notification.

"Y-yes, please. Brrrrrrr.'" She shivered. "This is a sweet place, Jim." She followed him into the kitchen.

"Thanks. It's small but perfectly formed, as they say." He smiled. He poured freshly brewed, steaming coffee into a mug for Felicity. "So, I'm *Jim* again, am I?" he asked, confused.

"It suits you better," she stated with a sad smile.

It's taken her long enough to figure that out. He grumbled under his breath. They wandered back through to the lounge and sat before the fire, silently. Felicity was hunched as if the weight of the world was dragging her down. Finally, Jim could wait no longer.

"So…to what do I owe the unexpected…erm…visit?" He would have said *pleasure* but considering he had spent almost the last three years getting over her it was not a word he could associate with Felicity any longer. She had caused him so much heartache. He couldn't go there again.

"I…I'm sorry to just turn up… I'm afraid I have some bad news, Jim, and I couldn't tell you over the phone. I just couldn't do that." Her lip began to quiver and her eyes glistened with welling tears.

"Hey…hey, what is it? What's wrong Fli…Felicity?" Jim put his cup down and slid to the seat beside her on the sofa.

"It's Daddy, Jim… He passed away just before Christmas… He'd been ill but had kept it quiet."

The news hit Jim like a blow to the gut. He inhaled sharply and ran his hands through his hair.

She twisted her fingers in her lap and glanced up briefly. "He had been receiving treatment for his illness but he didn't want Mum fussing over him." A sob broke free as the tears overflowed from her closed eyes and spilled down her face. "And he didn't want to worry me."

"Why…how…I don't…" Jim stood and leaned on the fire place. His stomach clenched into a knot and nausea washed over him. Edgar had been like a father to him. He had written several letters over the past year and had received light-hearted replies regaling Jim with details of the latest book he was working on. The last letter had been full of facts about George Leigh Mallory, the subject of his latest biography. It was the beginning of December when he had received the last letter. There was no mention of illness. *None.*

Felicity stood. "I shouldn't have come... I should've called you... I should've—"

Jim swung around and took her in his arms. "Hey, hey, shhh...c'mon, it's fine that you're here. I just wish I could've helped...or at least been there for you." He stroked her hair as she sobbed, his own eyes stinging with unshed tears.

~~~~~

Felicity relaxed into Jim's arms. It felt good to be there again. She had missed the feeling of being loved, *really* loved. Even though she knew that there was no way he could possibly love her now. Not after everything that had happened over the past few years.

"Felicity...I just want to ask you something." He pulled her away from his body and looked into her eyes, his only showing signs of regret and pain. She looked up at him, blinking through the blur of her tears. She had been doing a lot of crying lately, especially on the journey here. It probably showed. "Why wasn't I invited to attend Edgar's funeral?"

Felicity stepped away, her own guilt and regret pulling at her insides as she dropped her eyes to the floor. "I'm so sorry, Jim. I *wanted* to speak to you...to tell you what had happened, but Mum...she just insisted that you were kept away. She said it was too far for you, and that you wouldn't have come anyway."

"Hang on. You *know* how much I loved him. *Both* of you know that. You know I would've moved fucking mountains to be there! How could you let her keep me away? What is her fucking problem with me? I just don't get what I ever did to her." The volume of his voice rose exponentially with his evident anger. His fists clenched by his sides.

"Jim, I tried to convince her," Felicity pleaded. "*Honestly* I did. She was just so adamant. And she was grieving. I couldn't argue, Jim. That's why I am here now."

"Well, you can tell her a big fucking thank you from her favourite ex-fucking-son-in-law for taking away my chance to say goodbye to someone I fucking loved!" His anger-filled voice cracked as his tears flowed freely now. Felicity broke down again. She was a jellified mess. Her whole body shuddered with every pain filled sobbed.

~~~~~

Jim regretted shouting at her. It wasn't really her fault. Her mother had, yet again, interfered in their lives. He couldn't comfort her though. He didn't feel able. He just watched for a few minutes as she let all of her sorrow pour out.

Once she had begun to calm, he walked to the window where he looked out over toward the loch. The snow had begun to fall heavily and in the short space of time since Felicity had arrived. The road had completely covered. Unless she left immediately, it rendered her stranded. Looking over to the little island in the distance he could see that visibility was low and so realistically leaving now wouldn't even be an option. Plus, he could hardly kick her to the curb whilst she was in this state.

Great. Now what would happen? The snow had been predicted, but he had no clue it would get so deep so fast. He let out a long huff.

She stood and joined him at the window. She threw her arms up in exasperation. "Oh shit! What am I going to do now? I can't drive in this!" Her hands rested on her hips and she shook her head. "This is just perfect. Perfect," she sighed.

He continued to stare out of the window watching the glistening flakes floating down, down to the water, pavement and road below creating a sparkling white canvas as they settled.

Eventually he spoke. "Where were you supposed to be staying?" His voice was devoid of emotion, and he didn't turn to face his ex-wife.

"I hadn't booked anywhere… I figured I would just speak to you and then set off back home…maybe stay somewhere on the way home if I got tired."

"You can't possibly think it's a good idea to drive all this way and back again straight off." He snorted. "And anyway I'm afraid it looks like you won't be going anywhere." He turned to face her. "You can either stay here in ma spare room or you can walk down to the pub… They have rooms there." He made no attempt to convince her either way. Frankly, at this point he didn't much care.

"Do you have to be somewhere? Do you have anyone who is expecting you? I don't want to keep you from anything. I can stay at the pub if that's better. I don't want to cause you any problems," she rambled.

Jim clenched his jaw as he glanced at her. "Look, Felicity, I said you can stay. If you want to stay, then stay. I've got to go next door and open up the coffee shack. I'm late opening as it is." He turned and left her standing by the window. He grabbed his Arran sweater, scarf, and coat and pulled on his boots. "Make yourself at home. I only open until two on Saturdays through winter, but I doubt there'll be much demand today, so I'll be back later." He left the house, closing the front door behind him.

~~~~~

Felicity stared at the door. Jim had been so cold toward her, but she couldn't blame him for that. She had just broken his heart all over again. She was good at that, almost to the point of it being an art form.

After bringing her bag in from the car and making the decision to stay the night, she went upstairs to locate the spare room. Jasper followed closely behind as if he, too, appeared to be intrigued as to why she was here.

Jim's cottage was very pretty. The open fire gave the lounge such a warm cosy feeling. The stairs ascended from the lounge, and the kitchen/diner was to the right of the stairs. He had decorated the place simply but very tastefully.

Felicity opened a door to find what was clearly his room. The large, brass framed, double bed dominated the space. The bedding was pale blue and striped, and the walls were white. The pretty curtains matched the bedding and there was a thick, sumptuous throw blanket across the foot of the bed. She was impressed at how cosy and homely the cottage was. She scanned the room for photographs and clues as to what he had been up to in the last few years.

On a chest of drawers in the corner of the room, she spotted a collection of frames. She wandered over to take a closer look. There were photos of Jim and his parents, Jim and his kid brother, Jim and a mystery woman, and right at the back, Jim and Felicity. It was a photo taken at university on graduation day. They were laughing and holding each other. Seeing the photo brought a swell of emotion, and she left the room as quickly as she could.

The next room was a bathroom with a large roll top bath complete with a large hand held shower attachment. He had gone all out to make a luxurious room to relax in. It really was beautiful. The bath was big enough for two. She sighed and closed the door. The final door was the spare room. There was a white framed double bed with apple green and white spotted bedding. It was fresh and bright without being overly feminine, or masculine for that matter. She placed her bag on the floor and lay down on the bed, suddenly feeling drained both physically and emotionally. She covered her eyes with her arm and began to sob again. The rest of the bottled up emotion of the past few weeks over spilled and her body shuddered. Jasper had followed her and sat expectantly beside her head. She rolled over to face him and he tried to lick her nose.

"Oh Jasper… Why has it all gone so horribly, horribly wrong?" She nuzzled his fur and began to cry again. Eventually she cried herself to sleep with Jasper on the floor beside her.

~~~~~

"Felicity…Felicity…" She awoke to find Jim standing at the foot of the bed.

She sat bolt upright. "Oh heck, Jim, I'm so sorry, I must've dozed off." She rubbed her sore eyes.

"No need to apologise. Nothing's spoiling. You look like shit though." His face remained impassive.

"Thanks." He had never spoken words like that to her before and even though there was an element of truth in them, it hurt.

"I've made coffee. Want some?" He walked back to the door. "And I've made some food, too, if you're hungry." He didn't turn around but kept on walking and headed downstairs.

She got a terrible sinking feeling in her stomach. He *really* didn't want her here.

After Felicity had washed her face and freshened up, she made her way down to the kitchen where the aroma of something delicious tantalised her taste buds, making her salivate and making her tummy growl in anticipation.

"I made a steak pie. I hope you like that. If not I can rustle you up a sandwich." Jim stood at the stove ready to dish out the food.

"Oh yes, pie. That's lovely, thanks." She smiled and sat down at the little beaten up old table which sat against the opposite wall to the white pot sink. "I'll get out of your way as soon as the snow clears, Jim. I...I don't want to impose."

"Aye, well...you'll not be going anywhere for a few days. I've been listening to the local news. The roads are blocked. The snow's been pretty heavy all afternoon. There are severe weather warnings throughout this part of Scotland. And they're saying don't travel unless it's an absolute necessity." He didn't smile or show any emotion at all for that matter. Felicity felt increasingly unwelcome and uncomfortable. Anxiety and anger built inside of her. Why was he being so cold? What was the point?

She slammed her hands on the table and stood to face him. "Look, Jim. I know this is not ideal and I'm the last person you want in your house...*and* in your life...but I can't help the fact that I'm stuck here! I don't like it any more than you do. So would you just *stop* being so fucking cold and mercurial? I can't fucking deal with it right now! I *know* I hurt you. I can't take that back. I wish I could, okay?

I hate feeling like this! It's fucking awful. I can't deal with it! I can't deal with you treating me like some evil fucking bitch, Jim! It's not fucking fair! And I hate swearing and you've made me swear!" she screamed at him, her arms flailing as she went toward him, hell bent on slapping him, all of her pent up anger and frustration seeping out of every pore.

He caught her by the wrists before she had the chance to make contact with his face. "Have you finished?" he asked calmly, still holding her wrists but not tight enough to hurt her.

Her chest heaved as if she had just completed a marathon. He held her gaze, his eyes steady and his face too close to hers for comfort. She began to calm down as tears cascaded, leaving glistening trails down her heated face.

She sobbed. "I'm so sorry…please forgive me…for everything, Jim. I'm such a mess. I'm sorry for everything…so, so sorry." She rested her head on his chest and clung on to his shirt.

He encircled her in his arms and let her cry for what felt like an eternity. Being in his arms again felt like being home. A feeling which she knew there was no point acknowledging. He smelled of the same cologne that he always used to wear.

~~~~~

Jim stroked her hair. Having her here was unsettling. This was *his* place. There had been no memories of her here and that was a good thing. Not anymore. She looked great, beautiful in fact, despite the puffy eyes and dark circles. Her familiar perfume filled his nostrils making him feel melancholy as he was almost transported back in time to when he was *meant* to hold her in his arms. He stamped on the train of thought, bringing himself reluctantly back to the present. She shuddered in his arms.

He hated that he had been the cause of her tears. "C'mon…let's eat, eh? Before it gets cold."

She lifted her face from his chest. There was a huge wet patch of tears and mascara where she had been pressed against him.

She giggled. "Whoops….sorry Jim, I think you may need to wash your shirt."

He looked down and smiled in return. "Aye…looks that way."

~~~~~

They ate in silence for a while. Jim got up only to grab a bottle of red wine and two glasses. He poured them both a large measure. "Don't know about you but I reckon we need this," he said as he held up his glass to take a large swig.

Smiling, she did the same. "So…what have you been up to since we last saw each other? Have you…met anyone…special?" *Why the hell am I asking that? I don't want to know that!* He frowned at her as if to ask her the same question she was asking herself. But after thinking for a few minutes he turned the question on her.

"Why…have you? You know…met someone?"

She smirked at his avoidance of the question. "Not since Rory." She pushed her plate away.

He huffed. "I knew it."

"What do you mean?" She scrunched her face.

"I knew you'd end up with him." He pushed his own plate away now, his face very serious. "He was exactly your type."

"Jim, nothing happened until after you and I...until after...it was after we had split."

"So you say you've not met anyone *since* Rory? What happened with him?"

Felicity began to recount the not so pleasant details of her affair with Rory Fitzsimmons, which started in February 2010, the affair that, in effect, gave her a taste of her own medicine. And it was a bitter medicine to swallow.

Chapter 8

February 2010 — One Year After the Break-up

"Good afternoon, Mr. Hamilton. Are you on the lookout for another piece?" Felicity heard Franco Nilsson ask the tall, swarthy looking man as he perused the latest works on display in the gallery. She sneaked a peek around the wall.

"Ah, good afternoon, Nilsson. No, actually I'm on the lookout for your rather stunning International Art Dealer."

"Am I to presume you mean Ms. Johnston-Hart and not our intrepid Daniel Perkins?" Franco laughed at his own joke. The well-spoken client simply ignored him and carried on.

"Is she in?" He looked rather perturbed now as if he felt he was being deliberately delayed. As he was finishing his question, Felicity came through from the back room of the gallery carrying a briefcase and a file. Her heart began to beat a little faster when she saw Rory standing in the gallery. Rory was everything she wanted in a man (or so she thought). He was tall, good looking, ambitious, wealthy, and intelligent and to top it off he had a very prestigious career and a sports car.

Rory was a university rugby star and successful lawyer at Jenkinson-McLeary Solicitors. She had heard that he was hoping to make partner in the firm at a young age and that he worked long hours to ensure that he was first in line should the opportunity present itself. He was five years older than her and had made her acquaintance whilst purchasing artwork for his home and office from the gallery she worked at after leaving Oxford. He had followed her to her next gallery to purchase more artwork. She'd thought that perhaps he had a crush on her. Why else would he follow her to another gallery when Art and Soul had some wonderful pieces to tempt him? She had always thought him very handsome and charming. He was very tall, six foot five to be exact, a whole lot taller than she and four inches taller than Jim. He had very dark, almost black hair. He dwarfed Felicity and she quite liked it.

There had been a few coffee dates in the year since she split from Jim, but Rory had not made any attempts to kiss her or ask her out officially. He had hinted that he wanted her and had given her many compliments but seemed reluctant to take things any further. She had put it down to the fact that she was still *legally* married. He had offered her advice about divorce just after she had left Jim when he took her out for coffee on her request for his assistance. She had wondered for a while how she would feel underneath him in bed. Now that her divorce was final she hoped perhaps his attitude would change. Flirting with him had always been good, very exciting in fact. Even her mother approved.

"Rory! To what do I owe this unexpected pleasure?" She beamed at him from across the large, bright space.

"I was just in the area and so I thought I would come and insist on taking you out for a celebratory dinner." He gave her a lascivious grin. Under normal circumstances she would think him arrogant but this wasn't just *anyone*. This was *Rory Fitzsimmons*. No, she needed to make this one work. Her mother had met him at the gallery and had not stopped talking about him since.

She laughed. "I have nothing to celebrate though, it's not my birthday for two months…but funnily enough, I've just finished work. I'm on my way back to Polly's."

"Ah well you deserve to celebrate your decree absolute now that you're a free woman. Dinner is courtesy of yours truly. We'll go now." He was very insistent but she liked that. It made a refreshing change for a man to be so decisive and forthright.

"Okay, sounds good. Where shall we go?" Felicity blushed and tucked her hair behind her ear, realising that Nilsson was still observing their exchange.

"There's a delightful little Italian around the corner. Bella Roma? My friend Sal is the owner. I've booked a table for…ooh around about now." He said looking at his watch. Felicity made a bet with herself that it was an expensive designer watch. She would check later.

"Oh? And what if I'd have said no?" she teased.

"Pah! Don't be ridiculous. I knew you'd say yes, of course." *Hmm, okay a little arrogant.* She didn't comment aloud.

They made their way around to the Italian after dropping her briefcase and file in her car. Rory guided her into the restaurant, placing his hand at her lower back. Sal greeted them personally. He was a very handsome man with a goatee and floppy black hair. He seemed very friendly and made Felicity feel very welcome.

They chatted easily throughout their meal. And she managed to check out Rory's watch. *Yay! I was right.* She high-fived herself in her mind. Whilst they were finishing their drinks, Rory grazed her fingers with his own and gazed into her eyes. *This could be the night. Please let this be the night.* She prayed silently. Rory chatted briefly with Sal at the end of their meal and they said their goodbyes. Sal waved to her and gave the expected, "Ciao Bella!"

When they reached Rory's car he pulled Felicity into an embrace. "Right then, sexy. I want to get you home." The hunger visible in his eyes made her tingle. "I've wanted to kiss you for absolutely bloody ages but you were with that

John idiot, and as much as I hated him, I wasn't prepared to share."

That made Felicity uncomfortable. "Erm, his name is Jim and he wasn't an idiot—"

"He let you go, didn't he? That makes him a *prize* idiot in my book."

She felt a confusing combination of flattered and affronted at the same time, but his body was pressed up so close it was hard to think. "Now, come on. I want you in my bed."

"But…my car—" He stopped her mouth with a very full on, passionate kiss. She was rather shocked, but her legs weakened all the same. One hand held the back of her head and the other slid to her lower back, pulling her into him. *Gosh, so demanding.* She thought.

"Come on, sexy. You'll be staying at my place tonight," he insisted, thrusting his pelvis into her suggestively. She giggled like a teenager, eventually feeling rather silly, but the promise of what was to come hung in the air between them and she couldn't help feeling excited. Her car was locked in the compound behind the gallery and so she knew really that it would be very safe. She climbed into the passenger seat of Rory's sports car and he reached over and squeezed her thigh. Shivers traversed her body and she felt the heat rise quickly up her body and to her cheeks.

They arrived at Rory's stunning Georgian home and Rory came around to open her door for her. *Such a gentleman.*

Once inside the hallway of the house he closed the door and immediately grasped her in a strong embrace once again, pushing her up against the wall and invading her mouth with his tongue. She could hardly breathe and pushed him back. He released her and she gasped, her chest heaving.

"What's wrong? Have I got the wrong end of the stick here?" Rory was breathless too and a frown creased his brow.

"No…no…you just…surprised me. Can we take things a little slower, Rory? I don't mean to be a tease. It's just that I haven't…slept with anyone since…since Jim…well… Jim was my first so it's been a while."

He smiled and scooped her up in his arms. She gave a squeal as he did so. He chuckled at her reaction and proceeded to carry her up the first staircase.

"Rory! What are you doing?" She wasn't sure if she liked how things were progressing. She knew she found him very attractive physically and she *did* want to have sex with him, but he was maybe a little too dominant for her liking…or *was* he? She had somehow lost the ability to think straight.

"I think we should remedy your situation. Don't you?" He kissed her and smiled as he placed her back on her feet…in his bedroom.

~~~~~

She awoke at eight the following morning, naked in Rory's bed. She stretched feeling every muscle in her body ache. Even muscles she didn't realise she had ached. He had been very attentive. Completely different to Jim, but perhaps that was a good thing. The last thing she wanted was to be remembering Jim every time she made love with Rory. Although, calling it *making love* was perhaps a little optimistic. Rory had made her come twice, but he was a little rougher than she was used to, *fun* but rough. She hoped he had different levels of intensity otherwise she may struggle to function normally if their fledgling relationship made it past the starting blocks.

Rory walked into the bedroom carrying a tray of coffee and croissants. He was completely naked. She sensed that without a doubt he was *very* comfortable in his own skin. He placed the tray on the bed as she let her eyes roam over his body. He hadn't looked as she had imagined. He was broad and had fairly muscular arms and shoulders, which *was* to be expected as a former rugby player, but he was a little soft around his middle. He wasn't sculpted like Jim. Jim's abs were defined and his biceps were strong and rounded and his pecs... *Dammit! Why am I doing this to myself?* She shook her head to remove the unwanted invasion of images and pulled the sheet up over her breasts.

Rory pouted. "Awww, not fair! Pull that sheet back down! I love your tits. They're magnificent. You should just walk round topless all day."

She giggled nervously, unsure what she could actually say in response to *that* comment. Presumably that was his attempt at a compliment, but it was different to the compliments he had given her prior to their sexual encounter and she couldn't help feeling objectified.

He scratched the stubble forming on his chin. "In fact if you moved in with me I could just look at them all the time." He laughed.

Felicity inhaled sharply as if she had been stung. "I'm sorry, what?" She could have sworn he had just suggested that she should move in with him.

"Well...it's silly for you to live at Polly's really. You might as well move in with me. Then we can fuck all the time. Like bunnies. And I can look at your tits!"

All the talk of fucking and tits had begun to have an effect on him. He had that look in his eyes again. But it was having a *negative* effect on her. *Although he must have feelings for me, right? Surely he must if he's suggesting something so committed as moving in?*

"I...think it's a bit too soon, Rory. Don't you?" She found his humour very forward and very lewd. But she was willing to try to get past that. Perhaps if they got to know one another better first? "You can't just ask me to move in because you like my *breasts*." She emphasised her preferred word.

"Blah, blah. We'll talk about it later. Now come here my little love muffin and bring those gorgeous tits!" He pulled her toward him.

~~~~~

Against her better judgement, Felicity arrived at Rory's large, three storey Georgian home with her suitcases two weeks after their first *date*. Although he had asked her to move in rather quickly after they had started seeing each other, she had decided, with more than a little encouragement from her mother, to throw caution to the wind.

Penelope had almost had kittens, she had been so excited to hear her daughter had been asked to move in with such a wealthy, handsome, well-to-do man. She had thought it terribly romantic and immediately began trying to convince Felicity of the same. Eventually she had agreed with her mother and one morning after breakfast she had told him she would move in.

Expecting him to be overjoyed, she was a little shocked and tried to put out of her mind the fact that he said, "Yes, yes, it will better if you're living here, then I don't have to drive you home after we've had a couple of bottles of Rioja and a good shag." Laughing heartily as if there was nothing wrong in it. He liked to say *fuck* and *tits* quite a lot, which Felicity was trying to get used to, but it made her feel ever so slightly nauseated. But she resolved to make this work. She would change him. She *had* to.

He had helped her bring her bags in and had left her to it. He ordered a takeaway and opened a bottle of his favourite wine, a nice expensive vintage Rioja. Only the best would do for Rory. When they had got to bed that night, Rory had wasted no time in running his large, rough hands all over her body, even though she really just wanted to sleep.

She did something she had *never* done before and faked an orgasm just so that he would leave her to sleep. Sadly it didn't work. It just seemed to spur him on until he was on top of her seeking his own gratification. She felt rather like a bouncy castle with a puncture and yawned quietly on several occasions. When he was done, he kissed her on the nose affectionately and whispered, "Night-night wobbly arse. I'll wake you in the morning for round two." He squeezed her bottom, rolled over and went to sleep.

Perfect, night one and I'm already regretting this. But he was, on the surface, so right for her. She could look past his little idiosyncrasies. Couldn't she?

And so it went on.

She spent an awful lot of time on her own during the evenings and that was saying something considering she worked late herself. Some nights he didn't roll in until midnight, stinking of whiskey, and he always expected a quick fumble.

She began painting again, setting up a makeshift studio in one of the many spare bedrooms. She really began to enjoy it again. She hadn't realised how right Jim had been when he had told her a couple of years before that she wasn't herself unless she was painting. She began to work on a piece that just came to her. It wasn't from a scene she had memorised through the glass like the others she had painted in the past. This was a place she could see in her mind's eye. It felt familiar yet almost invented simultaneously; it was a place that she hoped one day to discover was a real place that she could visit, a peaceful, beautiful place where she could sit and breathe in the fresh air whilst feasting on the scene before her. But for now she would settle for putting the scene on canvas.

"Hi, wobbly arse! I'm home!" He shouted as he came in from the office at almost midnight one August evening in 2011. She was still painting in her makeshift studio. He came in and stood behind her as she worked on the piece. "Hmmm, not bad...not bad. Not as good as the stuff you sell in that gallery of yours but a nice little try all the same."

Patronising, insulting bastard. She cringed as he had slid his ice-cold hands up her T-shirt where, to his delight judging by the groan, he found she was braless. He began playing with her nipples as she tried to push him off and continue on with her piece. This so-called relationship just wasn't what she had hoped for or expected. There was no tenderness. In his opinion, showing emotions was for poofs and mummy's boys, as he so eloquently put it. She had realised awhile ago that it was going nowhere, but her mother's face just lit up every time they visited. And Rory knew how to charm her.

"C'mon, I'm really randy. I *really* need sex with my little sexpot. You know I make you feel good. Don't tease me, wobbly arse. Come on."

He ground his groin into her back making her over balance. She lurched forward into her easel, the paintbrush still in her hand. She landed on all fours, her paint-covered hands landing in the middle of her freshly painted canvas, smearing the wet paint, putting a hole in it and ruining the piece completely.

"Phwooooar...now that's what I like...you dropping on all fours and being ready for me as soon as I want it." He laughed dropping to the floor behind her and groping her breasts again.

She hit out behind herself. "You've ruined it! You stupid idiot! You've ruined my painting!" She pushed him back and stood up, tears welling up in her eyes. He stood, too, staring angrily at her, his fists clenched by his sides. "You idiot...I can't believe it...all that work...all those hours...you bloody idiot!" She shook her head as sobs broke free.

"Who are you calling an idiot, you bitch?!" He slapped her face, a loud crack resounding around the room. She stood open-mouthed gaping at him in utter shock, holding her cheek. It stung like crazy where his hand slammed against her jaw. He looked shocked at his own actions, but made no effort to comfort her.

She gritted her teeth and seethed at him. "I am going to collect my things and go," was all she could muster up the courage to say, scared he would hit her again if she were to say anything else.

He snorted. "Oh come on, wobbly arse. It was one little slap. And you've got to admit you were out of fucking line back there!" He followed her up the stairs into the bedroom.

Tears were streaming down her face making the sting even keener. She wiped her hands on some toilet roll to get rid of the excess paint and grabbed her suitcase from under the bed.

"I can't have hurt you. I didn't *mean* to hurt you."

She turned and saw regret in his eyes but it was simply too late. "Rory, please just leave me to pack," she croaked between sobs.

"You're such a moody cow. Do you know that?" He pulled the tie from around his neck and threw it onto the bed, slumping onto the mattress. "I mean, that painting wasn't that bloody good and look at you, all boo hoo hoo, you ruined my crappy little painting,'" he mocked.

She shook with anger. "Rory, please...just leave me alone."

"No I won't leave you alone." He sounded like a sulking schoolboy, whining because he'd been told to tidy his room. "I invited you to share my home... I gave you a room to paint in for fuck's sake! And this is how you repay me? By leaving?" He huffed. "Well, that's just bloody charming. Is this how you show gratitude, eh?"

She stopped what she was doing and turned to face him.

"Gratitude?" She snorted derisively. "Rory, I have lived here for almost a year and half. A year and a half of my life that I will *never* get back. In that time, I have spent more time with Madge, your cleaner, than I have with you. You come home late, smelling of alcohol and cigarette smoke and expect me to just part my legs for you, whether I'm in the mood or not. You *never* take me out. You *never* tell me you love me. YOU CALL ME WOBBLY ARSE FOR CRYING OUT LOUD!" she shouted at him.

"It's a term of affection!" He defended himself, obviously trying to laugh it off.

"You belittle the *one thing* I have had a passion for since I left Jim. And then to top it off, you push me into one of my pieces, ruining it beyond recognition, slap me, and then mock me for being upset!" She began shoving items of clothing, footwear, and toiletries into her case again. Her voice was loud and she knew she sounded strung out. "I'm an intelligent woman! I can't believe I stuck this for so long'" She laughed dryly at herself. "I will have someone call for the rest of my stuff as soon as possible." She stomped past him and down the stairs collecting her car keys from the hall table.

"That's it...you just sod off! You leave everyone, don't you? Don't stick to anything! Yeah well, I can get laid wherever and whenever I bloody want so you'll easily be replaced!" he shouted after her.

She stopped in her tracks and with as much venom as she could muster she shouted back, "Is that so? Well, for *your* information you fat pig, it helps if you know what to *do* with your *actual prick*. It's no use just *acting* like one!" She slammed the door behind her getting away from there as quickly as she could.

Chapter 9

Jim sat in a stunned silence once Felicity had finished regaling him with the delights of her failed relationship with Rory Fitzsimmons. Hearing about her sexual exploits with another man, especially such a disrespectful one, made him feel extremely uncomfortable. There was such a thing as too much information and this had certainly been one of those cases. He didn't quite know what to say and so silence seemed to be the best option until he could figure it out.

Eventually, he huffed out a long breath. "Shit...I can't believe he slapped you." He shook his head trying to allow this new information to sink in. "It's a good thing I didn't know about it at the time. I'd have killed him."

"I was just glad to get away from him. I was such a fool... I thought I loved him. He was wealthy. He had the huge house, the sports car, expensive suits. It was all a joke. They were all just *things*...things to make a statement, status symbols. He had no feelings for anyone but himself. Well, not until I left and he realised that he did actually love me in his own way. He used to call me at Polly's telling me he would kill himself if I didn't go back to him. Apparently, he was going to jump off London Bridge."

"And what did you say to that?" Jim enquired, frowning.

She smirked and covered her eyes with her hand. "I asked him if he'd like me to give him a push."

Jim burst out laughing. "Ahhh, such compassion... I love it!" He chuckled and she joined him in laughter.

"Well, you know…he was a big bloke… He might have needed a bit of a push outwards to stop him hitting his head on the concrete on the way down!" They both fell about laughing uncontrollably at the rather macabre discussion.

Felicity and Jim chatted late into the evening until she began to yawn. She was eager to ask him again about his love life, seeing as she had been so open about hers but she decided it could wait for another time perhaps.

"Hey, you look exhausted, Felicity. You should get to your bed," Jim told her as he placed their empty glasses in the sink.

She yawned again and rubbed her eyes. "Mmm, I think so." She stood to make her way to the stairs but turned. "You've stopped calling me Flick," she observed not making eye contact.

"Aye…just like you wanted. I've had to change a lot of things over the past couple of years, eh?" His face was impassive again as he spoke. He had also acquired the ability to switch off his emotions it would appear.

"Yes…yes I know you have… It's just that…I kind of miss being called Flick." She rested her head on the doorjamb as she felt a wave of sadness wash over her.

"Aye…well…goodnight, eh?" Jim appeared to be willing her to go to bed as if he wanted the conversation to come to a close.

She took the hint and went to bed.

~~~~~

Jim stepped out into the sub-zero temperature with a very reluctant dog in tow. He pulled his woolly hat down further over his ears and zipped his coat right up as far as it would go.

"C'mon, Jasper. I know it's cold, pal, but a dog's gotta do what a dog's gotta do." He scratched Jasper's head and began to walk, hoping that the cold air would clear his head of the fog, sadness, and perplexity that he was now plagued with thanks to the unwelcome visitor.

Jasper obediently followed close behind, stopping every so often to sniff the air. Jim paused momentarily and looked out over the water. The distant mountains were enveloped in snow and the little whitewashed cottages in the village were now camouflaged against the thickening achromatic covering. Although it was nighttime, the snow reflected the moonlight, making it feel earlier than it was. The icy air nipped at his skin and numbed his senses.

~~~~~

Back at the house Felicity lay awake replaying her last days of married life and how she had treated Jim. There was really no wonder he was struggling to be cordial now. She had put him through so much.

Full of regret and with the heaviest of hearts she allowed warm tears to fall as she rolled onto her side wondering if and how she could possibly make amends.

~~~~~

Jim awoke to the smell of bacon drifting up through the floorboards. His stomach grumbled appreciatively. It was clear that Felicity was trying to make herself useful. He stretched and lay there for a few moments longer until there was a light knock on his door.

The door was pushed open slightly but she didn't enter. "Ahem...Jim? Erm...I made breakfast." She almost whispered.

"Aye, I can smell it. Smells delicious. I'll be down in a minute, Felicity."

"Okay…I made fresh coffee too." She was silent a moment. "I'm afraid the snow's still really bad."

"Aye, it tends to stay awhile when it settles in. No bother. You'll just have to stay as long as the snow's here." What other choice did he have than to make it as amenable for them both as possible? There was no point in suffering through a negative atmosphere. It wouldn't change things.

"Thanks, Jim… I appreciate it." She rested her head on the door for a few seconds as if she was going to say more. She clearly thought better of it and walked away, returning to the kitchen.

A few minutes later, after pulling on a T-shirt and jeans, he walked in and was greeted by a plate of chunky bacon sandwiches. *Perfect*. His stomach made its desire known with another loud growl. He pulled up a chair and sat.

He cleared his throat. "Thanks for this Felicity. I don't expect you to wait on me whilst you're here though, you know."

"Hey, it's the least I can do, Jim. Tuck in and enjoy." She smiled taking a bite. It felt strange. Almost like they were still married and were on a mini break in a little cottage somewhere.

She chewed thoughtfully for a while. He watched her discreetly. It was obvious something was playing on her mind. Eventually she opened her mouth to speak.

"So…I told you about my failed relationship with Rory. What's your story since we split?"

Jim raised his eyebrows. "Whoa! Don't hold back, Felicity…ask away!"

She frowned as though she felt regretful. A twinge of guilt dug at him. He felt frustrated that she had even asked as it wasn't really a subject he felt comfortable talking about with her. He sat silently chewing for a number of minutes, trying to figure out what to say.

~~~~~

Felicity gathered the courage to look at him. Instead of the usual impassive mask, however, was a look of frustration…or confusion…some unreadable emotion. She wanted to take the question back. She was on the verge of apologising when he spoke.

"There is someone. Well, there *was*," he finally admitted. Felicity's heart sank. "She's not from around here. She travels around with a band. She plays the fiddle. They've stayed up on the campsite out back a fair few times. Mainly through the summer. Her name's Heather. We…get along really well, but we've never…ahhh…you know…we're not *together* as such."

"Oh…right." Felicity nodded trying her best to process the new information without showing her true feelings. "Where is she from?"

"She lives in the Borders. Near Jedburgh. It's a fair trek really. That's why we only see each other when she comes up with the Ceilidh band. I've got my work here and she spends most of her life on the road. They've done a few functions in the hotel along the way. The band is quite well known and very successful. They travel all over Europe in fact."

"Oh…gosh… What's she like…Heather?" Felicity asked, not really sure she should ask or indeed if she truly wanted to know but too intrigued not to.

"Ahhh, she's quite petite, slim, long dark hair, naturally wavy. Very pretty. Blue eyes." Jim looked almost wistful as he spoke. He drifted off into a kind of trance. Felicity wondered what he was thinking about…

~~~~~

August 2011 — Two Years and Six Months After the Break-up

"Hi, Heather. Have you guys got everything you need up there?" Jim asked the guest as she walked down from the small campsite at the back of his cottage.

"Aye, Jim. We're all sorted. We're not playing until tomorrow night so we're going to have a barbeque if you'd like to join us?" She smiled, her azure blue eyes sparkling with warmth as she spoke.

It was a warm August evening and perfect weather for a cook out. Jim and Heather had known each other for around a year now. There was a definite spark of attraction between them but both were shy. Heather inherently so, which was surprising considering her profession, but Jim's was an acquired shyness since his failed marriage had knocked his confidence.

The band laughed and chatted as they stood around near the brick barbeque that Jim had installed not long after moving in to the cottage. It was the perfect addition to his little campsite. The heat from the barbeque was welcomed now it was late evening and the temperature had dropped. Jim and Heather sat drinking bottled beer on the log bench also constructed by Jim, who had acquired many hands-on skills since the move. Heather shivered audibly.

"Hey, I heard that. Here you go." Jim slipped of his jacket and placed it around her shoulders.

"Thanks, Jim. You're so sweet." She smiled gratefully pulling the jacket around her. "Why are you not married?" The question was meant to be rhetorical but regardless of the fact, Jim opened up and explained all about Felicity and the divorce. Heather listened intently. It felt good to talk about things with someone who was removed from the situation.

"Wow. I'm surprised that happened to you. You're…such a nice guy. It doesn't seem fair." She shook her head in disbelief. Jim smiled at her comments. Why couldn't things between him and Heather be easier…less complicated. And why couldn't the distance be less? Eventually Jim decided to call it a night. Heather walked down to the house where the small shower block was situated.

"Thanks for the jacket." Heather said handing it back to him. As he took the jacket back, their fingers grazed. He took her hand and held onto it, weaving his fingers into hers.

He sighed. "I wish you didn't live so far away."

"Oh? Why's that, Mr. MacDuff?" She cocked her head to one side giving a half smile up at him. He stroked her cheek.

"I just…I think…never mind." He shook his head realising there was no point elaborating. Heather placed both hands on his chest and tiptoed so that her face was just below his. He gazed down at her, lowering his head until their lips were almost touching.

"Heather…how could this work? You live so far away and you travel so much I would never see you and—"

She placed her hand on his lips. "Shhh, Jim. Some things are just not meant to be, no matter how much we'd like them to happen. So…just kiss me."

With that he lowered his lips to meet hers. Her hands slipped up around his shoulders and his found her waist. The kiss was light but wonderful and over far too soon. Heather turned and walked back toward the campsite, looking over her shoulder and smiling at him, her long chocolate brown hair floating almost in slow motion as she walked. In that moment she reminded him of Arwen, the beautiful Elf from *Lord of The Rings*, and his heart ached just a little knowing that she would never really be his.

~~~~~

Felicity cleared her throat and then spoke to bring him back to her from wherever he had drifted off to. "You seem to really like her. Don't you think you'll find a way to make it work?"

"No. It wouldn't be fair to tie her down. She's not a homebody like me." He smiled as he spoke, his eyes tinged with sadness. "But I will say one thing." He looked directly at Felicity now. "Although I know I won't ever be with Heather, she's given me the hope that there *can* be someone else." He breathed out loudly. "When you and I split...I felt that I could never love anyone else...never let anyone else get close... Heather made me realise that I could. That it's possible. There *is* hope for me yet."

Felicity felt her eyes sting with tears. She hated herself for making him feel he couldn't love again. Although, hearing him speak about being with someone else cut her in a way she never prepared for. But it was always a possibility that he would have moved on. She had. Albeit temporarily.

~~~~~

Jim glanced over and saw a pained look in Felicity's eyes. He never intended his words to hurt her. He had to try and break this melancholy that had descended over them.

"Anyway, enough of that. Look, I'll have to work whilst you're here and...it's looking like you may be here a while.

I cannae leave the shack closed, I'm afraid. It's a lifeline for some of the villagers and I cannae let them down. What are you going to do whilst you're here?"

"Well…I have my laptop and so I could maybe do a little work…send some emails…do some research."

Jim laughed at this remark. "I hate to break it to you Felicity, but I'm afraid I don't have wifi *or* the Internet. I've never gone in for all the Facebook and Twitter stuff. And I just never saw the point in tapping away at a keyboard whilst my hands are still able to hold a pen to write my letters." He chuckled.

"Don't you write anymore? How do you not do that?! Writing was so important to you." She looked gobsmacked.

"Aye, I have a typewriter…and I've got a little word processor and a printer. They're pretty much obsolete but I get by. They're all I need really. No one is ever going to read my work. I only do it for enjoyment."

"Good grief, Jim! You're in the dark ages." Felicity laughed.

"Nope. I'm in the *peaceful* ages." He laughed, too. "Seriously though, what are you going to do? You'll be bored stiff, knowing you. You don't like the same books as me so that's a no-no." He pondered for a moment. "Hey I know! Why don't you paint? You can do it the kitchen…or the lounge…I don't mind."

"Oh yeah, because there just happens to be a branch of Atlantis Art Supplies up the road." She snorted, evidently thinking his idea utterly ridiculous given their location.

"Felicity…you're in the Highlands now, don't forget, artists on every street. Leave it with me." He gulped down the rest of his coffee and grabbed his coat. "Back in a wee while." He disappeared out of the front door before she could protest.

~~~~~

Felicity stared in the direction Jim had just left in. She hadn't painted in earnest since the debacle of the ruined canvas and Rory. She hadn't admitted this to Jim however. Whilst she was left alone, save for the pair of big brown eyes attached the panting head resting on her knee, she thought back to the scene she had been painting that day. She could recall the colours and shapes and began to imagine reproducing it. Her excitement began to build.

Whilst Jim was gone, she wandered around the house. She examined the books on the shelves in the lounge. It was so cosy in there with its log burner and gnarled railway sleeper mantle. The walls were painted a warm buttermilk colour complemented by the thick gold and burgundy tapestry curtains. *Judging by the weather I bet these are a Godsend*, she mused as she held the textured fabric between her fingers. His artwork consisted of architectural drawings of various random buildings that she had never heard of. She had to admit, however, that they made very interesting viewing. The detailing was incredible and gave a real feel of what each building must look like.

Jasper lay upon the thick pile of the deep red rug gazing up at her. Every so often he would wag his tail expectantly, but Felicity was too busy gazing into the crackling, dancing flames and thinking back to another time, a time when she and Jim had spent Christmas in a little cottage by the sea in Lincolnshire. She was completely mesmerised by the flames and caught up in the memories that almost an hour later Jim's entrance made her jump, snatching her back, rather cruelly, from her reverie.

As the door opened and he stumbled in, arms full of treasures, he brought along a freezing cold breeze of air, which diffused through the ground floor quicker than she could pull her cardigan zip up.

"Look what I got!" He sounded like the Jim she remembered from Uni. Excited and giddy. She scrambled to her feet from the squishy old gold tapestry sofa and to his side to examine the haul. His giddiness was contagious and she clapped her hands enthusiastically.

"Good grief Jim. How many artists do you know?" Her jaw dropped as he placed the goodies on the sofa. There were canvases, brushes, acrylics, water colours, palettes, an easel, all good quality too. He clearly knew some very generous people.

"Quite a few. Miranda Helliwell just along the road sells her art in galleries throughout the area. Max West just a little further along, and then along the other way Jilly McDougal, she's an amateur but bought all the best stuff when she started. All very nice people, all wanted to help."

Felicity was lost for words. "Wow," was all she could manage. She could feel her heart begin to pound as she thought about getting started. *How well thought of he must be here.* She smiled. He deserved no less.

~~~~~

Jim smiled widely as he saw the flames ignite in Felicity's eyes. He knew that look. He knew that hunger and had seen it in her a million times before. He *knew* she missed this, missed painting. It was a part of who she was; he had always said so. His heart swelled as he watched her, the huge grin on her face. It made him happy to know he had helped put it there.

"Look…I have an old pair of dungarees and a T-shirt that you can borrow to wear whilst you paint. They're scruffy as hell, but I only ever wore them for gardening or decorating. They're yours if you want them."

Her eyes lit up. "Oh Jim, thank you!" She flung her arms around his neck and kissed his cheek. He froze. "This means so much to me. I can't really explain…but…it just…thank you." She clung to him. The smell of her delicious perfume drifted into his nostrils again, clouding his judgement and mocking him for days gone by. He lifted his arms to hug her back, but instead patted her back like he would an old friend.

"Aye well, get set up whenever you're ready." He released himself from her grip. "I'll be off next door. Lots to do." He smiled awkwardly and left her to begin.

Chapter 10

The coffee shack had begun as just that, a place to grab a coffee to go, popular with tourists passing through but over the last year it had expanded and become the village store when the *actual* village store closed due to the owner's ill health. Jim stocked all the essentials needed for such a situation as the current weather. He stood outside looking out over the snow-covered street. It was strange how the thick blanket had dulled every sound, making it audibly quieter. It didn't feel quite as cold now. The snow had not only insulated sound but had acted as a duvet to the loch-side village too, although it wasn't warm enough for the snow to melt away. Not yet.

He opened the shack and switched the heat on full. A steady stream of customers filed in through the doors during the morning. During a lull, Jim stood rubbing his hands together in front of the heater. The radio played in the background. He stopped moving as the lyrics of *Distance* by Christina Perri Featuring Jason Mraz floated around the small space. He stood, eyes closed, and absorbed the poetry for a few minutes, feeling a lump form in his throat. Distance from Felicity was something he had both enjoyed *and* endured in recent years, but that had all changed now.

Jilly McDougal breezed into the shack with a pink nose, forcing Jim to swallow the lump and put on his customer-friendly mask. "Hi, Jim. Please tell me you have some kindling left." The friendly middle-aged woman pouted at him.

"Hi, Jilly. You're in luck. I only have a couple of bags left. Everyone must be making the most of their open fires in this weather and I haven't had a chance to stock up since the weather turned." He lifted up a net bag and passed it over to her.

"No wonder! And my fire at home is a true Godsend in this weather. It's blowing a draft under every door in my house. Oh, by the way, did your lady friend like her art supplies?"

"Aye, she did, Jilly. Thanks ever so much for your help with that." Jim felt his cheeks warm at her choice of words. *Lady friend.*

"Oh good. If it puts a smile on that handsome face of yours, I'm all for it." Jilly blushed a little. "Bye, Jim."

"Bye, Jilly. Thanks again."

Once she had gone, he quickly checked on his stock levels. They were getting lower by every hour he was open. Switching the coffee machine on, he quickly counted the number of packs of powdered milk, candles, matches, and bags of kindling he had left. There was nothing he could do about it. There was no way out of, or into, the village at the moment. Luckily the villagers all rallied around a neighbour in need.

Felicity walked in, Jasper following behind. Jim was surprised she wasn't inside the cosy cottage starting a master piece.

"Hi…what are you doing out?" he asked as he wiped the coffee machine down in readiness. He noticed she was wearing one of his thicker coats. She was buried inside it as it if were eating her alive. He smirked a little.

"What's so funny?"

He didn't answer.

She shook her head and continued. "I thought Jasper and I could go for a walk. It looked so pretty out. I'll start my painting later. Wow…nice little shop. I had no idea you had diversified. I thought it was just coffee and tea."

"Na. It evolved. The villagers needed it and so I obliged." He poured her a coffee to go.

"Ooh, thanks." She wrapped her hands around the paper cup and its corrugated cardboard insulator sleeve. "I borrowed a pair of Wellington boots and a few pairs of socks. I hope that's okay?"

He looked down at her giant man feet and couldn't help but laugh. She looked at her feet too and blushed her famous cerise pink, giggling. He thought she looked absolutely adorable. She sipped the steaming coffee carefully. "You really seem settled here, Jim. It's obvious you care a lot about this place…and its people."

"Aye. It's all I ever wanted. To be myself and to be relaxed in my surroundings." He spoke without turning to look at her. He baulked as the words left his lips feeling immediately guilty for the dig about their past. He hoped she hadn't noticed.

"You never liked London, did you, Jim?" she asked in a small voice.

Dammit, she noticed.

"I don't think I need answer that, do you?" He turned to her now, making his eyes stern.

"No…no need at all. Look, I'll see you later." She smiled sadly and set out, calling Jasper to her side. Jim felt a sinking in his stomach. He really would have to try and be less abrasive with her.

~~~~~

The snow crunched beneath the Wellington boots which felt like ships on Felicity's feet. Jasper cavorted in the snow like a pup, his stubby legs disappearing with every touchdown and his tail wagging frantically. The sky was a bright cornflower blue but the hue was deceptive, a direct opposition, in fact, to the icy temperature making Felicity's breath into clouds of humidity.

Although the cold made her lungs sting, she couldn't help but breathe deep. The air may have been icy but it was fresh. There wasn't a hint of smoke or engine fumes to fill the spaces where fresh, crisp air belonged. Happiness washed over her as she watched children playing at the opposite side of the road. Their snowman was dressed in all of their parents' finery, and Felicity wondered how much of it had been taken without permission.

On several occasions she had to duck to dodge snowballs as they were thrown from one side of the street to the other between *rival* gangs of friends, laughing and shouting. Each time was followed by, "Sorry, lady!", to which she waved, a gesture to inform that she wasn't bothered by their game playing. A woman was walking toward her with a yellow Labrador. She smiled as she approached Felicity.

"Ahhh, hello there! I'm guessing you must be Felicity, Jim's friend?" the older, grey-haired lady said as they were about to pass, the dogs greeting each other like old friends.

"Yes…yes that's right. How did you know?" Felicity was intrigued.

"Well, for one, you have Jasper and for two you are wearing what I'm presuming are Jim's clothes!" She laughed, her eyes examining Felicity's oversized attire.

"Oh, yes of course!" She looked down at the sleeve ends where her hands would normally be. "And you are…"

"I'm Miranda. Jim called to see me earlier to borrow some art supplies for you."

"Oh yes. Thank you so much. You've been so kind. Too kind to a stranger such as me."

"Oh no, no, any friend of Jim's is a friend of mine. You'll find that with everyone here. He's very well thought of." She smiled. "We all just wish he'd find himself a wee lady and settle down...have bairns...you know?" She smiled at Felicity, clearly unaware of her status as Jim's ex-wife. "Aye, well, best be off, Jess needs her walk and I need to get back to my painting." She began to walk again but stopped. "Come over for coffee and a wee chat whenever you like. Jim will direct you. It'd be good to talk arty things with a fellow artist." She smiled and carried on.

"I will...thank you."

Felicity made her way back to the coffee shack. She could see Jim in the distance standing outside chatting to one of the villagers. Since her arrival, she had noticed that he looked so much more relaxed than he had done during the last year of their marriage. He looked younger and more bohemian. His beard was fuller but it suited him. Before, he was in the realms of designer stubble but now he had a full goatee. His hair was still thick and in shoulder length, shaggy layers, but it was smattered with flecks of grey now. He looked so comfortable in his chunky jumpers and scruffy jeans. He wore them well. He had always been a very attractive man and the attraction was still there, unfortunately. He had filled out too, but she had noticed that it was all muscle when he had removed his jumper the day before and exposed a little of his torso causing her mouth to water. He looked up and waved.

~~~~~

Jim watched her tramping toward him in her oversized clothing. "Nice walk?" he asked as his neighbour walked away complete with his bag of kindling.

"Yes, very bracing. Had to dodge a few snow balls." She laughed. There was the smile he remembered from years ago and that almost musical, infectious laugh. Her features had relaxed. "Were you planning anything for dinner? If not I thought maybe I could treat you to a nice meal at the hotel?"

He thought about it for a second. What harm could it do? They were two adults, admittedly with a complicated history, but nevertheless they were past all that. "Oh…aye…aye okay. That'd be nice. They have a nice menu. I don't eat there often. No point with it just being me." He shrugged. "Anyway, I'll be home in around an hour, so why don't you go get yourself showered and ready. You may still have to wear my Wellies. Snow's quite deep…and you look so fetching." He chuckled. He couldn't help but tease. Her cheeks coloured.

"Hey, cheeky!" She hit him playfully. "I'll go and get sorted and see you soon." Jasper dutifully followed Felicity back next door to the cottage.

~~~~~

Thankfully when they arrived at the Shieldaig Hotel, the fire was already roaring, giving a cosy, amber glow to the bar area. They hungrily perused the extensive menu in silence. Once their food was ordered, Jim brought a bottle of Pinot Noir over from the bar. A kind of shyness fell on the pair as they sat together in romantic surroundings but without the romantic attachment.

Felicity sighed, suddenly, as they sipped their wine. "Where did it all go wrong, Jim?"

"You want to talk about *that* now?" Jim was confused at her choice of conversational topic.

"It's on my mind I suppose."

Jim sighed and pondered a moment before speaking. "I didn't fit into your world." He shrugged. "And you wanted to find someone who did. I wanted you to be happy so I let you go." Jim gave his verdict in a nutshell. She visibly cringed at his matter-of-fact admission.

"So you take no responsibility?" she asked, frustration etched on her face.

He rolled his eyes. "Aye, well, I suppose I was to blame for the fact that I didn't fit into your world. But I loved you, Felicity. More than anything. It just…wasn't enough for you." He took a gulp of his wine, suddenly feeling too warm.

"You had so many possibilities ahead of you though, Jim. You graduated with a *first* from Oxford, for goodness sake. Why didn't you do something with it? Where was your ambition?" She took a large gulp of her wine. "I got so frustrated by your lack of ambition." She shook her head.

Jim clenched his jaw. "Felicity, you seem to forget that you had enough ambition for the both of us. Was it not enough that I supported everything you did? I never missed a function. I even wore suits!" He laughed incredulously. "All I wanted was to love you and have you love me enough. I guess it wasn't meant to be, eh? Like you said back then."

She shook her head. "I did love you. I was crazy about you. But…" She fiddled with her napkin. "I think I listened to my mum too much."

He thought he could see regret in her eyes.

"Your mum? Aye, she wasn't my biggest fan, eh? And still isn't by all accounts."

Felicity snarled. "Yeah, well, she's a total fraud."

"What do you mean by that?" Jim was intrigued by her harsh statement.

"Something I found out at the will reading. Something she had kept from me all these years."

Jim leaned forward unable to hide his interest. "Which was…"

"Her name. The stupid woman changed her name just to impress."

"Eh? Sorry, I don't follow?" Jim placed his elbows on the table. But before she could go into any detail their food arrived.

"Oh lovely. Smells delicious and I'm famished," she informed the waitress with a sweet smile.

"Enjoy." The young woman smiled back. "Hi Jim, how's Jasper?"

"Hi Sally, oh, he's fine. He's missing you. Be sure to pop round and see him soon, eh?"

The young woman blushed and tucked a stray strand of mousy brown hair behind her ear. "Oh, I will. Been a bit busy lately with my studies but I will pop round," she told him. She left them to their meal.

"Gosh do you know everyone?" Felicity asked.

He stabbed a piece of steak and held it to his mouth. "It appears so."

~~~~~

They finished their meal and headed back out in the freezing cold evening, back to the cottage. Felicity bent to fiddle with her boot, grabbed a handful of snow, and threw it straight at Jim's head. It hit with a thud and splattered into his hair.

"Whoa! You little swine!" He laughed, bending to seek his own ammunition. She dodged and caught him square on the back of the head with her second snowball.

"Right, that's it! This is war!" He picked up a huge handful of snow and ran toward Felicity, who tried to run away but slipped and landed on her bottom in the snow, thanks to the ridiculously large Wellington boots she was wearing. She let out a scream and Jim's assault struck. Snow slid down her back under her oversized coat and stuck to her hair. Jim slipped, landing half on top of her, and they both laughed, gasping for air as they lay in the snow-covered street.

They made eye contact and suddenly their position was not so funny. She searched his eyes as he breathed out puffs of breath, which clouded as the warm hit the cold.

Slowly his smile faded. He closed his eyes tight and leaned closer. She held her breath. She felt sure he was going to kiss her. But instead he leaned his forehead on hers and sighed, clenching his jaw.

"Come on. Let's get in where it's warm," he whispered. He shifted and held out his hand to pull her up. Feeling surprisingly disappointed, she took his hand and was immediately pulled to her feet. They brushed the snow from their clothes and went inside, both disappearing into separate bedrooms to change and emerging at the same time in their comfy clothing.

"I'll open another bottle of wine, eh?" he said as he headed toward the stairs.

She followed him and curled up in the old armchair beside the fireplace.

"Jim…this chair is the same as that scratty old thing Charles had in The Book Depository," she called through to the kitchen

"Aye…that's cause it *is* the scratty old thing from The Book Depository." He smiled as he walked back into the room. "It was my parting gift from Charles. He said it wouldn't look right without me sitting on it." He chuckled.

"Awww, that's so sweet." She felt a lump lodge in her throat and bit her lip to abate the threatening tears.

He poured them both a glass of wine and sat on the floor in front of the blazing fire. Jasper came and spread himself across Jim's legs.

"Ahem…earlier, you mentioned something about your mum but didn't finish telling me. Do you not want to talk about that anymore?" he tentatively asked, afraid that perhaps she had changed the subject deliberately.

"Hmmm. She drives me to distraction, Jim. Honestly, I let her influence me far too much when I was younger."

"I'm sorry but I have to agree with you there. I hope you don't mind me saying this, but she really was impressed by status and *things…possessions*. Your dad was completely different, so accepting. To be honest, I often wondered how they stayed together so long." Jim let the words fall from his mouth and then cringed. "Shit, Felicity, I'm sorry I shouldn't have—"

"Shouldn't have what, Jim?" she laughed bitterly. "Shouldn't have spoken the truth?" Her face became flushed with anger.

"What did she do to you that's so bad?" He was all ears now. Clearly Penelope had irked her daughter in some way…and badly it would seem.

"Well, she always used to tell me that I could do better…you know…when you and I… Jim, I didn't agree with her."

He raised his eyebrows. "Hmmm. Not at first, eh?"

"That's just it. She used to go on and on about social standing and making something of myself. She's made it her life's work to ensure that I get the very best. Including boyfriends. She turned her nose up at anyone who wasn't Oxbridge educated or about to be Oxbridge educated. She used to instil in me how important it was to be seen in the right places, to wear the right clothes, to have the right car, the right job. She even insisted I keep my own name when you and I married."

"I knew she was behind that." Jim shook his head.

"Well…it turns out that Mrs. *Posh-knickers* lied all along about her own upbringing! She always told me that my grandparents were wealthy but died in mysterious circumstances, and that's why she never received her vast inheritance."

"Aye…that's right…that's what you told me."

"Well…on the day of Dad's will reading it became very clear that *Penelope*…" She made inverted commas in the air. "Wasn't all that she seemed."

"I…I don't really get what you're—"

"*Janet.*"

Jim's face scrunched in utter confusion. "Felicity…what are you talking about? Who is Janet?"

"Janet is my mother, Jim!" Felicity was clearly angry. Her face flushed and her chest heaved. "She lied all along. About…everything!"

Jim rubbed his forehead. "You're going to have to explain. I'm sorry, I'm just confused."

"Not half as confused as I was. Right, where do I start? Probably the beginning, eh? Okay…she was born in the East End of London to a very poor family. She was christened Janet Mason. When she was seventeen she went on a job interview in the centre of London at a hotel and got the job as a receptionist. On accepting the job, she began telling people that her name was Penelope Brandon. She met Dad at the hotel when he was a guest. She lied to him, too." Felicity shook her head as she spoke the incredulous truth.

"She told Dad, and me for that matter, that cock and bull story about my grandparents when it turns out they both died quite young and left her nothing because they *had* nothing. There were no suspicious circumstances at all. She had basically disowned them through shame. She was ashamed of her own parents because they were poor, Jim. How sad is that? How cruel? Dad never met her parents. I have no idea how she managed to pull off the story for so long about being so wealthy."

Jim gaped in shock. "How did you find all this out?" He couldn't quite take it all in.

"The solicitor had found it out when he was doing the paperwork for the will! He called her Janet at the will reading. She went white. I wondered why. Afterwards I asked for an explanation. She broke down and told me everything. She cried such a lot and kept saying she was sorry. But afterwards it was as if everything was wonderful and she felt better for getting off her chest. Bloody great!" Felicity snorted derisively.

"Off her chest and onto my mind. Honestly, Jim I was so, so angry. I feel like I don't know my own mother. She lied to me all those years and then tried to make me *into her*. And it nearly worked. Thanks to her I lost my marriage…and…my… You weren't just my husband, Jim…. You were my *best friend*." She covered her face with her hands and her shoulders began to shudder as the pent-up anger and frustration connected to the ridiculous situation began to overflow.

Jasper jumped up as Jim moved forward to comfort Felicity. He held her wrists in his hands and pulled her hands away from her face. He looked into her sad gaze. She threw her arms around his neck. On his knees before her, he cradled her and allowed her to cry. Her anguish was palpable as she shook with the violent sobs that wracked her body. Jim stroked her hair as she cried.

Eventually, when she had calmed, he held her face in his hands and wiped her tears away with his thumbs. "Hey, you've been through such a lot lately. I'm angry with her, too. I'm angry that she put us in this situation. It was a horrible thing to do. No mother should do such a thing. But...she's still your mother and I guess deep down she thought she was doing the right thing. Don't let yourself get bitter and twisted about this, Flick, eh? It's not worth the stress. Just rise above it and move on. We both need to do that."

"Jim?"

"Yeah?"

She smiled. "You called me Flick."

He closed his eyes for a second. "Oh...sorry...I mean Felicity."

"No...I liked being Flick." She managed a small smile. She had liked being Flick and all it had entailed. "It takes me back. You know, to when you and I were actually okay."

"Aye...that's a long while ago, eh? But that's just it, Flick. We can't go backward...only forward."

"Oh...shit...I've just remembered. I have something for you." She jumped up from her chair and hurried upstairs, returning soon after with a large brown padded envelope.

Jim looked on in bemusement. "What the heck is that?" He scrunched his nose.

She sat back in the chair. "It's for you. It's from Dad. It was in the will that I bring it to you...personally." She sniffed.

"What is it?" Jim took the package. It was sealed very well.

"It's an incomplete manuscript. The last one he was working on before he passed away. He wanted you to have it. The solicitor said he would prefer it to be delivered by hand."

Jim held the package with both hands. "That's...really sweet. I have a little piece of him right here now. That's..." He stared at it, emotions washing over him and the sting of tears becoming apparent in his eyes. "I'll treasure it...always."

Jim made his excuses and went to bed. Felicity followed not too long after, to her own room.

~~~~~

The manuscript lay unopened at Jim's bedside. He was touched by the gesture. He would cherish this gift, would keep it sealed until he felt better equipped to read it. There were too many things going on right now. He drifted into a dream filled sleep.

Chapter 11

Jim opened his eyes and looked to his right. Felicity was stroking his bare chest delicately with one finger and watching him intently. When their eyes connected she pulled herself up to him and kissed him gently on the lips.

"Hey sleepyhead…I've been waiting for you to wake up." Confused, Jim tried to speak but she stopped him with a deep kiss. Her tongue slipped into his mouth and her hands caressed his chest and neck. It felt good to be with her again, like this. The room was glowing, bathed in the bright, early morning sunlight. Felicity sat, slipped off her white cotton nightie and straddled his torso. Her breasts were so beautiful in this light.

Still feeling confused, but deciding not to protest, he reached up and caressed her. She placed her hands on top of his as he worshipped first one beautiful, ambrosial mound of flesh and then the other. She moaned and let her head roll back. She gazed down at him, smiling. Her eyes warm. The ice had melted. She manoeuvred her body over him until he felt himself slide inside her. He gasped and closed his eyes. As she moved, he let out a deep groan.

"Jim…Jim…*Jim!*"

His eyes snapped open and he sat bolt upright. It had been a dream. *Fuck!* He cursed inwardly. He had let her get inside his head. *Not good…not good at all.*

"Jim, are you okay? You were moaning in your sleep and I was worried." Felicity stood outside his closed door.

"Err…yeah…yeah I'm fine…just a nightmare!" *Huh, I got that fucking right.*

"Oh…okay. It's nine o'clock. I'm making coffee. The sun's out." She spoke again through the door.

"Aye…thanks…I'll be down in a wee while," he replied, rubbing his hands over his face.

He took a cold shower and tried his best to rid himself of the images from his dream. When he was done, he made his way downstairs. Felicity was by the window. *Oh great.* The sight of her made things worse. She was standing in front of her easel with his dungarees loosely falling off one shoulder and a pale pink, cropped vest top underneath. It was the type she used to wear for working out and he could see the curve of her waist. *Oh god*, he moaned inwardly. He loved that part of her body, that feminine curve. She already had paint on her cheek. Lust struck him again, an overwhelming desire to just throw her to the ground and climb on top of her. He had to leave the room.

He clenched his jaw and made his excuses. "Ahem…just getting my coffee," he called, his voice breaking as he said it. Then he began to snigger. He felt like a silly teenager lusting after his art teacher or something equally as ridiculous. *C'mon man, pull yourself together! She's your ex-wife, remember? EX!*

When he had gathered himself he went back to the lounge to peer over her shoulder and look at the painting.

"Wow, that's really beautiful, Felicity." he said, genuinely impressed at the familiar looking scene on the canvas. He felt a little disappointed that he had called her Felicity again. It felt so formal. But *she* had made it that way. And it was for the best to keep the familiarity at bay.

"Do you think so? It's the same scene I painted that time at Rory's…you know, the one he destroyed?"

"Aye. It's really beautiful. It looks…really familiar."

"No…no it's an imaginary place. I've had it in my head awhile and I felt I needed to paint it. I wish it *were* real. I'd love to climb into the view." She smiled as she stood back to view what she had done so far.

"I'm not opening up today, so I thought I would take Jasper for a walk. Leave you to your painting," he said trying to figure out why the painting on the canvas pulled at him so.

"Okay, that's fine. I really want to get it done this time. I don't think it'll take me long now I've made a start. I'm really passionate about it. It won't leave my head until I get it done." She smiled at him.

He raised his hand up with the intention of wiping away the paint splodge from her cheek but changed his mind. "You've got some paint…" He gestured to her face.

She laughed. "Oh…that's always happening. I get a bit carried away." She wiped at her cheek with the back of her hand and in that moment Jim's heart ached. She looked more beautiful when she was painting than at any other time. Her eyes sparkled with life and vitality. Her face glowed. She really was exquisite. He'd always thought so. They shared a gaze for a few moments but Jim broke the spell by turning away.

"I'll…ahem…be off now. Leave you in peace."

~~~~~

Felicity's heart sank. She saw something in his eyes but couldn't decipher it. She wanted more than anything to make amends for how she had treated him. She would love to be his friend again. But would he let her?

~~~~~

As he walked along the seafront, Jim noticed that the snow was beginning to turn to slush. The day felt warmer and this would all mean the end of Felicity's little sojourn to Shieldaig. He felt a pang of sadness but knew that it was for the best really. It had to end sometime. *He* had to return to normality. He didn't have to like it but he knew it was going to happen.

He trudged through the snow for hours and was no longer feeling the cold. He had seen a few villagers out and about and had a couple of little chats along the way. As he walked back to the cottage he saw, in the distance, a snow plough. The children were out in force waving at the welcome visitor, who was about to create a lifeline to the world beyond Shieldaig. This would mean schools would re-open and he would be able to receive stock deliveries for the coffee shack once again.

After a couple of hours, he returned home to find Felicity even more bathed in paint than she was when he had left. The fact made him smile. He was amazed at how she had managed to cover herself in splodges but not land a drop on the carpet or furniture. There was something a little too comfortable about her being here and it unsettled him to think so.

"You're back. Did you have a nice walk?" She didn't look up from the canvas.

"Aye…very fresh. Fancy a coffee?" he asked as he removed his cold outdoor garments. Jasper resumed his usual place on the rug in front if the fireplace.

"Oooh, yes please! I'm gasping. I haven't stopped since you left. It's coming along nicely," she called. Jim came back through whilst the kettle was heating. He gasped when he saw the portrayal of the stunning, imaginary vista on the canvas before him.

"Wow, Felicity…it's…it's beautiful…truly beautiful." Her paintings always took his breath away and made him feel quite emotional. He swallowed the lump in his throat and walked quickly back to the kitchen. He recalled the first time he had seen one of her completed pieces.

~~~~~

November 1998 – Ten Years and Three Months Before the Break-up

Thursday evening had come around quickly. Thursday was their night, a night when Flick and Jim spent some time alone together. They had only been an official couple for a few weeks and everything was still in its rosy glow of lust, passion, and new love. Jim had been to collect fish and chips from the van that stopped just off campus and they smelled delicious. He tapped gently on Flick's door.

"Hi, you." She smiled at him as he leaned in for a sensuous, lingering kiss. He brushed her bangs back from her face and chuckled at the stunning vision before him. "What?!" She feigned hurt.

"You do make me smile…you have paint on your nose, chin and forehead. In fact you've even have it in your hair." He kissed her again.

"Oh, it always happens." She smiled. "I get quite carried away! Anyway, come and see." She pulled him by the arm and led him to the easel over by the small window. "Ta daaaaaa." She waved her jazz hands, proud of the painting before her. Jim stood open mouthed as his eyes strolled over the canvas. The painting was of a man and a woman, not unlike themselves, kissing by a tall leafless tree in a wintery looking meadow. Although the subject matter could've been construed as somewhat cheesy and clichéd, the brushwork was stunning and the sentiment, much to Jim's surprise, actually brought a lump to his throat.

"It's beautiful, Flick. The people look familiar." He winked at her, sliding his arms around her waist and kissing her neck. She shivered.

"You think so? Can't think why," she purred, sliding her arm up behind her and around his neck. "The scene is one I saw through the glass on the train when we went to the coast last weekend but the people..." She turned and kissed him again.

Suddenly, he nipped her bottom playfully, making her squeal. "C'mon, I'm starving, and I mean for *food* for once!" He laughed as he handed her the fish and chips, wrapped in paper, their mouth-watering, salty and vinegary aroma wafting through the small space.

~~~~~

Shaking himself back to the present again, Jim poured the boiling water into the mugs for himself and his ex-wife as he pondered awhile on the painting of the couple in the meadow. He had no idea what happened to it. *He* didn't have it. He would have to find out...maybe...or maybe that would do him no good whatsoever.

Chapter 12

The following day brought bright blue skies and sunshine. It wasn't exactly tropical but it was enough to almost complete the thawing process. Felicity's painting was just about complete and Jim knew that she would be leaving soon. Considering that fact produced mixed emotions. On the one hand, he could resume the status quo that existed prior to this intrusion; on the other, he *would* resume the status quo that existed prior to this intrusion! *Hmmm. Two sides of the same coin.* The direction of his thoughts concerned him. He needed her gone.

When he had showered and made his way downstairs, she was standing in front of her easel making some additions to her canvas. Her eyes lit up when she saw him.

"Hey...sleepyhead! I've been waiting for you to wake up." Her words produced a flashback to his vividly erotic dream from a couple of nights before and he gulped, lost in his thoughts for what felt like an age, as he pictured her naked on top of him. He shivered and shook his head as if shaking away a snowfall. "You look like you've seen a ghost." She frowned.

"Ahem...erm...no... Sorry, just...waking up, I suppose," he stuttered as he tried to shrug her comments off. *A ghost? No. But a vision of the past, most definitely.*

"I'll make coffee if you like? Then I thought maybe we could take Jasper for a walk. I'll cook tomorrow night but I thought maybe we could eat at the pub again tonight?" She chatted as if all was normal, as if she had just somehow slipped back into his life. The snow on the roads had gone.

The roads were clear. What was she playing at? He still couldn't find it in his ruptured heart to trust her.

"Erm…yeah…okay, whatever," was his feeble response. Why couldn't he just ask her to leave? After all she did have a life and a job to go home to.

They sat drinking coffee and staring at the scene on the canvas as if it was an actual vista and they were sharing it on top of a hill somewhere. Myriad thoughts raced through his mind. He struggled to organise them rationally into any semblance of normalcy. He felt it best, therefore, to remain taciturn. He could see that she kept glancing sideways in his direction. She, too, appeared to be feeling the same awkwardness. She opened her mouth to speak but as she did the phone rang. Jim jumped up to answer it. *How does the phrase go? Saved by the bell?*

"Yes…hello?" His face scrunched and he felt sure that she could hear the yelling down the line. In fact the whole of Shieldaig could probably hear it! "Whoa…whoa! I've done no such thing! Yes she *is* here…but she *chose* to come here. She *is* an *adult* you know. Oh just shut up, will you… I'll put her on." He thrust the receiver at Felicity who, with a bemused look, took it.

~~~~~

"Hello?"

"Felicity? Darling! I've been so, so worried. Why on *earth* are you there with *him*?" Penelope sounded almost hysterical.

"Oh…it's you. Mother, stop being so melodramatic. I came here to do what I should have done before Daddy's funeral."

"You shouldn't *be* there! You know what will happen. He'll brainwash you into going back to him!" Penelope's hysteria increased and so did Felicity's annoyance.

"For goodness sake, Mother, it's not like he bloody kidnapped me. How did you get this number?" She could feel the crease between her eyes deepen.

"I had to…to…practically *beg* Charles to give it to me!"

"Oh great. Poor Charles." She covered the receiver and whispered to Jim "You had better call Charles. Mother's been harassing him, I'm afraid. Sorry." She cringed and Jim shook his head. He looked very angry and his jaw twitched. Poor Charles. This was the last thing he needed.

Felicity continued to bark back at her mother whenever she could get a word in. On several occasions, she held the receiver away from her ear as the volume became too intense.

Eventually, temper got the better of her. "Mother! Just stop! You of *all* people cannot talk about being manipulative and *bad* for people! *You* wrote the book on deceit. And *no* for your information Jim and I are *not* back together. Not that it would be anything to do with *you* if we were. I was snowed in here. The snow is melting and I will only be here a couple more days. Satisfied? Well, quite frankly, I don't care whether you are or you aren't. This is *my* life! Do you hear me? *Mine!* I intend to live it by *my* rules from now on! Goodbye." She pressed the hang up button and threw the phone onto the sofa with such a force that it broke.

With her chest heaving, she covered her mouth. "Oh, shit!" Her eyes widened in horror. Jim stared at his broken handset. "I'm so sorry, Jim!"

He just shook his head and left the room. He headed upstairs to use the handset in his room to contact Charles but the phone rang again.

"Ignore it!" Felicity called to him, "It could be her again!"

He ignored her and answered.

"Oh Jim, old boy, are you okay? I tried to call earlier but it was bloody engaged for ages!" Charles sounded stressed and concerned.

He sighed. "Aye…I'm okay."

"Did Dragon Lady call? She called here, and when I wouldn't give her your number, she bloody turned up in the bloody shop and made a right old bloody scene in front of customers! I was bloody horrified, old chap."

Jim rubbed his eyes as he shook his head. "Shit, I'm so sorry you had to go through that, Charles. It was unfair of her to involve you."

"No, no. It's fine. Is Felicity still with you?"

He rested his elbow on his knee and his head on his hand. "Aye, Charles. She won't be for much longer though. I can't handle this anymore. Her being here is too…just too…*hard*, you know?" Jim sat with his back to the door.

~~~~~

Felicity's heart sank as she heard his words. She had climbed the stairs to see who was calling. He clearly wanted her gone. She understood why. She made her way back downstairs in order to avoid any further awkwardness if he found her loitering outside his room. She sank into the sofa and leaning forward, placed her head on her folded arms. Tears trickled, unfettered, down her face from where she had felt the colour drain at Jim's words. She felt lost, desolate almost. This was *not* how things should have gone.

He eventually came down stairs. She wiped her eyes and gave him a sad smile as he stood looking down at her where she sat.

"Jim…look… I'll gather up my things and leave. The snow has pretty much gone…and…"

"Aye…the road was clear of snow yesterday. You could've gone then." His tone was harsh.

She thought that it felt like the first time she left him. Only this time she was reluctant. Her heart twinged in her chest, a real physical pain that made her reach up and run the area.

Jim winced as if he had realised he had been too hard. "Look…stay until tomorrow, eh? You'd be better getting an early start…it's almost two o'clock and…well…you'd be better going tomorrow." Jasper approached the pair reticently and Jim crouched down to fuss him.

Felicity's eyes began to sting once again with the threat of more tears. She desperately wanted to stay awhile longer, but couldn't express this to Jim, who had clearly come to the conclusion that she had outstayed her welcome.

If only she could stay a couple more days…maybe then she could get him to forgive her? But how? She had no clue when she thought about it. The scars ran far too deep. She rued the day that she ever listened to her mother. Jim had been her best friend for so long and she had lost that. Whenever anything good had happened in recent years, Jim had been the first person she thought about calling. *Thought* about, but never actually plucked up the courage.

She stood, thinking it best to say something. "Jim…I…" Her lip quivered as she searched for the words that might go some way to express how she felt. But the words failed her. She shook her head and Jim left the room.

Chapter 13

Felicity had retreated to the guest room. She lay on the white framed double bed and glanced around thinking that if she lived here she wouldn't change a thing about this room with its apple green bedding and driftwood picture frames. When things had settled down, somewhat, and both had taken time to calm and have a little space, there was a knock on the door of her bedroom.

"Yes?" she called.

"I'm taking Jasper out again…do you…maybe…want to come?" Jim replied through the closed door.

"Oh…no…no it's okay," she croaked and cleared her throat. "I…I don't want to get in your way any more than I have, Jim."

There was a light thud as if he had rested his head on the door. "Look…I *want* you to come. I have something to show you," he insisted.

"Oh…okay. Give me five minutes." She sat upright, a smile pulling at her lips for the first time since the incident earlier. He went quiet and she figured he had left her to get ready. She grabbed her jeans and sweater. Then pulled on the socks that she had borrowed and stifled a giggle at how ridiculous her size four feet looked in something belonging to size ten feet.

~~~~~

The late afternoon sun was low and cast that familiar amber glow over the picturesque little village. Jim, Felicity, and Jasper headed up the lane leading away from Jim's

street. The snow had been melting and mixing with the
mud causing a dirty grey slush to form. The gentle breeze
was bringing the blood to the surface of Felicity's cheeks
and nose, making her look blushed. She dutifully followed
Jim up…up…further away from home. Her hands
remained in the pockets of her oversized thick fleece lined
coat. Jim strode ahead with Jasper keeping close. Every so
often the dog would stop and glance back as if to check on
her. When he stopped, he wagged his tail almost in
encouragement as they trudged up the sloping ascent.

"Jim…where…are…we…going?" Felicity panted.

Jim was keeping quite a pace and she was out of breath.

"We're nearly there. I just thought it was important to
show you while the light's good." He knew he hadn't really
answered her question. He stopped walking. "Look."

She eventually caught up and stood beside him. She
inhaled sharply as she looked out. "Jim! It's…it's my
painting!" Her hands covered her mouth and her eyes were
wide like saucers as she looked over the valley below them.
Snow still covered most of the sheltered area but the trees
were positioned almost identically to her supposed *imaginary*
view.

"Isn't it breath-taking?" Jim turned to her. His heart
pounded and his head was filled with a million different
emotions all vying for the surface.

"Oh, Jim. It's…I can't… Wow." Her garbled words
came out in a breathy whisper. They stood side by side,
looking down to where the trees lined a little loch or pond.
It was hard to tell as they were quite high up. The
mountains in the distance created the perfect backdrop to
the vista, their rocky surface still dusted in the sparkling
white, frosty layer.

Jim nodded and smiled and without turning to face
Felicity said, "I know how it happened now… Many years

ago when we were packing to leave uni...you and I went through my old childhood photos. I came here with my Mum, Dad, and Euan on holiday when I was about eight. My dad took the photo and I always treasured it. I'd completely forgotten about it and always wondered why I was so drawn to this place. I haven't looked through those photos since you and I did all those years ago. I can't believe it stuck with you too...but clearly it did... You painted it, Flick." He paused to glance at her.

She stood with tears glistening in her eyes as she listened and realisation appeared to dawn on her. He must have been right. There was something distinctly magical about the place, otherworldly even.

Jim took a lung full of the crisp, wintery air. "I come up here in the good weather usually. Flask of coffee, blanket, and a good book. I read for a wee while and then sit and drink my coffee, just staring at the view. It's the closest thing to paradise I can think of."

He turned his head slightly and smiled warmly. "When I saw your painting I couldn't figure it out, but then I came up here and I realised. It's...it's like you'd been here before. But then again you *have*...in a way. We shared the memory back at university and you couldn't get the place out of your mind...you said so. We'd both just forgotten why that was."

He turned now to look at her fully. She turned to face him with anticipation in her wide eyes as if she was wondering what would happen next. He stepped toward her but then something flashed through his mind. He couldn't do this...not again. His heart wouldn't take it. He turned away, his jaw clenching, as he tried to get a handle on his emotions. At that moment, Felicity's mobile phone rang.

"Oh good grief…who would have thought I'd get a signal up here?" she mumbled. "I only charged it because I thought I was going home and might need it." She looked blankly at the handset in her hand. "I don't even know why I brought it out with me to be honest. I've enjoyed the peace and quiet."

Jim gestured toward the buzzing handset. "Aren't you going to answer it? It might be important." He knew his voice was flat. He'd shut down again and was back to the emotionless state that he'd managed to maintain for most of the past few days. Self-preservation.

"Oh…right…yes, I suppose I should." She lifted the handset to her ear. "H-hello? Felicity Johnston-Hart speaking." She stepped a few feet away. Jim inadvertently listened to the one sided conversation.

"Really? Oh my. That's incredible, Franco! I can't quite believe it…it's just quite sudden…I know…yes an amazing opportunity. Oh yes most definitely…I see…yes…oh right. So when do you need to know by? Gosh…that soon? Oh…okay, leave it with me…yes, I'll be home in the next day or so, weather permitting… Thanks Franco…see you soon, bye." She hung up and looked over to Jim. She looked stunned and the colour flushing her cheeks had paled significantly.

"Are you okay?" Jim asked, keeping his face blank, an expressionless mask.

She frowned. "Yes…yes…fine…just got some thinking to do, I suppose." She stared off into the distance at the stunning view once again.

"Oh? How come?" Jim was intrigued now.

"Well…I've been offered a job in New York. Starting in a month."

His heart sank. "New York? Wow...sounds like a fantastic opportunity." He tried to sound bright, breezy, and positive but failed miserably.

"Yes...yes it's fantastic. But...I just have two days to think about it." She turned to Jim again. "It's not long, eh?" He could tell her smile was forced, and he could see pain in her eyes. Why, he didn't really know but the enthusiasm she should have been feeling just didn't appear to be manifesting itself.

He cleared his throat. "No...no it's not long at all really. But you've always dreamed of working in New York. Right back when you first joined the Art world it was always a dream of yours. What is there to consider?" He knew what he wanted the answer to be, but the answer never came. She just stared blankly over the beautiful view. After a few silent moments, he touched her arm. "We should get back and eat. You've an early start in the morning, eh?"

"Yes...we better had."

They walked slowly back toward home. Jasper covered twice the distance, running away and then back to them again, his tail wagging frantically.

~~~~~

Back at the house, Felicity disappeared to her room to pack the rest of her belongings whilst Jim concocted something that smelled delicious down in the kitchen. She wandered down when she was finished and leaned against the doorframe in the kitchen.

"Mmmm, something smells good," she said as she watched Jim working.

"Aye, I made us a nice beef stew with a hint of red wine. It'll be ready in around an hour." He smiled back over his shoulder. He looked more relaxed now. His dark hair was deliciously shaggy and he wore his favourite Soundgarden T-shirt with his tattered old black jeans that had almost faded to grey. His feet were bare. She watched his sculpted arm muscles as he worked. His backside looked good in those tired old jeans, too. He hadn't lost his draw for her. She still found him so very attractive. It was almost an invisible pull that had only faded with distance temporarily but was back with a vengeance in the close confines of the cottage. She allowed herself to hope that when she left it would fade again. But deep down she knew that wouldn't likely happen.

~~~~~

The table was set and the wine bottle stood in the middle, a little of its contents sacrificed to the stew. Just as Jim put the plates on the table, the lights went out. Felicity jumped.

"What's happening?" Her voice wavered, and if Jim wasn't mistaken, he'd swear she sounded scared.

"Don't tell me you're still afraid of the dark, Felicity?" Jim chuckled.

"Ahem...no...course not. I just can't see what I'm eating...that's all." There was annoyance in her tone, but he had a huge grin on his face. It was wrong to find pleasure in her discomfort, but thankfully the lack of light meant she couldn't see.

"It's just a power cut. Hang on...I have some candles...here...somewhere." He fumbled around in a drawer. "Ahhh, gotcha." There was a crackle and suddenly the faint glow of candles began to brighten the room. Jim placed tea lights on every surface. "Thank goodness for IKEA, eh?" He chuckled again. "It's funny, whenever I go to that place I always seem to come away with a bag of tea lights or a few pillar candles. *Now* I know why."

Felicity giggled. "Gosh, I thought I was the only one who did that." She looked around the room. "This is nice, actually…the candle light," she said as she sipped her wine.

"Aye…kind of…ah, never mind." He shook his head.

"Kind of what?" she asked.

"Och, I was going to say *romantic* but…I don't know…didn't feel like the right thing to say." He shrugged.

"Ah." She smiled.

"Sooo…any more thoughts on the new job? How did it come about anyway?" He decided to gloss over the awkward pause that hung in the air.

"Well…the guy who was heading up the new gallery in New York…a guy called Chester Withers…he's had a kind of…nervous breakdown by the sound of it, poor thing. It must be the stress. To be honest though, from what I'd heard, he'd been losing his touch. His last few acquisitions weren't up to standard, and Franco was unhappy but couldn't really do much. Anyway…when Chester got too bogged down with the stress he walked…or he was fired…I'm not that sure. Anyway, Franco wants me to take over as soon as possible."

"And if you say no?" Jim chewed on a mouthful of beef as he spoke.

"Don't know…I suppose they'd advertise. Someone would snap it up. I'm very lucky to be offered the position."

"Franco clearly has faith on your abilities," Jim offered, positively.

"Oh yes. There's no doubt about that." She cringed at her response and added, "Yikes, did that sound terribly conceited of me?" Her fork was halfway to her mouth.

He winked. "Aye…but you're allowed."

Felicity hit his arm playfully. "That's it…I'm full to bursting!" She patted her tummy as she leaned back in her chair. "It was delicious. Thank you."

"Aye…it was rather good, wasn't it?" he said pushing his plate away.

Felicity giggled. "Humph…now who's the conceited one?"

"Touché." Jim laughed. "Come on, let's go sit by the fire. I'll do the dishes in the morning when I can see."

~~~~~

The pair retired to the cosy lounge where the fire and the addition of a few tea lights gave a warm glow to the room. They sat in silence with the remainder of the bottle of wine in their glasses. The flames were quite hypnotic in their dance around the large lump of wood they surrounded. Jim watched Felicity as she watched the flames. Her loose knitted top had slipped down off her shoulder revealing her collarbone and the curve of her slender neck. He felt an aching deep inside and reached out absentmindedly to touch her there.

She turned quickly to look at him as if shocked by the tender contact. "Jim?"

He looked into her eyes. They looked like they were on fire as the flames were reflected back at him. He placed his glass on the table beside him and took her glass from her hand placing it next to his. Without stopping to think things through, he took her hands in his and kissed them both. She inhaled sharply as his eyes stared deep into hers.

He leaned forward until their mouths were almost touching, anticipation building deep in the pit of his stomach. Her breathing had become a series of short inhales and exhales. He knew she felt it too, whatever the hell *it* was. Before he had time to consider the consequence of his actions he took her mouth with his. His hands slipped into her hair and his tongue into her mouth. She returned the kiss with as much fervour as it was being given, breaking away only to remove her top, revealing her beautiful, naked breasts. He stifled the groan bubbling up from within and pulled her to him. He kissed her again, feeling her softness again his hard chest.

~~~~~

Felicity's body ached for his touch as it had since she arrived at his door a few days ago. He didn't disappoint her, caressing her face, neck, arms, and breasts. There was a hunger in his eyes that she had missed so, so much.

She tugged his T-shirt over his head and stroked her hands down his torso. His body was still the most sensual thing she had ever touched, smooth skin over taut muscles. He laid her backward effortlessly and removed her yoga pants and panties until she was lying there, bared in front of him, waiting, anticipating, *hoping.*

He lowered himself onto her and kissed her neck. She groaned, grasping at his back and running her hands slowly downward as he shivered under her fingertips. His jeans were soon discarded along with the other items of relinquished clothing. Neither said a word. Their eyes remained locked unless one or the other was closing them to revel in the ecstasy of their caresses. *Now do you see Jim? Now do you get it?*

His now prominent desire pressed against the apex of her thighs as he rocked his pelvis back and forth, mirroring her movements. She lifted her legs and wrapped them around him and it was then that he thrust inside her. The air escaped her lungs in a breathy moan as she accepted him. Still neither of them said a word. Their bodies were connected in the most intimate way and they revelled in it. He bent to her breasts and took a tightened bud in his mouth, pulling it deep. The moan that this elicited seemed to spur him on. He stroked her face tenderly and kissed her with such passion. Felicity felt the tightening deep within her as her orgasm quickly began to take hold and she grabbed at Jim as she was overtaken by the most delicious sensations and emotions coursing through her body. It felt good. It felt amazing.

She felt like she was home.

~~~~~

Jim felt her tighten around him as he moved between her thighs, and he felt completely overwhelmed, lost in her, captivated. He gasped and groaned, locked intently onto her fiery blue gaze. As the pressure built, he nuzzled her neck, his movements becoming more urgent and rapid, nibbling and sucking at her tender flesh. The most exquisite sensations radiated throughout his body until he climaxed, shattering into a billion microscopic pieces, grasping at her hair with one hand and the other lifting her up onto him by her buttocks. He didn't say any definable words, just noise, desperation-fuelled noise.

He collapsed onto her and she clung onto him. He was still inside her and he didn't want to leave. It had felt so good, so very right despite how wrong it had been. A sinking feeling set in and he knew immediately he had made a terrible mistake. This wasn't meant to happen. They were over a long time ago. *His* feelings didn't count. They never had. And he couldn't stand to go through losing her again. It had taken years to get over her and—whom was he kidding? He had never fully gotten over her.

~~~~~

She held him as he laid there, his heart pounding against her. She was desperate for him to realise how she felt. She hoped that now she'd made it clear. *This* was where she wanted to be, in his arms. This was the only place she had ever been truly happy. If only she could voice it, say the words.

The fire had begun to die down as they lay there, still saying nothing. She stroked her fingers lazily up and down his spine as he remained inside her, his body slowly returning to normal. But he shifted and stood suddenly, clearly unable to make the eye contact that had been so direct only moments before.

He pointed awkwardly toward the stairs. "I'm going to…take a quick shower and then I…I think I'll turn in," he announced.

She tried to ignore the uncomfortable feeling churning within and pushed it away. They had just shared such intimacy for the first time in years. Of course it would feel strange. "Okay…I'll be up soon." She smiled.

When he had left the room she gathered her clothing together and slipped them back on. Her muscles ached in the best possible way. She never thought that being with him again could be possible. And she had never expected that it would feel so right. She had hoped but never really expected it. But he had instigated it so there was hope. Wasn't there? It must have meant something…surely?

She finished off her wine and blew out the candles. The cottage wasn't a scary place, but she really *didn't* like the dark. Much the same as she really didn't like flying. The thought of taking the job in New York preyed on her mind for a few moments until she pushed that aside too. She went upstairs, and finding that Jim had finished, she climbed into the shower. The bathroom was still steamy. Once finished, she tiptoed along the short hallway, opened the door, and slipped into bed, naked. Beside Jim.

Chapter 14

When Felicity awoke she was alone. She felt a little disappointed, as she had rather hoped for a repeat of last night's passionate lovemaking. Because that's what it had been...hadn't it? She heard Jim clattering about downstairs. She guessed he was in need of a hearty breakfast after the night before and smiled at the delectable memories as she stretched. She refused to think there could possibly be any other reason for his absence.

Once she had showered and dressed in a comfy sweater and jeans, she went downstairs to where he stood. He was at the sink finishing off the dishes from their wonderful evening together. She slid her arms around his waist and kissed his shoulder.

"Good morning, you," she whispered, nuzzling into him.

"Oh...good morning, Felicity," he replied rather stoically. She felt him tense under her arms. He paused, keeping very still as if afraid to move. "I've made...some porridge. It's keeping warm on the cooker." He pointed in the direction of the stove. "There's syrup...or...or I have jam?"

"Oooh, yummy. Thank you." She felt his eyes on her as she almost skipped over to the cooker and dished some of the gooey mixture into the bowl that he had left out for her. She drizzled golden syrup on top and sat down at the table. "So...did you sleep well?" She grinned.

His face remained the usual impassive mask. "Aye...I did, thanks. Ahem...what time are you setting off?" he asked avoiding eye contact. He took a sip of the coffee in his mug.

She stopped eating and looked up at him. "Oh...I...erm... Oh," was all the response she could manage. She bit her lip as confusion and embarrassment washed over her whole body, followed by hurt. She felt her cheeks heat.

"It's just that it's eight o'clock now, and I think you should get a good run at it...you know...so you don't get caught in traffic," Jim stated, rubbing his forehead and appearing unsettled by her reaction.

Her eyes began to sting yet again. "Yes...yes...I suppose I should get going." She stood to leave the room. Her chest hurt and she felt light headed.

"Are you okay? You've gone pale." Jim's face was filled with concern.

She nodded vehemently. "Yes...I feel a bit...dizzy that's all. I think I stood up too quickly."

Jim nodded his understanding. "Aye...well finish your porridge. You can't leave on an empty stomach, eh?"

"Suddenly, I'm not hungry anymore." She left the room and went upstairs.

She sat on the edge of the bed, feeling a mixture of anger, pain, and sadness. He didn't get it. But how could he? He was so fucking dense! Maybe it had meant nothing to him? The anger began to rise inside her as she grabbed her things together. She stomped downstairs, dragging her case behind her.

Jim was standing in the lounge, leaning on the mantle when she entered the room. He looked up and met her gaze. She couldn't read the emotion she saw there. Was it regret? Was he about to ask her to stay?

Staying as calm as she possibly could, she kept eye contact. "Right...I'll be going. You don't have to put up with me any longer," she stated coldly.

"It was no bother really." His smile did not arrive at his eyes.

She turned to leave but stopped with her back to him. "Just answer me one thing, Jim... Why did you make love to me last night?" Tears of anger combined with hurt welled in her eyes, causing her vision to blur.

Jim frowned as he stood up straight, his fists clenched by his sides. "You were leaving anyway, Felicity. You have a life to go back to." His frown deepened. "And...isn't...isn't that how you and I say goodbye?" She turned to look at him. He actually looked confused. She took a deep breath. *Revenge. Of course. It was revenge.* How cold and calculating could a man be?

"You...you bastard," she whispered. "I never thought you were the kind of person to keep score. You've been waiting for this opportunity...haven't you?" She began to physically shake. The tears overflowed but she didn't care anymore.

He held his hands up in surrender and stepped toward her. "No...no, Flick. That's not—"

"Save your breath, *James*," she interrupted, uninterested in any pathetic explanation he had to offer. "That's how you want to play it? Fine. I'll be sure not to think of you when I'm in New York. I mean...why would I waste my time?" She opened the door and stormed out without looking back.

~~~~~

Jim stood frozen to the spot. He was completely baffled. *What the fuck just happened?* He couldn't understand her reaction. She didn't love him…did she? No! *She* had left *him. She only came here out of guilt! Last night was about history and pent up feelings of lust…it was about goodbye…not love.* He snapped to his senses and was determined to stomp to the car and have this out with her. *She left me, for fuck's sake! How dare she act like I'm the one in the fucking wrong?* When he arrived at the curb, she was half way up the road, driving much too fast. He watched until she was out of sight and then he went back inside and slumped onto the sofa.

"I just don't get it," he told Jasper. "*She* left *me* and now *I* feel like shit? I just don't understand, Jasper. We both wanted that intimacy last night. I've been fucking *dreaming* about her, for fuck's sake. I could tell she wanted it, too. *Just sex*…that's all she wanted. She made it clear when she left me the first time that she didn't *love* me," he rambled at the dog who looked on with his ears back as if unsure how to react to his master's loud voice.

Jim wandered around all day trying to figure out what on earth had gotten into Felicity. He vacuumed, scoured, scrubbed, and did several loads of laundry. Still he couldn't figure out a plausible reason for her behaviour. *It's not as though she came here to win me back.* He snorted at the thought. He decided to take Jasper for another long walk.

The snow was all but gone. But it was a bitterly cold day. Jim and Jasper walked up to the viewpoint he had shown Felicity. He felt sad as he looked out across the valley. She had left the painting propped up against the wall in his guest room. She obviously didn't want it after all that work. But it was beautiful. He wanted to hang it but felt sure that he would be overtaken by sadness whenever he looked at it. Just as he was when he looked out at the real thing now.

He returned to the house after an hour and a half of brisk walking in the cold January air. The lounge was chilly.

After he had built a fire, he went upstairs to change into his joggers and a sweater. Maybe lifting weights would help? Before he made his mind up he noticed the brown padded envelope on his nightstand. Picking it up, he examined it. It was written in Edgar's own handwriting and had evidently not been opened since Edgar himself had sealed it. Jim took it down the stairs with him. Once he had made coffee, he opened the envelope.

Inside the contents were neatly tied with a red ribbon, rather like the legal documents of a solicitor. There was a thick wad of paper, which he presumed was the manuscript of the incomplete book on George Leigh Mallory. Underneath the ribbon was an envelope addressed to Jim, again in Edgar's handwriting. Jim slid his finger along the seal and took out the contents. Awash with emotion, he began to read.

Dear Jim,

If you are reading this, I am no longer with you. I instructed my solicitor that no one but no one must open this letter, except for you. My dear boy, I can only apologise for the fact that, no doubt, you were excluded from my send off by my wife. It pains me to be sitting here knowing that this will undoubtedly be the case. She has some ridiculous notion that you are bad for my girl. How one could surmise such nonsense when one only has to know you to understand how much you cared for (and probably still do) my Felicity.

Please forgive Felicity. For she, too, has the ridiculous notion that my busybody of a wife knows what is right and wrong for her. The well-known phrase 'Mother knows best' sticks in my craw, old boy, I can tell you. The day you were forced out of my family was one of the saddest in my life and as my illness took over me my one real pleasure, apart from seeing my daughter, was awaiting your wonderful letters. You have a way with words, son.

This brings me on to the manuscript enclosed. Now I know you want none of the fame and fortune of becoming a well-known writer, even though your talent is beyond that of many published writers I have read, and so I present to you an opportunity to, ironically, become my ghost-writer. I would very much like for you to finish the manuscript and forward it to Geoffrey Haddington, my editor, who has been instructed to await your contact. If you choose not to take this opportunity, however, know that my opinion of you will not deteriorate. I regard you with the highest esteem and always have. Please remember that.

Now, onto my main reason for writing to you from beyond the grave. Hmm, that's a strange thing to write when I am still here! Anyway, I digress. Felicity has not been the same since she jettisoned you from her life. I can only liken it to a light being switched off. Her eyes don't sparkle the same anymore. She's lost her...how do you put it? Va-va-voom! I have to say that is a word I never thought I would write! Anyway, I am digressing again!

A week ago, after I had been honest with Felicity about my illness and the fact that I wouldn't be around for very long we had a heart to heart. I asked her to be truthful about your break up. Jim, she broke down and sobbed. She cried for about fifteen minutes and I just held her. When she had calmed herself down I asked her again. I would like to share with you what she said.

Felicity felt that she had something to prove to her mother. She felt that she had to be seen as a successful, wealthy woman who was going places. The crazy thing is that I already saw that in her. But her Mother, who has always been critical, had standards that she set which were impossible to meet. I know things about Penny that would make all of that seem a little ironic but I am sure they will come out soon enough, if they haven't already. Penny, for reasons known only to herself, didn't feel that you fit in with this inflated sense of importance she had for material things; and quite rightly too. You are far better than that.

Felicity confessed to me that you were her soul mate. You were her best friend. She convinced herself that these things were not important. She did so to gain her mother's acceptance. I cannot tell you how sad and angry this makes me. I sincerely hope that Penny can live with herself for the damage she has caused.

Despite all of this I too must admit to being a fool for love. No matter how much my wife meddles and interferes I cannot help but love her and I know that she loves me too, deeply. I know, also, that she wants the best for her daughter. She is just misguided as to what that entails. I have spoken to her recently about you and think she may be realising what she has done. This has made her angry. But this anger, whilst outwardly expressed in a way that hurts others is only dealt with as such because to turn it in on herself would destroy her. The guilt she feels is eating away at her and she has no idea _how_ to deal with it. I am sure she will have protested at Felicity coming to see you, through pride.

Now, what I am about to impart came directly from Felicity's own mouth…she still loves you. I will write that again in the hope that it sinks in. Felicity _still_ loves you, Jim. She has remained in-love with you all along. She just pushed the feelings down until she too believed they were gone. Her heart is broken. She realises now that she made a terrible mistake in letting you go but she will not and cannot bring herself to tell you of this as she feels sure that she has hurt you to a level which is beyond the powers of forgiveness. And so I am doing so from wherever I have gone. I know you can forgive her because I have forgiven Penny. When you love someone as much as this it is all you can do.

Now, I requested that Felicity should deliver this package to you personally if you had not been allowed to attend my funeral. If she has in fact delivered it and she is still with you when you read this letter then please don't be upset with her if you were not informed about my passing until after the funeral. I can assure you it will not have been her decision to not invite you. If she is still with you I would like you to take a long look into her eyes and see the truth. <u>You are meant to be together</u>.

If Felicity is no longer in Scotland I would like you take a long look at yourself in the mirror. Ask yourself if you can forgive this misguided young woman and if the answer is yes, I want you to get in that battered old Land Rover of yours and drive down to London to take back what should never have been broken asunder.

She feels that you and she have some connection that goes deeper than 'normal' love. She dreams of you often and a place where you and she stand looking out over a valley surrounded by trees and mountains. It sounds very much like some of the places you have described in your beautiful letters to me, Jim. You are two souls which are incomplete without one another.

Please, for the sake of you both go to her. You will never be complete with another. I think you know this.

I will close now as I am feeling rather tired and emotional. It pains me to know that I may never hold you in my arms again, Jim. But know this. I have loved you since my daughter brought you home. You and I had an affinity just like a Father and his son and that is what you have always been to me. My son.

With much love
Your Father
Edgar

Chapter 15

Jim's shoulders shuddered as he sobbed. His face was wet with hot tears. Jasper sat beside him with his head resting on his knee. The information contained in Edgar's letter both shocked and saddened him. He had blown it. There was no way things could work out now. Any chance there may have been to reconcile with Felicity had died. *The way she looked at me as she left.* He groaned. *How could I have been so stupid? So blind?* There was no point chasing her down. None.

He sat, drumming his fingers, his knee bouncing up and down as it often did when he was frustrated. He re-read the passage over and over where Edgar told him that Flick still loves him. He mulled it over in his mind and then read it again.

He picked up the phone. "Miranda? Hi, it's Jim. I need to ask you a favour. Any chance you can look after Jasper for me? I need to go to London." Miranda was intrigued but Jim didn't elaborate. She agreed to take Jasper in the next day. Jim dashed up the stairs and grabbed an overnight bag. Once done, he picked up the phone again.

"Charles? Yeah, hi. I need to ask you a favour. Can I stay with you for a couple of days? Great! Thank you sooo much. I should be down tomorrow afternoon, I'll explain then." Jim sat back with a face-splitting grin fixed firmly in place.

He looked down at Jasper and scratched the top of his canine friend's head. "Nothing ventured, nothing gained, eh, Jasper?"

He had no clue what he would say to her once he arrived. He had no clue whether she would even speak to him. He wondered if he should call Polly in advance and see how the land lay as he felt sure that Flick would have called her to let her know she was on her way home. But then again, even if Polly said he mustn't come, he would still get in the Landy and head off to London to see for himself. *Why waste time on pointless phone calls then?*

He decided he would get an early night and rise at around six, pack some sandwiches, and set off. He figured he could make most of the journey without stopping. He resolved that he would only stop if absolutely necessary, that way he could maybe meet her from work and they could go somewhere neutral to talk things through. That was it. All planned. He breathed a sigh of relief, leaned back, and closed his eyes.

Suddenly he bolted upright when he heard a loud rhythmical knock at his door. His heart leapt. *Shit! Maybe she came back?!* He hurried to the door and yanked it open, almost pulling it off the hinges in his excited rush.

"Ta daaa!" A tall, lanky man threw his arms around Jim.

"Euan?!" Jim shouted, hugging his brother back. "Shit, Euan, why didn't you call? I could've picked you up at the airport!"

"In that ancient old shed you call a car? No thanks! We hired something a lot more civilised, didn't we, Tar?" he asked over his shoulder. The petite frame of his girlfriend stepped sideways and opened her arms out to Jim.

"Hey! Tara! You look amazing, come here." Jim scooped her up and swung her around and then pointed to his brother. "And you, you great heathen, you leave my lovely Landy out of this. She'll go on forever. She's done me proud all these years and there's plenty of life left in her yet."

"Yeah, whatever you say! And get off ma woman, you hairy lout!" Euan punched his brother's arm playfully.

"God, it's so good to see you both, come in!" Jim stepped aside as his brother and potential sister-in-law entered his tiny cottage.

"Geez, bro. I'm sure this place gets smaller." Euan laughed. His last visit had been the year that Jim had moved in and he had been overwhelmed by the size of the property compared to the one he and Tara shared in New South Wales.

"Aye but there's only me and Jasper so it does us just fine." He went through to the kitchen to make coffee for his guests. "So, how long are you staying?" he asked, cringing as he remembered his letter from Edgar and the plan to chase after Flick.

"We're here for a month, mate! A whole month!" Euan beamed at his big brother.

Shit. That would mean that Flick would be in the states when they left. *Shit, shit shit!* What could he do? His brother had flown all the way around the world to be with him. He couldn't just leave and dash off to London/USA on a whim. It wouldn't be right.

"That's great." It *was* great. It was wonderful. He would just have to have a major rethink.

The evening was filled with chatter and catch ups. The brothers joked around like old times and Tara listened intently whilst the two regaled her with stories of their childhood in Dumbarton. They told her these stories whenever they got together. She rolled her eyes frequently and smiled as they carried on regardless.

Euan and Tara updated Jim on their latest hobby, windsurfing. Jim was slightly envious at that. It was something he had always wanted to try but had never had the courage. As the evening wore on, Jim cooked a large pan of Spaghetti Bolognese and a garlic baguette. The wine flowed and so did the conversation. At around midnight, Euan stretched and yawned. He looked down at his gorgeous girl who lay across him, fast asleep.

"I'm bushed, Jim. I think I'll turn in if you don't mind, eh?"

"Aye, you know where your room is, bro. I'll make breakfast when you get up so don't rush, eh?" The brothers hugged and Euan scooped up his girl like a little china doll and carried her up to bed.

~~~~~

Jim couldn't sleep. He lay awake almost all night trying to figure out what to do. He could call her…but that would be impersonal. He wanted to see her face and discuss things properly. He would have to wait. *It may mean a flight to the USA but so be it.* Eventually he drifted off into a fitful sleep.

Sleep didn't carry him away for long. He was in the kitchen making coffee at eight the following morning when he decided to call Charles and explain that his visit was cancelled.

"What was your reason for coming all this bloody way, old boy?" Charles enquired, probably guessing that there was more to this than just a social visit.

"It's a long story, Charles, but to give you the abridged version… Flick brought me an incomplete manuscript as requested by her Dad via his will. In the envelope with it was a letter. Edgar said in the letter that Flick still loves me."

"Bloody hell! Do you think it's true? Or *another* bloody lie?" Charles asked in his Charles-type way.

"Edgar wouldn't lie. He says she told him I'm her soul-mate, that she has always loved me, that she regrets how things ended between us."

"Well, it was her bloody doing, old chap. You weren't going to bloody chase her down were you?"

"I wanted to at least talk to her, you know? I need to know if she still feels that way, although after how things ended when she was here this week, I am guessing I've blown it."

"But Jim, I thought you were over her? You spent so long putting things in place to help you bloody move on."

"Aye, I know…but…I can't help myself."

He went on to explain to Charles what had happened the night before Flick left. How they had ended up sleeping together and about her reaction the next day when he treated it as just sex. He felt quite ashamed as he spoke, realising that this was the first time he had ever done something as callous. It wasn't meant to be callous. He had simply misread every single signal. The stupid thing was he had been completely oblivious to the signals and the looks until now.

Charles sighed. "Oh, Jim. You bloody fool. I'm sorry but you are." Charles was right. He was a bloody fool, for so many reasons. The conversation came to a close and Jim sat with his head in his hands.

"So, she was here? And she still loves you, eh?" A familiar voice came from over his shoulder making him jump.

"Fuck, Euan! You scared the shit out of me! How long were you standing there?" Jim didn't bother to hide his annoyance that his brother had been listening in.

"Long enough, bro." He pulled out the chair opposite Jim and sat down to face him. "Look, Jim, you've spent the last two years…no…longer, getting over that bitch—"

"Do *not* call her that." Jim's tone was harsh and he spoke through gritted teeth.

Euan held up his hands. "Sorry, sorry…I just can't believe you're thinking of going back to her after what she did to you. She messed with your head and broke your fucking heart! Are you seriously going to give her a chance to do it again? I thought you were over her?"

"Euan, you don't know how I feel. I miss her. I never stopped loving her. I tried, believe me, I did. But she's not someone you get over easily." Jim rubbed his forehead. The brothers sat in silence for a while.

Euan helped himself to coffee and sat back down at the table. "Jim, please…give it some time, eh? Think this through. I like Flick. She's a great girl, as long as she is not breaking your heart. At first, I was so chuffed for you. She was gorgeous, funny, a talented artist like I have never seen before… Does she still paint by the way?"

Jim stood and without saying another word, went upstairs to collect the canvas from his room. He returned and without speaking turned the piece around to show his brother.

"Bloody hell, Jim! That's beautiful." Euan gasped. "Why is she wasting her time chasing millionaire's money and other artists when she could be getting recognition for her own talents?"

"I have no idea, bro. She loves to paint. I've never seen a sexier, more beautiful woman than Flick when she paints. She lights up. It's a wonderful sight." Jim sat, clinging on to the canvas.

His mind drifted to her standing by the window where the best light was, easel set out before her, paintbrush in her mouth like a rose in the mouth of a flamenco dancer, hands on hips. He remembered the sensual curve of her bare flesh just peeking out through the side of the over-sized dungarees.

Euan snapped him out of his daydream. "What ever happened to all her other paintings? You know? The ones she did when you were together?"

"She left them behind at the house. She didn't seem to care about them. But I did. I kept them. I even brought them here when I moved. Some are under the bed in my room and the smaller ones are in the loft. There was only one that I couldn't find. One she painted of the two of us."

"What a waste." Euan shook his head. He was right. So, so right. Flick should be the one whose art was on display in galleries. Someone should be selling *her* art, not the other way around.

"Aye…total waste, bro. But she thinks she's happy in what's she does now. The trouble is, I don't think she really knows what she truly wants, thanks to her mother." Jim went on to explain all about Penny, aka Janet, and her advice to her daughter. Euan was aghast. He shook his head.

"Why would you do that to your own daughter? Does her happiness mean nothing to that witch?" Euan didn't particularly hold back.

"I think, deep down, she *thinks* she *is* doing what's best for Flick. I suppose me being unambitious and in a *dead-end* job didn't help matters at the time. And I'm not sure things are any better now."

"Fuck that, Jim! You have your own home and a business. Two businesses if you count the campsite. What more does she want? Just because you're not rolling in cash and famous doesn't make you unworthy."

Jim nodded. "I know that…and you know that…"

"I just think you should take care, Jim. She's hurt you before. What's to stop her doing it again?"

Jim shrugged his tense shoulders. "Nothing, Euan. That's the thing. She could stomp on ma heart again, and I think I would just go with it if it meant I got to be with her for a little while."

"You *idiot*!" Euan smiled, shaking his head. "You really love her, eh?" Jim just nodded. "Well, do me one thing, okay? Wait until we've gone home before you go running off and catching a plane okay?"

"Aye...don't have much choice, do I?" Jim ruffled his brother's hair like he used to when they were kids. Euan whacked his hand away. He still hated it.

Chapter 16

Felicity pulled up outside Polly's late in the evening. She was exhausted from her long journey down from Scotland. She had stopped several times when her emotions had got the better of her and tears blurred her vision. Throughout the whole journey back to London, she played the past few days over in her mind. No matter how much she thought things through, she couldn't realistically blame Jim for his treatment of her. She just felt disappointed that he had chosen to act that way.

Once inside Polly and Matt's three-story Georgian town house, she heaved a sigh of relief and dropped her case by the coat stand. Polly came through from the kitchen, took one look at her, and opened her arms. Felicity fell into her friend's warm embrace and began to sob yet again.

"Oh, sweetheart. What on earth happened up there? I've been so worried." Felicity didn't answer right away. She just poured out all of the raw emotion that she had left inside her, soaking Polly's cashmere sweater through with warm, salty tears. "Come on, let's go through to the lounge... Matt, bring Flick a glass of wine darling!" she called to her husband.

Matt brought the glass, squeezed Felicity's shoulder, and left the girls to talk. Polly handed a rather pretty tissue box to Felicity and waited for her to calm down enough to speak.

"Oh, Polly...what have I done to him?" She sobbed. Polly held Felicity's hand and gently stroked the back of it.

"Sweetie, that's all in the past. Surely he wasn't still holding a grudge, was he?"

"No…no…he was lovely, for the most part. Distant and guarded, but lovely. He let me stay when I got stranded because of the snow. He cooked for me. He even borrowed painting supplies from his friends so that I wouldn't be bored." She sighed. "But he clearly has a visceral fear of getting hurt again. There's been no one serious since me. He met someone lovely by the sound of it, but she apparently lived a fair distance away and he used that as an excuse to not take things further. He won't allow anyone to get close and it's my fault entirely."

"I…don't understand. What went wrong?" Polly tucked a stray strand of hair behind Felicity's ear. "You only went to tell him about your dad."

"Oh, Polly…things were going so well. I felt like I was making amends. I apologised. We talked so much…about everything…and then last night…last night we made love." She covered her face with her hands.

"You did *what*?!" Polly didn't attempt to hide her shock, sitting bolt upright as she spoke. "Oh no, sweetie. But…but…how come?"

"Oh, I don't really know to be honest. We kind of got caught up in the moment. There was a power cut. I don't like the dark…and…well…one thing led to another."

"But Flick, darling, we talked about this. You know how vulnerable you are about Jim. We talked about how you would protect yourself, honey. You're still so deeply in love with him that sex was *bound* to complicate things."

"I know. I just didn't think long enough to stop myself. And I wanted to be with him so much. I think that, on some level, I naively thought we would get back together. That making love to me would make him realise he still loved me. But then this morning….he was…he said…he repeated back to me the line I said to him on the day I left."

"Which was what, Flick?"

Felicity could see the colour in Polly's cheeks. She was angry.

"That it was how he and I say goodbye." She rested her head in her hands feeling rather ashamed.

"Ah."

Felicity had made her friend aware of most of the detail behind her decision to leave Jim at the time it happened. Polly had been honest and said that she didn't completely agree that leaving him was the right thing to do, but she stood by her and vowed to always be there for her in her time of need.

This was that time.

"I broke his heart so severely, Pol, that he hasn't had a proper relationship since. I've ruined his life. I can't bear it. He was my best friend in the whole world. My soul-mate and I broke him." Tears began to fall freely once again as Felicity absorbed the weight of her actions.

~~~~~

A while later Felicity awoke with a start. She sat bolt upright when she realised the room was empty. She was covered over in a cream faux fur blanket on the sofa where she must have fallen asleep. The clock above the mantle told her it was the early hours of the morning. She switched off the table lamp and made her way up to the third floor that she rented, as a whole, from Polly and Matt. Today of all days she was happy of the living arrangement that had been in place for a long while. Things had only changed, temporarily, when she had moved in with Rory. Prior to moving in with Polly, Franco Nilsson had found her a stunning loft apartment to rent. It was near the main gallery and was very modern, bright and airy. When she viewed it she decided it was far too big and impersonal, and she thought she would feel lonely there. She didn't need to try living there to know it just wasn't her. She hated it. Living with Polly and Matt and having friends around when she needed them, like now, was a blessing.

Matt and Polly were always expressing their gratitude for the extra income from letting out their third floor, which was to all intents and purposes a small apartment in its own right. Interest rates had risen substantially since they bought the large property, and they had struggled to pay the mortgage during the period when Flick had moved in with Rory. The fact that there was no separate entrance was all that would have stopped them subletting it to a stranger, so the arrangement worked well.

The little apartment was decorated in creams and beiges, very neutral. There was a main room, which acted as a lounge with a beige chesterfield style sofa, dining area with a café style dining suite in chrome, and a kitchenette where Felicity was able to cook for herself. Off the lounge was a decent sized bathroom with separate shower cubicle and through another door was a double bedroom with built-in wardrobes. Research had told them this area would have been maid's quarters when the house had been built originally. But it suited Felicity quite well. For now.

Considering Felicity's penchant for art, the walls were pretty bare. She had a few photographs of herself with Polly at university and her family but no artwork per se. In her bedside drawer, she kept one framed photo of herself and Jim. It was taken during their first Christmas as a married couple and was beautiful. It was in the drawer so that Felicity could avoid the emotions that seeing the two of them looking so happy evoked, but she knew it was there for the moments when she felt stronger. Even though this was not one of those occasions, she couldn't help lifting it out of the drawer and thinking back to Christmas 2003…

December 2003 – Five Years and Two Months Before the Break-up

The tree was quite small but stood proudly in the corner of their pretty little lounge by the fireplace. They had bought most of their ornaments from Covent Garden. Luckily they both favoured the more traditional ornaments and white lights. Not the flashy, headache-inducing, multi-coloured lights, No, they agreed, white lights that stayed nice and still so as not to cause migraine or a huge distraction whilst they watched TV or kissed for hours at a time. It looked beautiful.

Flick and Jim sat in front of their tree on Christmas morning opening gifts from friends and family, which were mostly of the couples variety—house gifts such as matching Mr. and Mrs. mugs, His and Hers robes and towels, sweet little penguin salt and pepper pots, kitsch but cute, etc. Flick had bought Jim a beautiful, leather bound notebook with his initials embossed on the front for his poetry and book ideas, which he had loved. Jim handed a small gift bag to Flick and her eyes lit up. *Small gifts are always more exciting,* her mother always told her. *They usually contain diamonds!* She doubted it on this occasion, as money was tight. But she didn't really care about diamonds.

With the sound of Bing Crosby playing in the background, Flick opened the bag and took out the velvet box. She opened it slowly, prolonging the anticipation. Jim chewed on his nails, as if he wasn't sure she would like the contents.

Flick gasped. "Oh, Jim! It's beautiful!" She flung her arms around his neck and kissed him fervently. "I just love it. I'll never take it off. Put it on me." She handed Jim the beautiful chain, which had a simple heart-shaped pendant hanging from it.

As he fastened it around her neck, he said, "It's white gold you know. Not silver. I couldn't afford platinum…but now you know you will always have my heart."

Flick turned to face him. "Jim that is the most romantic thing anyone has ever said to me. I'll treasure it and look after it always."

As soon as the words had left her lips, he had kissed her tenderly.

~~~~~

January 2012 — Two Years and Eleven Months After the Break-up

Back in the present day, Flick sat on her bed holding the photo of her with Jim. *Didn't do a very good job of looking after his heart, did you?* She chastised herself regretfully. She trailed her fingers down the image of Jim's handsome face, kissed it and placed the frame back in her drawer.

Chapter 17

The morning after his brother's surprise arrival, Jim sat drinking coffee in the kitchen. He played over in his mind all the things that Euan had said. His brother was, quite rightly, against Jim chasing Flick down. He got it. *Totally.* But Euan didn't fully understand the way he felt about Flick and the impact she'd had on his life. Euan had said that if it were him, he would convince his big brother that there were plenty more fish in the sea and that he should do himself a favour, go fishing and move on. Jim took it all with a pinch of salt. It was great to have him around, but he couldn't help wishing he could just get in the car or on that plane and go to her. *If Euan knew I felt this way, he would be so upset.* Jim began to feel a tad guilty for wishing the time past.

Euan and Tara finally roused from the land of slumber and joined Jim at the table. They kept whispering and looking at each other. It was clear there was subterfuge afoot. Jim didn't ask. He waited until one of them plucked up the courage to speak.

Euan apparently could hold his tongue no longer. "Jim…we've had an idea…tell us to butt out—"

"Butt out." Jim smiled snidely as he interrupted his brother.

"Okay, I deserved that. Seriously though, I've been thinking…that is, Tara and I have been talking…and…we think you should do something with the paintings. Flick needs a wake-up call."

Jim scrunched his face in confusion and shook his head in protest. His voice was sharp as he spoke. "What do you mean? You're not suggesting I throw them away are you? Cause if you are—"

"No! Don't be daft, Jim! Not at all. Quite the opposite." Euan raised his hands in submission. "We think maybe you should try and get them into a gallery. Don't you have any connections with anyone she knows?" Euan looked hopeful. "Or maybe that gallery she used to work at before? You know, an exhibition of her *own* work. Maybe if she sees that she can make it as artist in her own right, she'll feel able to come back here to be with you. It's the perfect location for an artist."

Jim contemplated for a few minutes whilst Euan stared expectantly.

After a long silence, Euan spoke again. "Look…I hope I haven't crossed a line Jim…it was just a suggestion."

The cogs in Jim's mind were almost audibly turning. "Actually…it may be a good idea." He rubbed his chin as he thought. "I could try to find someone…" His words trailed off as he disappeared into his own mind.

"Anyway, I'll leave you to decide what's best to do about it. Like I said it was just an idea." Euan smiled at Tara who slid onto his lap, closing the distance she had apparently been keeping in case fireworks ensued at her partner's suggestion.

"I never thought I would hear myself saying this, bro, but you may have had a fucking brilliant idea for once in your life." Jim's face lit up with a wide toothy grin.

"Cheeky sod!" Euan punched Jim's arm playfully. Jim cried out in pain whilst chuckling simultaneously.

~~~~~

After breakfast Euan and Tara decided to get some of the wonderful Scottish fresh air available to them and took Jasper along for the stroll. Jim decided to rummage through a box of items belonging to Flick that had been discarded at their marital home when she left him for her new life. He was pretty sure there was a little black address book in there. She had purchased a PDA and had copied all the numbers over, rendering the little book useless. He wasn't sure until now why he hadn't just thrown it all out. Maybe things *did* happen for a reason.

On locating the book he opened it and thumbed through to the *F* page. Sure enough, there it was, the telephone number of one Julian Forster, Flick's first protégé in the art world. Jim sat back on his haunches as he remembered his first encounter with the unlikely star...

~~~~~

January 2007 — Twenty-five Months Before the Break-up

"It's all bollocks, you know." A voice from beside Jim rudely tore him from his reverie.

Rather taken aback by the harsh comments of the stranger, Jim turned quickly. "Excuse me?"

Waving his arms around at their surroundings, the man continued. "This. It's all pretentious bollocks. *They* make it about money." He gestured in the direction of Flick and Franco Nilsson. "But all I want to do is paint and have someone appreciate my art."

Smirking at the truth of the man's words, Jim said, "Aye, I think I could be inclined to agree, mate." He nodded and took a swig of his Jack and Coke.

The man held out his hand. "Julian Forster." Jim reciprocated and the pair connected in a firm handshake.

"Jim MacDuff."

"Aren't you Felicity's partner?" Julian enquired.

"Husband."

"Ah…but she doesn't have your name," Julian observed.

Flinching at the comment, Jim took another swig of his drink. "Long story."

"Hmmm. I bet that's a load of pretentious bollocks, too," Julian said dryly.

Jim laughed. "Do you know what, mate? I think you just hit the nail on the head."

"Come on, Jim. I say we go and make the most of the free bar." Julian suddenly perked up.

"Aye. Why the fuck not?" Jim followed the artist as he led the way to the place where Dutch courage could be acquired on tap.

"She used to paint you know," Jim offered as he caught sight of his beautiful wife, who was busy networking, smiling, and flirting as she did, without realising it.

"*Used* to?" Julian's response told Jim that he couldn't imagine painting being something discussed in the past tense.

"Aye, she gave up when all this started." He took another gulp of his Jack Daniels, neat this time. He hissed as the heat from the amber liquid slid down his throat.

"Shit. How could she give it up? With me it's…it's who I am." Julian watched Flick too now, shaking his head as he spoke. "I know you shouldn't let such things define who you are, but with me it…well it just *does*," Julian explained.

"Aye, well, with Flick it clearly is *not* the case," Jim concluded.

"Does she miss it?"

"She never talks about it. Not really. It's a shame though. She was bloody good at it. And I used to love watching her paint." Jim smiled absentmindedly as images of a paint-covered Flick flashed through his mind.

"Huh. What a bloody waste."

"Aye…you can say that again, mate."

After that particular meeting, the two men found themselves at several other gallery and art world functions together. Finding solace in each other's company they would stand at the bar uncomfortably attired in their suits, drinking and complaining about how plastic some people were.

~~~~~

January 2012 — Two Years and Eleven Months After the Break-up

Jim was trying to formulate the plan that his brother had conjured up the idea for. Even though he had found a number for Julian Forster, he was in no way sure that Julian would even still have the same mobile phone. People these days seemed to change their gadgets like they did their underwear. *Nothing ventured, nothing gained*, he reminded himself. as he picked up his phone and dialled.

"Hel-lo?" came the response at the other end.

"Hi, is this Julian Forster?" Jim asked tentatively.

"That all depends on who wants to know," replied the stern male voice.

"I…don't know if you'll remember me…my name is Jim MacDuff. We met—"

"Jim! Of course I remember you. My partner in the crime of hating all things plastic. How could I forget? How the hell are you, mate?" Julian's voice perked up at the realisation.

"Great, thanks, Julian." Jim's voice wavered and he cringed at the sound of it.

"Call me Jules, please, all my friends do. What can I do for you?"

"Look, you know how I told you that Felicity used to paint?"

"Yeah…I still don't get how she could give it all up to sell other people's work."

"Well, that's just it. I need to ask your advice…and maybe a favour, too."

Jim went on to explain about his divorce from Felicity, their recent meeting, the letter from Edgar, and that he wanted to ask his professional opinion about Flick's paintings.

"Wow, mate that's some serious stuff. And you'll never believe this but I'm in Inverness right now! I've been painting for fun again. London just consumes and digests you until there's nothing left to give. I have to get away every so often to remember why the hell I started painting in the first place. How about I meet you in the city next Friday, and I'll take a look at the pieces?"

"Jules, I would be eternally grateful, mate. Thanks so much."

"No worries at all. I can see why you love it up here so much, Jim. The Black Isle is stunning beyond words. I've rediscovered my passion for painting Scottish scenery again. I think Felicity would be crazy not to jump at the chance to come back. I'll do everything I can to help, mate. Don't you worry."

Jules agreed to meet him at a pub he had discovered in Inverness the following Friday. He asked Jim to bring a selection of Flick's artwork along for him to look over. It was all set. They would meet at noon in Johnny Ray's pub. Jim felt a rush of excitement at the thought of doing this for Felicity.

~~~~~

On return from their walk, Jim filled Euan and Tara in on his plans to meet with Jules. Tara got quite giddy.

"I can't believe you know Julian Forster! *The* Julian Forster!" she squeaked. "He is *so* famous in Oz! His artwork is just...transcendent," she announced, dreamily, to the two baffled looking men opposite her. She blushed, reminding Jim of how Felicity used to do the same, so easily. He smiled at the memory.

"Aye well, whatever you say, Tara. I just know he likes to paint nice pictures!" Jim laughed. "And he sounds keen to help me out on the little mission."

~~~~~

Friday morning was thankfully dry, making the transportation of Flick's paintings somewhat easier and less risky than anticipated. Jim and Euan loaded up the Land Rover with a selection of Flick's canvases in a variety of sizes. They were mainly landscape paintings of scenes she had painted from memory following car and train journeys. Jim loved that about her. She looked out through the glass and saw the beauty out there in ways he could never do. She made even industrial landscapes beautiful. He loved that she painted from memory. She did set up her easel and paint what she saw before her, too, but her best works were taken from her mind's eye. That way she could put her own interpretation into the colours and breathe life into the dullest of scenes. Each piece had a personality of its own. Each showed the untapped talent that Flick had quashed and hidden away from view for far too long.

Tara and Euan hugged Jim as he prepared to leave. He was starting to feel the nervous energy building inside him.

"Phew...I'm shaking like a leaf," he informed the couple who stood with arms around each other.

"You'll be fine, Jim. Flick is very talented. Julian will see that right away," Tara assured him.

"Yeah and I bet he has loads of contacts. You need to get him on side, Jim." Euan looked as nervous as Jim felt.

"Don't worry, bro, I intend to make something out of all this. I've got to. Wish me luck, guys."

"Oh, we certainly do, bro." Euan turned to his girlfriend. "Come on, you. We've got the house to ourselves all day and I'm as randy as hell." He picked Tara up and turned toward the cottage, carrying her caveman-like whilst she squealed.

"Ever heard the phrase *too much information*, little brother?!" Jim called after him, laughing when Euan made a rude gesture with his middle finger.

~~~~~

Jim arrived at the agreed meeting place right on time. His palms were sweating as he walked through the doors and scanned the pub for a sign of Julian. Someone waved frantically at him from a corner table. Jim didn't recognise the man with the full beard until he got closer and realised it was, indeed, Julian Forster.

"Jim, mate! Great to see you!" Julian grasped Jim in a manly bear hug, nearly knocking him off balance.

Jim laughed. "Jules, good to see you, too. I almost didn't recognise you."

"Yeah, that'll be the fuzz, I guess?" Julian scratched at his hairy chin. "I got sick of being all clean-shaven and proper so I thought, sod it, I'm going to grow a beard."

Jim pointed at his own chin. "Well, I can say nothing, mate." They both laughed. The pair agreed that the need to be clean-shaven was not a necessity in this day and age.

"What's your poison, mate? I'll get you a drink." Julian headed for the bar as he spoke.

"Ah, just a shandy, thanks. I've got to drive home after this." Jim sat down at the table.

Julian returned and placed the shandy in front of Jim. "So, you guys split, eh?" Julian looked saddened at the news. "Mind you, I have to be honest, mate. I always thought you were a bit of an odd couple." Jim felt hurt at his words and it must have shown in his face. "No, no, don't get me wrong. I'm not saying there was anything *wrong* with *either* of you," Julian backtracked. "No, it was just a…I don't know…strange coupling. She was so ambitious and clean cut and you…well, you're so laid back and…*normal*."

"Gee thanks. Is that supposed to make me feel better?" Jim took a large gulp of his shandy.

"See, I don't really get my point across with words. That's why I'm not a writer like you." Julian's eyes betrayed the guilt he felt for what he had failed communicate. "I just felt that she kind of overshadowed you back then. You looked like you hated being at the gallery events. Am I wrong?"

Jim paused for thought but conceded that he was quite correct in his assumptions. "Nah, I used to hate those things. But I loved her, Jules. I would have done anything for her, you know? Still would and that's my downfall. She's my weakness. I think I'd forgotten that until I saw her again and I mucked it up." He rubbed his hands over his face.

"So now you're trying to win her back?" Julian asked.

"Well, I don't really know what I'm trying to do, to be honest. Things didn't end very well when she left to go back home, and I seem to have misread all the signals. I just…I want her to be happy. It's what I've always wanted."

"And you think that getting someone to display her work is a way to do that?"

"Jules, when you see the paintings, I think you'll agree that she can't just leave her talent behind. It's like she's lost sight of who she really is. If I'm honest, I want the girl I fell in love with. And that was the Flick who paints amazing, heartfelt pieces of stunning artwork. Not the woman who jet sets all over the world discovering other artists and selling *their* work, no disrespect, mate. I wouldn't mind but she absolutely *hates* flying." Jim looked pleadingly into Julian's eyes. "I want *my* Flick back, Jules. I at least want to try, and then even if it doesn't work out I know that I've done *everything* I can."

Julian nodded, but then after a pause he huffed a long drawn out breath, as is preparing to deliver bad news. "But, Jim, what if she doesn't want to be that person anymore? What if she is angry at you for doing this?"

He looked directly into Julian's eyes. "It's a chance I have to take." His resolve was firm.

"Right then, mate, let's have a look at these paintings!" Julian clapped his hands together and stood with determination.

~~~~~

The two men stood in the car park looking at the artwork in the back of the Land Rover like they were doing some dodgy, underhanded deal. Jim glanced around nervously hoping that some passer-by didn't see them and call the police.

"Bloody hell, Jim." Julian gasped. "I can see what you mean." He shook his head. "This girl is wasting an amazing bloody talent!"

Jim let out a huge sigh of relief. He wasn't aware until that point that he had been holding his breath. "You think so?" He bit on his bottom lip and fidgeted, tying his fingers in knots.

"*Think* so? I *know* so, mate." A wide grin spread across Julian's face. "And I know just the person to show them to." His expression changed to one of concern. "The only trouble is our Felicity Johnston-Hart is well known throughout the art world. If her name is on them or on the exhibition everyone will know it's her and she'll find out what's going on before we have time to finalise things."

"She never used to sign the fronts of her pieces. I think that was another sign of her feelings of inferiority. You'll find her signatures are on the back."

"Well that's a good start…so all we need to do is decide what name to put down for the artist presenting the exhibition." Julian looked skyward as if the answers could be found up there.

Jim's brain whirred with ideas. A grin spread wide across his face.

"Flick MacDuff," was all he said.

Chapter 18

February 2012 - Three Years After the Break-up

New York was cold. Flick hadn't been prepared for quite how cold it would be. It was almost Valentine's Day and she was in the Big Apple all alone.

Again.

Once she accepted the position at the New York gallery, Franco had insisted she fly out early. She had jumped at the chance to escape and get Jim out of her mind once and for all. The gallery was looking amazing, and she had settled in okay since making the journey at the beginning of the month to begin her new position. The only problem was: the getting Jim out of her mind part wasn't quite working.

She had hoped and prayed that he would turn up on her doorstep demanding that she stay with him. She knew it was unrealistic to wish for such things. But a girl could dream. It never happened and so with more than a little trepidation she accepted the role and decided this had to be a fresh start.

The first couple of days in the big city had been a blur of finding her bearings and meeting her new staff. Everyone had been lovely but a little cautious to begin with. She understood their reticence at welcoming her as Chester's replacement but did her best to be friendly and approachable. Yet here she sat, at her paperwork covered desk wishing she had a romantic evening to look forward to.

"Hey, Felicity. You look deep in thought there." A female voice dragged her from her sadness. She smiled as she turned toward Lia, her personal assistant—formerly

Chester's personal assistant. She was a strikingly beautiful brunette with a figure that most women would give their eyeteeth for. And the annoying thing was she was kind of sweet, too. "Penny for them?" Lia cocked her head to one side, smiling.

"Oh, I was just depressing myself with the fact that I'm once again in New York for Valentine's Day and I'm totally alone." Felicity sighed. She shook her head as if to rid herself of the melancholy. "Oh, pay no attention to me. I'm just being a sissy." She forced a laugh.

"Not at all. It must be hard being away from your husband." Lia looked sympathetic.

"Ah…well…I'm actually *divorced* from…the love of my life," Felicity mumbled her reply. Lia looked shocked.

Understandably so.

She pulled her lips in between her teeth and frowned. "If you don't mind my asking…if he's the love of your life how come you're divorced?" Lia's confused expression was no surprise to Felicity.

She rolled her eyes. "Long story. Too long and drudgy to bore someone I hardly know with it." Felicity turned back toward the paperwork she had been staring at earlier. Not working on, just *staring* at.

"Well, why don't we remedy that? How do you feel about going for a drink across the street after work with me? I usually meet some friends there, but they're out of town for Valentine's, go figure. So it'd just be me and you. We could work on that someone-you-hardly know issue." She smiled warmly. Felicity looked to her again. She turned her eyes to the ceiling as if trying to work out if she were free. Who was she kidding? She was nothing *but* free.

"Okay. Thanks, Lia. That would be lovely."

"Great! Shall I come get you at six thirty? I know you tend to work way past five and I have some stuff I need to get finished too, so…"

"Yes…although it may be a little after that. It's four now and I have lots of things to work through. The acquisitions paperwork has been left in a bit of a state." She huffed, rubbing her eyes.

Lia cringed. "Is it that bad?" She looked uneasy. "Can I help with anything?"

"Yes, I'm afraid it *is* that bad and no, thank you…I need to get this done myself. The figures are just not adding up, and I need to call Franco with a full report by the end of the week. Lucky me, eh?"

"Okay…well if you need anything…even if it's a coffee, just holler." Lia smiled warmly.

"That's really kind, Lia. Thank you."

~~~~~

Right on cue at six thirty, Lia came back to Felicity's office and tapped on the door. "You ready yet?"

"Hi. Almost. Give me fifteen more minutes…make it twenty." It was Felicity's turn to cringe. "Oooh, I'm sorry, Lia it may be more like twenty five."

"Hey, don't worry. I'm all done for today, but I have my eReader. I'm reading a really good book." She held her hand up in a dramatic gesture to talk behind it. "It's a little steamy, if you know what I mean. The lead male is sooo hot. Scottish and tattooed. Plus he's a little rugged and has a potty mouth." She sniggered. "So I think I'll just sit in the break room and wait on you." She turned on her heel and walked away.

Scottish and rugged, eh? Go figure.

Mick's bar was beginning to fill up when they arrived at seven. Despite its name the establishment was quite upmarket and was viewed as one of *the* places to be seen around the city. Lia waved to the bartender to get his attention and he came right over.

"Hey, Steve. This is Felicity. She's *British*. It's her first time here at Mick's." Lia bombarded the man with useless information. He turned to Felicity and his smiled broadened. He had a look of Joey from the series *Friends*, and she half expected him to raise an eyebrow and feed her the line the character was most was most famous for. Instead and much to Felicity's disappointment, he lifted his chin in a move of acknowledgement.

"Hey British. What's your poison?"

Felicity felt her cheeks heat. "Oh…Jack and Coke?" She had no clue what to order and for some reason Jim's favourite drink was what sprang to mind.

"Comin' right up." He turned to prepare her drink order. Felicity looked toward Lia who was now grinning from ear to ear.

"Is he cute or what?" She nudged Felicity playfully. She couldn't deny that there was something attractive about the man. He was very muscular. His hair was tousled in that *just got out of bed* way and he did have a very nice smile. But she didn't really care how good-looking he was. He wasn't Jim.

The two women found an empty booth and took their drinks over, claiming it as their own. Felicity was relieved to finally be getting to know someone else in the city. It was beginning to look like the start of a lonely and isolated life for her. Lia seemed nice and was only a few years younger than herself. She seemed like the type of person Felicity could be friends with, even if she did look like she had walked off a movie set or the cover of a swanky magazine.

A true New Yorker by birth and upbringing, Lia knew all the best places to eat, the best places to visit, and the best places to meet eligible bachelors. Felicity smiled at her comments about the single men of New York and hoped that maybe one day she would be able to meet someone. But right now the idea of someone new was so far off in the future that it didn't need to take up valuable space in her mind. Her mind was crammed full as it was.

They chatted easily for a good couple of hours. Lia Cole was surprisingly an only child. Felicity found this strange as she just looked and acted like someone who would have lots of siblings watching her back. This was not the case. She loved art. That was clear and had studied art history at college much the same as Felicity. That was their common ground. They talked about their favourite artists for hours. Lia had a boyfriend but was quite cagey on the details. All she did ascertain was that he was quite a lot older than Lia.

The conversation centred a lot on Felicity and her life. Surprisingly she had found it easier than normal to open up about her past with Jim. Lia had point blank decided he just wasn't good enough for her. But she just didn't know him. Felicity had to change the subject.

"So tell me, Lia, what happened to Chester?" The former manager of the art gallery had allegedly had some sort of break down, but Felicity had met him several times whilst working for Franco and he always seemed so together.

Lia shifted uncomfortably in her seat. "Oh, you know, work pressures...he let things get on top of him." Felicity thought she noticed her cheeks colour as she spoke. Perhaps she felt somehow responsible? Poor Lia.

"But he was so...controlled. I find it hard to believe he just gave up."

"Yeah well, he just got so wound up about…stuff, that something had to give. I guess it was his health and sanity or his job." Lia shrugged but didn't make eye contact. There was something in the way she spoke that just didn't ring true. They sat in silence for a few moments whilst Felicity mulled things over. Eventually she put it down to the alcohol.

"So, Felicity, are you going to date whilst you're here?" Lia quickly changed the subject back to Felicity's single status again.

"I seriously doubt it for the moment. I really want to get a place to rent and get the gallery organised and…maybe in a few months…who knows." Felicity stirred the ice around her glass.

"That's a shame…there's a gorgeous guy at the bar who is *totally* checking you out." Lia giggled.

Felicity felt the heat rise in her cheeks again as she slowly shifted her gaze and looked over to where the man sat. He smiled and raised his glass to her. She turned away abruptly.

Lia leaned over the table toward her. "What's wrong, Felicity? He's a good-looking guy. Just relax and have some fun with it."

Steve from behind the bar came over to their table with two more drinks. "Ladies…Compliments of the mafia type sitting at the bar." Steve smirked as he placed the drinks down in front of the two women.

Felicity shook her head. "Oh. No, no, thank you but please tell him I don't accept drinks from strange men."

Lia snorted with laughter. "What are you five? He's not some pervert offering you sweeties, little girl." She mocked and Felicity felt sure she was crimson by now.

"Hey, it's okay, British. Poured them myself. He never got to lay a hand on them, so they're good," Steve informed her.

Feeling somewhat cajoled into the situation, Flick accepted the drink. "Well tell him thank you." She glanced over to where the man sat again. He was very attractive. Clean shaven, short, dark almost black hair, and olive skin. He looked Italian. He looked stunning.

"Back in a sec," Lia announced rising from the table.

Felicity panicked. "Where are you going? You can't leave me!"

"I'm going to the bathroom. You have to stay here in case someone takes our booth. It's getting busy in here. I won't be long." She walked away.

Felicity looked up to see the handsome man walking toward her. God, he was not only gorgeous, but ridiculously tall and well-built too. *Oh shitty, shitty, shit.* Why did this stereotypical, Italian hunk want to hit on *her*, for goodness sake?

"Good evening, I wanted to say thank you for accepting the drink I sent over. It's not something I usually do and I could see that you hesitated. I don't blame you *cara mia*. You are very sensible and I apologise if I offended you or worried you in any way." Yup…Italian…and gorgeous…and nice. *Dammit!* Guilt washed over her as the man turned to walk away.

"Wait." She spoke before thinking. The man stopped and turned back to her. "Erm…I should thank *you*…for the drink, I mean."

"You are most welcome *cara mia*. I was watching you and felt…drawn to you. Forgive me." It was a cheesy line but, boy, close up he was rather stunning, as she had presumed he would be. He held out his hand. "I am Vitale De Luca…and you are?"

"Felicity Johnston-Hart. Pleased to meet you, Vitale."

"The pleasure is all mine I can assure you. Are you here on holiday with your...husband?" the rather beautiful man enquired. Felicity caught herself looking at his lips and inadvertently licked her own. He smiled as if he saw.

"N-no...I'm working here at the Nilsson-Perkins gallery. It's a new role and I haven't been here long." She gulped as the man slid into the booth opposite her, never taking his gaze from hers.

"I thought as much. If I had seen you before I would have remembered. Sei un gioello."

Oh God, and now he is talking in Italian... I'm done for.

"I'm s-sorry, I don't speak much Italian." *Idiot, you don't speak any sodding Italian!*

Vitale smiled wider this time, revealing a set of perfect white teeth. Not perfect in that fake veneer type of way. No, these were his own, perfect white teeth, sitting in his own delicious mouth, behind those full luscious lips...

"It means you are a jewel...a gemstone." He cringed and shook his head. "I must sound like a...what do you call it? Cheese monster?" He bowed his head and his self-deprecation was sweet.

Felicity couldn't help but smile. "Not at all. I've never been called a *jewel* before." She realised she was twisting her hair around her fingers. *Oh for goodness, sake woman get a grip.* She released the strand and straightened.

"I would very much like to take you to dinner. Would you consider this maybe?" Vitale asked, looking hopeful and smiling at her reactions.

"Oh...I don't know...I'm not looking for—"

Vitale's smile faded. "No, no. That's fine. I pounced on you the moment your friend left. You are new here and this is the last thing you need. Cheese monsters coming on to you...I understand." He stood to leave just as Lia returned.

"The offer was very sweet." *Stupid, stupid, stupid woman.* She was mentally beating herself up as guilt washed over her. "I don't mean to offend you."

Vitale reached and took Felicity's hand. "Not possible *cara mia.* You have brightened my evening simply by speaking to me. I give you my card." He released her hand. "Maybe once you are settled you can give me a call and I can cook for you? Not Italian though. I will not betray my mother's memory. My Italian cooking is terrible! No, I will cook for you the best Paella you have ever tasted. I don't know any Spanish people I could offend by doing so." He laughed and she couldn't help but laugh, too, at his admission.

"That would be lovely," she replied. As she took his card from his hand he held her fingers in his.

"Until next time." He smiled warmly, his dark eyes sparkling. "Have a wonderful evening ladies." He turned and walked away.

"Wowee, lady! He was so freaking hot I thought my panties would melt!" Lia fanned herself. "Are you going on a *date*?" She tapped her fingers together giddily.

Felicity shook her head. "No, he asked and I declined." *Again, stupid!*

"Seriously? Are you crazy?" Lia's wide-eyed expression told Felicity all she needed to know.

"Yes…I think it's official." She said putting the card away without looking at it.

Chapter 19

February 2012 – Three Years After the Break-up

Jim looked after the rental car as it disappeared into the distance. He waved one last time to his brother. Seeing Euan and Tara together had made him realise just what he had been missing with Flick. A smile spread across his face at the thought of his plans for the exhibition. She *had* to realise she was meant to paint after this, *surely*? Shivering, he went inside and closed the door to the sub-zero temperature that had set in once again overnight.

He scratched Jasper's head. "Come on, boy. I need a cup of Joe after that cold out there." He walked through the cosy lounge where the fire was just about dying down and into the kitchen.

Today was going to be a pretty major step on the technology front. He needed the boost of caffeine for what would, no doubt, be one hell of a confusing experience. Ram and processor speed, broadband router this, that, and the other. It was all Greek to Jim, but he had decided that Edgar's book needed to be finished using the most up to date equipment if he was going to do it justice at all.

After two cups of fresh coffee, he donned his warm fleece and waterproof walking coat and climbed into the Landy. He set off for the nearest retail park—which wasn't actually that near—in search of a laptop computer. *Oh…and a printer…of course I'll need a printer…and some paper…and something to keep it all in…bloody hell this is going to be expensive!*

After being bombarded with overly complicated information and looking at a gazillion different laptops—that actually all looked pretty much identical until they all blurred into one—he exited the store weighed down with boxes and bags galore. The young male sales assistant clearly knew his stuff, which highlighted the exact *opposite* about Jim as he was bamboozled with memory sizes, running speeds, and graphics cards.

The young guy—oddly called *Guy*—had assured him that, in this day and age, it was a *crime* to not have Internet access. The teenager had gaped at Jim for what felt like an hour when confronted with the news that he had just never had the Internet installed. He had only *now* acquiesced to its installation, deciding that Flick would probably want to have this…if she moved in…no, no, *when* she moved in. *Stay positive, MacDuff.* It may be temporary whilst they figured things out, a kind of trial period, a holiday if you will, but he was determined to do everything in his power to ensure that she had no reasons to *not* move in.

Guy had given detailed instructions as to how to set everything up when he arrived home and that he needed to call his telephone provider to set up the Internet connection. He had thrust a business card into Jim's hand, telling him to call if he got stuck, and then he had given him a look of sympathy. Jim felt ancient and about two inches tall, but had to admit the information was a jumble in his mind. On arriving back at the cottage, he unloaded his purchases, rolled up his sleeves, and set about the arduous task of joining the 21st century.

Firing up the laptop was quite exciting. Of course he had used computers before, but had always favoured the old fashioned way. There was something soothing about the click, click of a typewriter and burrr-ing of the winder that made him smile. But here he was tapping away at the keyboard of his flashy new laptop, feeling quite proud of himself for succeeding.

~~~~~

The manuscript pages sent to him by Edgar were wonderful. Jim had always loved the gentle flow of Edgar's prose and having this opportunity to write and be published whilst being able to remain in the background was just mind-blowing. He had gone through Edgar's myriad notes with a fine-tooth comb and felt well equipped to do the work justice. It would keep him occupied whilst Julian put everything in place over in Glasgow. He made a start as soon as things were set up and gave himself a pat on the back for getting it all to work first time. *In your face, Guy.* He mentally stuck two fingers up at the barely-out-of-nappies-patronising-to-the-core sales assistant.

Julian rang later on that day. "Jim, mate! How's it going? You started writing that book yet?"

"Hi, Jules, yeah. I made a start today when I'd finished setting up my new laptop." Jim couldn't help but smile to himself with pride again.

"Ooh, get you joining the techno-age. You'll be Tweeting next." Julian chuckled. *Oh no I bloody won't.* "Great, great stuff. Anyway, I'm glad you took him up on it. It'll do you good to be writing again. Look, just a quick update. The guy I mentioned at the gallery, Jean-Paul Fabron? Remember? He absolutely *loves* the paintings and he has agreed to a three month exhibition!" The excitement in Julian's voice took it up an octave.

His enthusiasm was contagious, and Jim felt giddiness bubbling up from his boots. "What? Really?" He sat up straight, silently fist bumping the air and mouthing the words, *Get in!* "That's fantastic news! Thank you so much, Jules. Thank you."

"Hey, it's no problem, mate. She's so talented it's worth it to see her get the notoriety she deserves. Now, I need to talk to you about getting her to come over." Julian's voice became serious. "I have to be honest, I think *I* need to be the one to go over to New York, Jim."

Disappointment washed over Jim, his mood plummeted. "You? How come? I…I wanted to go see her."

"I know, I know. But I think we need to keep it anonymous right up to the point where she walks in and sees it. I can go over there and pretend to have an amazing find for her. She'd go for that."

"Aye, I know but—"

"What would *you* say if you went? That you loved her and had taken her most private works and slapped them all over Glasgow to show her just how much? Think about it. What if she's angry? She could be. I think that me getting her here is the best idea. Once she sees the exhibition she *will* be bowled over mate. She couldn't possibly be angry when she *sees* them up there."

Jim acquiesced. After all it did make more sense. But he couldn't help the heaviness he felt over it. "Aye, okay. So what's the plan?"

"Right, so here's what I'm thinking. I go over and tell her I've made this amazing discovery, but that I'm keeping it anonymous so that no one else can see the work before Nilsson-Perkins. She'll go for that. I'll tell her to book a flight and come over so that she thinks she's coming on business. You'll be hiding in the wings, so to speak, when she arrives for her private showing. Et voila! She adores you once she finds out how amazing the paintings look and that *you* have been instrumental in arranging it all!"

Jim thought for a few moments, his heart already pounding at the plan. "Okay, so when are you going out?"

"I think next month. The exhibition will start in April, and so she'll have a month to make arrangements and get herself over here. Sorted."

"And what if she refuses?"

"Not a chance, Jim. I know Felicity of old, mate. She's like a dog with a bone when she sniffs new talent. I only have to think back to how she was with me. Talk about bloody tenacious. She wouldn't leave me alone until I'd agreed to work with her. She's bloody good at her job, Jim, even if she should be painting instead. And I think that I can lay it on thick enough to make her completely intrigued."

"Okay. Great. Keep me posted, eh?" Jim didn't like how much he had been manipulated in one day but had to agree that in Julian's case, he was right.

The call ended and Jim went back to Edgar's book. Thanks to his new link to the World Wide Web, he had been able to do his own research for the book and it was coming along well even though he hadn't really been working on it long. He made a call to Edgar's editor to let him know he had taken up the challenge. Geoffrey Haddington had been a long-time friend of Edgar's and was delighted to receive Jim's call.

"I'm so glad you decided to do it, Jim. Edgar thought the world of you and he was so hopeful that you would take it on, but I was under strict instructions not to bother you if you chose not to. Bless you for doing this."

"Oh no, don't thank me. It really is an honour. And I thought the world of him, too. I miss hearing from him. But I feel closer to him whilst I'm working on his book, if that makes sense." Jim felt his cheeks heat at his sentimental admission.

"Perfect sense, Jim. And thanks to you Edgar will live on through this final work. I can tell you with all honesty that he would be so very proud of you. He often spoke of you and how much he missed you being around. I'm sure you know this but…he thought of you as a dear son. And he knew that you would do a good job. Again, thank you."

The older man's words brought a lump to Jim's throat but he felt good when the call was over. If he had been in any doubt over completing the book, those doubts had melted away completely now.

Chapter 20
February 2012 – Three Years After the Break-up

At the end of their evening, Felicity and Lia made their way out of the bar and hailed a yellow cab. Lia was dropped off at her apartment block that looked nothing like the one inhabited by Monica and Rachel on *Friends*. Felicity couldn't help smirking at her own naiveté. She really was going to have to readjust to the *real* New York and stop living in the imaginary version she had learned from TV. She had been to The Big Apple on business on several occasions but living here and seeing where real people lived...well, it was a different thing entirely.

The gallery, and the bar, were only a short cab ride back to the rather plush, well known hotel where Franco had insisted Felicity stay for a while until she found somewhere more permanent. It was very elegant and elaborate but it was the kind of place you needed to experience *with* someone. Not alone. And she was oh so alone, feeling that ten times more when she arrived back there on an evening and had time to herself. Time to think and reminisce.

~~~~~

Whilst on the way back to her hotel suite, Felicity rode the elevator with what appeared to be a newly married couple. They kissed and fondled each other with little regard for their fellow passenger. Felicity rolled her eyes as the young man held the woman in a possessive embrace and nipped at her neck with his teeth, completely oblivious to Felicity's presence. Thankfully, she left the elevator before they went any further. She felt like she had been temporarily thrust onto the set of some erotic movie and was annoyed at the fact that they blatantly ignored her coughs whilst trying to draw their attention to the fact that they had company.

Finally, she reached the sanctuary of her luxurious and over-the-top suite. Falling back onto the plush sofa, she switched on the television, and of course, there it was on the screen, the well-known movie where the girl looks across at the empire state building just as it lights up with a heart and she realises that her Mr. Right is probably waiting for her at the top. Jeez, the whole city was mocking her very presence.

Grabbing her bag, she rummaged around in it until she found the card that Vitale had given her. She read it with interest. *Vitale DeLuca, Managing Director, DeLuca Pharmaceuticals*. Wow. He was a big wig alright. M.D. of a drug company. Obviously a drug company that was doing quite well judging by his expensive suit.

She placed the card back in the bottom of her bag as Jim suddenly sprang to mind. Okay, so he wasn't Italian, dark or mysterious. But he was warm, sexy, and hilariously funny. Passionate…yes, he was that, too. She groaned as she realised once again that she had blown it with him.

She resolved to focus on work. Romance was something she could, would, and *should* live without. Jim was someone she would have to learn to let go of.

Work.

That was the answer.

~~~~~

Monday morning was bitterly cold. She was beginning to become accustomed to this February, New York weather. The skyscrapers went a little way to shielding her from the icy chill, but she still wished she had a little more appropriate clothing. She would have to go shopping.

Shopping in New York.

Alone.

Blurgh. She could ask Lia to accompany her. That would probably be best, as Lia would know the best places to shop. Although after Friday, she was unsure as to how much, other than art, they had in common.

She sat in her office thumbing through some more of the paperwork that Chester had made a pig's ear of. Lia had called and asked if she wanted to join her for lunch but she had declined. Sarah, the receptionist who was heavily pregnant, had gone to her prenatal visit, and Kyle, the other gallery assistant, had met his wife and daughter for lunch, and so the gallery had been closed for an hour. Not something Felicity would usually do, but on this one occasion, when everything was just so disorganised, it didn't feel that it mattered too much.

Her head was throbbing, and typically, she didn't have any headache pills with her. She decided to go and raid the cupboards in the break room and see if someone, anyone was either around to give her some or had left any in a drawer or cupboard. She hunted through half a dozen drawers but to no avail.

A door through the break room had intrigued her for days now. She hadn't noticed it before last week, but when she asked Lia what was through there, she was told it was just a stock room where old damaged, paintings were kept ready for insurance claims. *How many damaged items could there be to warrant a whole room?*

This was not something that had ever been an issue before. Not something she had heard of. Not something that was needed in the London gallery. It was becoming so *very* clear why Chester had been let go, and she knew that as the new manager, it would be her job to deal with damages and insurance. *Oh joy.*

She decided as no one was here to give her lame excuses it was time she took a look in that storeroom. Wondering what the hell *else* Chester had done. It *had* to be him. Lia had seemed sympathetic to him. She showed some kind of misplaced loyalty. But Lia was just a nice girl who would do anything for anyone. She must have respected her former boss a great deal. At least *she* had some admirable qualities, which is more than could be said for the man himself.

She tried the handle but the door was locked. Incensed that as the manager of this gallery there were rooms she couldn't even access, she rifled through drawers looking for a key. None materialised. With her anger increasing she decided that *someone* must have a key. Lia wasn't due back for an hour, and so Felicity nervously went to her desk first, feeling guilty but also entitled to look in that room. No key there. Next she searched Sarah's desk and then Kyle's. *Nothing.* Back to the kitchen, she rifled through the drawer nearest to the door once more. *Nothing.* One last-ditch attempt found her on a chair sliding her hand along the top of the door frame. *And bingo!* Sure enough there was a key secreted on the top of the frame amongst the dust bunnies. Why were the contents of this room so protected when they were damaged stock? She took the key down and decided to try the door.

The key fit, and with trepidation at just how much money Chester had seemingly lost for the company, she dreaded what was behind the mysterious door. She flicked on the light switch and walked in. She gasped, covering her mouth with her hands, as she saw several stacks of paintings. *There must be thousands of dollars of damaged canvas here!* Her heart raced. What the hell had caused this? How could Chester have been so lacking in care? How the *hell* would she explain this to Franco? He would go all out to ruin Chester who was already ill by all accounts.

She flicked through the canvases to see if any could be salvaged. But confusion washed over her. She shook her head and went back to the start. *What the—?* She pulled out canvas after canvas, which showed no damage. Not in any way. *So why?* She froze when she pulled out two canvases she recognised as pieces by well-respected artist Edward Vincent, who was known for producing valuable *one off* paintings. So why were there two canvases here which were identical? And more to the point why were there two of *this* painting when *she* had sold the original to a wealthy businessman in London? Looking closer she inspected the signature and numbers denoting that this was, indeed, a one off. Oh no! They were copies! Forgeries! Gathering speed she flicked through the canvases again.

Copy after copy marked up to be one off original pieces. Copies of paintings that were worth tens of thousands of dollars, and considering how many of them were here in this room, it would amount to millions of dollars. *Forgery. Oh. My. God.* Her heart rate increased further and she began sweating. Someone was using *this* gallery to sell forged artwork. *Shit! This can't be happening!* She quickly closed and locked the door taking care to leave everything as it was. She needed to think. Who knew about this? Who was in on it? Did Franco know? Surely not. Franco was a genuine man with a passion for originals, *especially* one off pieces. There had to be an explanation that didn't include Franco.

She returned to her desk and stared at her phone. Who could she trust with this? She snorted. Of course, *Jim* would be the only one she would trust with this kind of thing. He was sensible and level headed. *He* would know what to do.

She picked up the receiver but immediately put it back down. She couldn't just call him out of the blue. That would be ridiculous. She felt like she was ready to scream.

She surmised that Chester was somehow involved but couldn't prove that yet. Considering she was an Oxford graduate from Hampshire, this kind of thing was relatively new to her, and she had not one single clue as to how to go about solving such a crime. She was no detective. And she could be implicated in this, too, if the criminal behind it found out she knew. This was not good. *So* not good.

Suddenly, Lia breezed in. "Hey there. Brought you a cupcake from the little bakery across the street. They are sooo delicious." She rolled her eyes as she spoke.

How sweet. Lia had worked here awhile. She would know wouldn't she? If dodgy dealings were going on? Or would she? She had been sympathetic to Chester before. But she was so nice. Maybe she just felt sorry for him? She couldn't possibly be aware. "You okay, Felicity? You don't look too good. You're…real pale." Lia's eyes showed her concern.

"Erm…no…I don't *feel* too good. I think I have a migraine coming on." She rubbed her temples.

"I have some pain pills." Lia stepped closer to Felicity's desk. "I could bring them to you."

"That would be great… Yes, please, Lia." Felicity nodded but it hurt to do so. Lia disappeared and quickly returned with the tablets and a glass of chilled water. Felicity downed two of the tablets and took a large gulp of water. "Thank you so much."

"Maybe you should go home… I mean back to the hotel? You look so very pale. We can manage here. It's been quiet all day."

As much as Felicity hated to admit it, Lia was right. Plus she needed to distance herself from her discovery for a while and think. Formulate a plan. She stood and wobbled, the pain in her head causing the dizziness and a wave of nausea to wash over her. She grabbed her bag by the strap, but everything fell out as she did.

"Here, let me help you there." Lia crouched to put the items back in Felicity's bag. "Come on, I'll walk you out and hail you a cab." Lia put her arm around Felicity's waist.

"You're being so lovely. I do appreciate it." Felicity smiled.

"Hey, that's what friends are for." The two women walked toward the exit.

Lia hailed a yellow cab and waited until Felicity got inside okay. She instructed the driver where to go and waved goodbye to Felicity. "I'll call you later," Lia called with the look of concern still in place. Felicity held her hand up in a wave but was struck by dizziness again as she turned her head.

Back in her suite, she sunk onto her bed, not really knowing how she managed to coherently pay the driver and make her way up to her rooms. The events of the day had just about knocked her sideways, but she couldn't think about it now. She decided to let sleep take her and she would think more tomorrow. Thankfully sleep came quickly as the pain pills kicked in and she drifted off.

~~~~~

A phone was ringing somewhere. Felicity opened her eyes and carefully sat. She realised it was her cell phone that was in fact making the noise. She clambered of the bed and stood. Her head felt much better but there was still a dull ache at the back of her skull that reminded her of why she was here and not at work. The room was dark apart from the light of the lamp in the corner. She fumbled around and managed to find what she was looking for.

"Hello?" she croaked.

"Finally!" Lia sighed heavily at the other end of the line. "I was getting so worried, Felicity. I was ready to send for paramedics or something. How're you feeling?"

"Oh…you know…fair to crap." She yawned.

"Well, do you want me to come over and look after you? I have nothing planned. I could bring you some food up?"

Bless her. "No, no, it's fine, Lia. Probably better if I get some more sleep. I feel completely drained." She rubbed her head again. "What time is it?"

"It's after eight. I wanted to give you long enough to sleep off the migraine. Do you get them often?" Lia's question stopped Felicity for a moment.

"Do you know… I don't remember the last time I had one. It's probably over a year ago now." Felicity actually *knew* the last one she had was on the day she left Jim.

"Well, something must have triggered it. I think you should consider seeing a doctor. I can recommend one if you'd like me to. But for now, get some more sleep and stay home tomorrow if you feel bad. Honestly, Felicity, we can manage without you for a couple days."

"That's very sweet, Lia, but I have a serious job to do at that gallery. I can't afford time off."

Lia sighed. "Okay, you're the boss. Sleep well. You have my cell. If you need anything just call, okay?"

"Okay, thanks again, Lia. I really appreciate it." She hung up.

~~~~~

The next time Felicity awoke it was to the sound of her alarm clock. With trepidation she lifted her head, anxiously awaiting the thud, thud, thud of her headache. Thankfully it didn't happen. Pulling herself to a sitting position, she suddenly remembered what had caused her headache to get so bad in the first place. She let out a long groan. She had to *really* think through what to do next about their little stash of art forgeries, and to ensure it was dealt with as soon as possible but without any innocent parties being implicated.

She climbed into the shower, turning the dial as hot as she could stand it. Maybe she could scald some ideas into her brain and wash the remnants of the issues down the drain? Neither of those things happened. *Dammit.* She readied herself for work, blow-drying her blonde hair roughly and pinning it up into chignon. She applied a little makeup and put on her charcoal grey pantsuit. She was ready.

When she arrived at the gallery, Sarah was already there, making a pot of fresh coffee. She smiled at Felicity as she arrived. "Good morning, Felicity. Kyle called. He'll be a little late in."

"Okay. Is everything alright?" Felicity enquired.

"His daughter is running a fever and his wife is suffering with morning sickness, so he has to run his daughter to see the paediatrician."

"Oh dear. I hope she'll be okay." Felicity's concern was fleeting and she felt a little guilty. But she needed to get into her office and formulate some kind of plan.

Lia arrived carrying her staple take out black coffee and a bran muffin in a brown paper bag. She poked her head around Felicity's door. "Hey. You're looking much better today."

"Thanks I feel it. Lia…can I speak with you for a moment?"

"Sure…this sounds ominous. You look serious." Lia's brow furrowed as she walked in and began to walk over to the chair opposite Felicity.

"Close the door first please," Felicity requested. Lia looked very worried.

"Uh-oh…am I in trouble?" Lia placed her cup and bag on the desk.

Felicity smiled as warmly as she could. "No, nothing like that. I need to speak to you in confidence. A serious matter has come to my attention."

Lia frowned. "Oh? What serious matter?"

"Lia…you know the storeroom at the end of the break room?"

"Yesss? The *damages den* as I like to call it…what about it?" Lia looked confused.

"I went in to assess how many damaged pieces there are. I'm trying to get a very broad picture of what needs to be dealt with…you understand?"

"Yesss?" Lia was still looking confused.

"I made a rather startling discovery," Felicity informed her.

Lia's mouth dropped open and she leaned forward. "Really? How much damaged stuff was in there?"

"None. Not one damaged thing, Lia."

Lia touched her hands to her face. "What? I don't understand? Where's it all gone? Chester said it was in there—" Lia now looked panicked. Her face had coloured up red.

"No, no there *were* pieces in there. Just not…*damaged* ones."

Lia shook her head. "I'm sorry, Felicity. I don't remember Chester dealing with them *all* before he left. I may be coming across dumb here, but I don't get—"

"Forgeries, Lia."

"I'm sorry? What?" Lia's face paled, and her eyes widened like a startled animal.

"I found row upon row of forged pieces. Copies. I know this because there were several copies of *Jagged Heart* by Edward Vincent, a one off piece that I sold in London to a very private millionaire businessman and *that* one was the original. I took delivery of it in person from the artist himself."

"Are…are you accusing *me* of having some kind of involvement in this?" Lia's face continued its colour journey, this time it went white and her eyes became glassy.

"No! God, Lia no don't be silly! Not at all." Felicity shook her head vigorously, and Lia heaved a sigh of relief.

Lia visibly relaxed. "Phew…I really thought I was in seriously deep shit for a moment there."

"No. But I think I *do* know who is involved."

"You do?" Lia looked inquisitively at Felicity.

"I think it may be Chester."

Lia laughed loudly. "Chester? No way! He was so…*straight laced*. Honestly. He would never do something like that, Felicity…I swear it."

"Think about it, Lia. He was letting the pressure get to him. He was making lots of mistakes. He was in over his head. I think we need to speak to Franco."

"No!" Lia spat making Felicity jump. "I-I mean, no, he wouldn't do that." Desperation filled her voice. "There must be a mistake. Why don't we do a little bit of detective work? We could figure it out between ourselves, then decide what to do? I'll help. Wouldn't it be better to go to Franco with more evidence than a room full of fakes?"

Felicity thought about it for a moment. Admittedly, it would be better to go to Franco once they had more evidence. And she couldn't just go accusing someone simply because he was suffering with his health. Perhaps

Lia was right? They could do some digging around and see what they could find out.

She sighed. "Yes, maybe you're right. Maybe we should do a little digging. I don't really know where to start."

"Okay, look, I know Chester. We worked together a hell of a long time. He was a good friend. I could, you know, do a little subtle digging with him. I could arrange to go see him."

Felicity shook her head. "No, Lia. I can't risk you being in any danger."

"Look, like I said, I know him very well. He's *not* a violent man. He's sweet, gentle, and kind. He wouldn't hurt me. I promise you that."

Felicity pondered again. "Okay…if you're sure you know him well enough."

"I do. Leave it with me. If he is in on it, I can assure you that I'll be able to tell." Lia seemed determined to help Felicity get to the bottom of this.

"Great. Well…let me know when you've been in touch with him, okay?"

"Sure." Lia stood. "Oh, I'm sorry is that all?" Lia asked turning back to Felicity.

"Absolutely. I think that's enough drama for one day, don't you?" Felicity rolled her eyes, trying to make light of a very dark situation.

Chapter 21

March 2012 — Three Years and One Month After the Break-up

The art forgeries weighed heavily on Felicity's mind and somehow the whole situation made her homesick. Being in New York wasn't all it had been cracked up to be. Since discovering the stash in the storeroom, Lia had been meeting with Chester to try and wheedle information out of him. Her reports back to Felicity were telling her that things were on track. Felicity wanted things to move along faster as this matter needed to be dealt with and over.

Soon.

"Look, I can't just rush in there and say, *Hey Chester, were you selling knock off art work when you were at the gallery?* He would run for the hills and then where would we be? If he *is* involved we need to be gentle, Felicity. He isn't well and he needs to be treated with kid gloves."

"I know…I get it…I do. I'm just worried that the longer those things are here, the more chance there is that we could *all* be implicated too." Felicity shuddered at the thought.

Lia nodded. "I know. But that's why we need the evidence to stack up. So *we* are *not* implicated."

Felicity felt like a schoolgirl sulking because she wasn't allowed to tell a secret. What Lia was saying made sense. She just wanted the matter out of her headspace.

"I'd better go. I'll be late for my appointment with the realtor." Felicity stood to leave.

"Are you sure you don't want me to come along? I know the best places to live and if the realtor tries to rent you somewhere gross or in a bad area I could be there to get your back?"

Felicity shook her head and smiled at the gesture. "I'm a big girl, Lia. I think I can handle apartment hunting."

~~~~~

Maddison Kennedy met Felicity outside the first apartment block. It was an older building but not quite as old as some of the buildings in London. It had character but she just wasn't sure. Although she did need somewhere to live. She decided it would be best to keep as open a mind as she possibly could manage. After walking up two flights of stairs, Felicity realised just how unfit she had become. *Why…is…there…no…elevator?*

"And here we are. Number two fifteen. Come on in." Felicity followed the petite redhead into the flat. She had to stay a couple of steps away so as not to be knocked out by the overpowering perfume that Miss Kennedy wore. "As you can see it's open plan, much the same as most of the apartments in the city. It has that old world charm, don't you think?"

"Erm…yes…I suppose so." *If by old world charm you mean wallpaper that Noah himself could have chosen, wiring of death, and a peculiar smell of cabbage.* She walked around the room. The kitchen area was small and dingy. Someone had painted the cupboards in a dark green for some strange reason. The lounge area had fitted bookshelves, which were probably the nicest thing about the place. There was only just enough room to put a small table by the window.

"Come on, I'll show you the bedroom." Maddison oozed enthusiasm. But Felicity guessed that she would do the same if showing her a cardboard box by the roadside. *Occupational hazard.*

"Bed*room*? Singular?" Felicity enquired.

"Ah-huh, that's right." Maddison's face dropped.

"Ah. Therein lays a problem. I need a *two*-bedroom apartment. My mother will come to visit at some point, and I don't think I can ask an old lady to sleep on my couch." Although that idea did appeal just to see the look on Penelope's face. "And I don't relish the thought of giving up my own bed either.

"Oh. Okay, let's go to the next place. It's only a couple blocks away. I'll drive us."

"Great...thanks." Felicity cringed at the thought of being in a close and confined space with perfume-girl.

As they left the building, Felicity's cell phone rang. She excused herself and answered the call.

"Hey, how's the apartment hunt going?" Lia's voice trilled down the line.

"Oh...it's not. No luck so far." Felicity sighed.

"Well I have news that may cheer you up!" Lia sounded giddy.

"What news?" *Please let Chester have confessed to everything and be willing to give himself up.*

"You have a visitor waiting here for you," Lia sang.

Felicity's heart jumped into her throat. "Who? Who is it? Is it Jim?" She was filled with hope.

Lia's voice dropped sympathetically. "Oh...no, sorry. It's Julian Forster. You know, *the* Julian Forster...famous British artist?"

Felicity laughed without any real feeling. "I know Julian, Lia. I discovered him, remember?"

"Whoops, sorry. Anyway, he says there's no rush. He says he'll go across to Mike's and have a drink while he waits for you."

Felicity wondered what on earth Julian was doing in New York. His exhibition here wasn't until later in the year. "Tell him I'm on my way."

Feeling a sense of relief for her nostrils, Felicity informed Maddison that an urgent appointment had come up. "I really should get back. He's flown in specifically to see me, and I can't keep him waiting," she lied. She had no clue why he was here. It was a social call for all she knew, but it gave her the excuse she needed to get away from Miss Perky-Perfume-Pants and find another realtor, one who actually listened to her clients and maybe didn't bathe in eau de toilette before leaving the house. Phew!

At that point, Maddison made her confession. "That's probably not too bad a thing. All the apartments I was going to show you were one bedroom. I was given incorrect information. My sincere apologies, Ms. Johnston-Hart. Let me get back on the case and I'll be in touch."

They shook hands and Felicity hailed a cab to Mike's.

~~~~~

Fifteen minutes later, after fighting through the bustling metropolis that is New York City, Felicity walked through the doors of Mike's bar and scanned the room searching for her friend.

"Felicity!" came a voice from the direction of the bar, and she looked to see a tousled and bearded man walking toward her. He was dressed in dark blue jeans, a lighter blue shirt, and big tan-coloured boots. His signature long black trench coat was unfastened, and he had a striped Edinburgh university scarf draped around his shoulders. In his left hand he carried a woolly hat that looked far too long to fit any human head.

"Julian! Hi!"

He pulled her into a warm bear hug, towering over her even in her four-inch heels. "Come on, let's grab a drink. What can I get you?" He kept his arm around her shoulder as they walked over the bar. Steve, the regular bartender was nowhere in sight. Instead Gino, an older man, was working the daytime shift.

She sighed. "Just a mineral water please. Got to be back at work this afternoon."

Julian ordered their drinks and guided Felicity to a booth toward the back of the bar. The place was surprisingly busy considering the time of day. But it was a popular place.

When they had made the small talk associated with two friends who haven't seen each other in a while, Felicity cut to the chase. "So, what brings you to la grosse pomme?" She sniggered at her own terrible French accent.

Julian laughed, too, rolling his eyes. "Ah, well, therein lays a tale Ms. Johnston-Hart. I have something for you."

"Ooh, I love presents. Gimme, gimme." She held her hands out.

"Not so impatient, honey. I can't *give* it to you directly as such. You have to come and see it."

She narrowed her eyes at him but kept her smile in place. "Hang on. Are you being smutty? Because if you are—"

"Good grief, no!" He laughed. "No offence but my heart belongs thoroughly in the clutches of another. No this is *work* related."

Felicity sighed. "Oh. I got excited then." She took a sip of her iced mineral water suddenly wishing it were wine.

"Don't sound so disappointed. I can assure you, you will *love* this." Julian wiggled his eyebrows.

"Okay…tell me then." Suddenly, paying full attention to Julian, she leaned forward across the table.

"Okay. So there I am looking through some paintings belonging to a friend when I come across these *amazing* pieces by an unknown artist!" His eyes sparkled as he spoke.

Felicity's interest peaked. She loved to discover new talent. "Tell me more. I like the sound of this."

"I *knew* you would." He winked. "Okay, so I'm not at liberty to reveal the artist's identity yet. She's quite shy, and we feel that until you've seen her work and decided whether you think Nilsson-Perkins will be interested, we should keep that snippet quiet."

Felicity's face scrunched in irritation. "That's a bit unorthodox, Jules."

"Yep, yep, I'm aware of that. But you trust me, don't you?"

"Of course."

"Right, okay then. What else do you need to know?"

"Well…I've ascertained the tiny detail that the artist is female…so…where is she from, who are her influences? What does she paint? How old is she?"

"She's from the South of England. Her influences are the greats, Monet, Manet, myself." He dusted at his shoulders in a boastful manner and with a glint in his eye. "She paints the most amazing scenery. But she doesn't just *paint* the scene. She brings it to life in the most remarkable way. And the way she uses light…" Julian rolled his eyes back as if in some kind of euphoric state. "I'm telling you, Felicity, she is *the* next big thing."

"Hmmm. Well, I suppose you should know, having been that very thing yourself, eh?" Felicity poked his arm playfully across the table. "She sounds great." Her eyes glazed over a little as she felt a surge of emotion.

"You okay Felicity?" Julian sounded concerned and his expression told her the same.

"Sorry, yes. Just a little melancholy… Things have been a little tough lately and…well, I used to paint. I think I miss it. Being here makes me see that and hearing you talk about this young woman makes me feel a little envious. What I wouldn't have given for someone to have said that kind of stuff about my work… Oh well, what's past is past… Just ignore me." She waved her hand dismissively and cleared her throat as she shook her head. "Right, so when do I get to meet her?"

Julian seemed to be stifling a smile. "That's the thing. She won't fly. I need you to come to Glasgow and see her work."

She narrowed her eyes. "But you said she was from the south and why can't she fly? I *hate* flying and still do it."

He opened and closed his mouth as if struggling for what to say and then finally said in a rush. "It's a medical condition…yeah, she's awaiting clearance for flying, but it'll take too long if we wait. And she can't risk trying. And yes, she *is* from down South, but lives and paints in Glasgow just now."

She eyed him suspiciously for a moment. But his expression was blank. "Okay. When do I need to come out?"

He audibly exhaled a huge breath he must have been holding. "Great! Okay, you really need to fly out in April so it's not long. I have the details of the exhibition I'm setting up, right here."

He handed her a piece of paper with details scribbled on it. She cringed. "Gosh, Julian, you should have been a G.P with writing like this!" She laughed. He blushed.

"Good job I'm an artist then and people only have to be able to read my autograph."

She rolled her eyes. "True."

Julian and Felicity spent the next hour catching up and eating a late lunch, which she decided she needed. He was only in New York over-night, and so they hugged and parted agreeing to see each other next month in Glasgow.

~~~~~

Back at her hotel that night, Felicity felt lonelier than ever. She contemplated contacting Lia but decided she had leaned on her enough since being here. She pulled out a box from her wardrobe that she had made sure to keep with her when most of her other belongings had gone into storage.

It was a box of keepsakes, things of sentimental value, things she knew would make her cry. She didn't look at the contents of the box often. In fact, for her own sanity, she chose to avoid looking inside the box at all costs. She had only brought it to the hotel as the thought of it being piled up in some storage unit made her feel physically sick. They were *her* memories after all. Little pieces of her heart were hidden in the contents of this box.

Seeing Julian had made the sense of homesickness much more vivid, almost palpable. He was a connection with home. He had been her first big discovery and was the only person from her art world life that Jim had any friendship with. They'd got on really well and knowing this made her miss Jim even more now that she had seen Julian. It was silly really. It wasn't as if they were *best* friends. It was a tenuous link when all was said and done. But it was a link and it made her heart ache.

Tentatively removing the lid from the box, she looked inside. Folded pieces of paper, photos, movie ticket stubs, and a little teddy bear. The beautiful white gold locket was in there somewhere too. She pulled out the first piece of paper.

You are my soul, my love has no destination without you
You are my breath, I breathe but dust when we're apart
You are my warmth, chills sear me when you're gone from me
You are my friend, my love, my passion; you are my heart.

The poem Jim had written for her on their first Valentine's Day apart was the first thing she came across. She'd been in New York and he had hidden it in amongst her clothing in her suitcase. She had cried silent tears when she'd read it then; now was no different. Here she was in New York without him once more. Only this time he wasn't waiting at home for her return.

Chapter 22

March 2012 – Three Years and One Month After the Break-up

Jim's eyes were fuzzy, and when he looked at the clock, he was surprised to discover it was eleven in the evening. He had been trying to keep his mind off Julian's visit to New York. He said he would call as soon as he could with news, but as yet no call had come through. He was hoping this lack of communication wasn't a negative thing. But he just couldn't be sure.

Would Felicity see right through the plan and figure out who was behind it all? Would she believe every word that fell from Julian's mouth? She had no real reason *not* to believe him. But she may think it was odd. Who would blame her?

He shut his laptop down and resorted to making a cup of hot chocolate and clearing out the fire grate. It was a very cold March evening and the fire had been on the go most of the day. He had let it die down a couple of hours earlier, thinking he would write for another ten minutes and then go to bed. That hadn't happened and now he could see his breath when he exhaled.

Sitting in the lamplight huddled under a fleece blanket on his sofa, he began to doze off. He fought sleep as best he could, but every few minutes he jerked his head up after drifting ever closer to the land of slumber.

Suddenly the phone rang. Jim dived across the sofa, almost causing himself broken ribs in the process as he landed on the hard arm and grabbed the hand set.

"Hello? Jules?" He panted.

"Hi Jim! You sound like you've been jogging, mate." Julian laughed

"Hardly. It's gone eleven here." He tried but couldn't keep the annoyance out of his voice.

"Yeah, sorry about that. I've just got back to my hotel from seeing Felicity."

"And?" He didn't even try to hide his impatience.

"She fell for it, mate! Woo hoo!" Julian yelled down the line.

Jim's breath left his body in one quick huff. "Thank fuck for that!"

"Err, I think you mean thank *Jules* for that." Julian laughed triumphantly.

"Aye! That as well!" Jim chuckled. "How did she seem?" *Please say she talked about me non-stop and misses me terribly.*

"She looks amazing, Jim. I won't lie to you. I mean *sizzling* hot. You're one lucky dude, I tell you. Want to know something funny?"

"Always," Jim replied

"When I told her about our mystery artist she got all misty-eyed and said how much she missed painting."

"What? Really?" Jim was shocked but very happy with that little nugget of information.

"Really. She's so talented Jim, but she doesn't even realise it. She just hasn't got a clue."

"Aye, you're right." Jim chuckled. "Honestly, Jules, I can't thank you enough. I really appreciate all of this. You're sacrificing a lot for me."

"Nah. I'm sacrificing nothing. She discovered me and now it's my turn to help her dreams come true. Honestly, I have nothing better to do with my time at the moment. The cash is rolling in nicely and I'm all finished on the pieces for my next big exhibition, so this is giving me something to focus on…and to be truthful, I've found it quite exciting, all this cloak and dagger subterfuge. It's a break from my normal routine."

"Aye, well, it means the world to me, all this." Jim suddenly felt emotional, so he cleared his throat and said his goodbyes.

He shuffled up to bed, but felt wide awake. A new flood of adrenaline coursed through his veins. He just hoped that he hadn't left things too late. He'd wanted to go to Flick as soon as he had read Edgar's letter, but then with the arrival of his brother his plans had been scuppered. He'd lost confidence. Simply turning up now that she had gone to New York was not an option. She would be in her element there. The last thing he wanted was to fly all the way out there to be shot down in flames. No, this was the best way. This way he had a different life to offer her.

~~~~~

Early evening, Felicity sat watching mind numbing reality shows on the TV in her suite. She was bored and miserable. She was contemplating calling room service when her telephone rang. Perhaps Lia had come to her rescue again.

"Hello?" she answered in a less than enthusiastic tone.

"Ms. Johnston-Hart?" the young man on reception asked. *Well, who else would it be you utter muppet? I am alone up here. As usual.*

"Yes, this is she."

"Ah, good. There is a gentleman in reception to see you." Her heart fluttered. Who on earth would be here? Julian was going home. Unless his flight was delayed or he decided to stay to do some sightseeing, "Ms. Johnston-Hart?" the young man spoke again.

"Oh, yes sorry. Did he give a name?" she enquired.

"Yes, he says he is Vitale DeLuca."
Ohmygodohmygodohmygod!

"Erm…did he say what he wants?" She glanced into the mirror at her reflection. *Hmm, hair in a ponytail, no make-up, yoga pants, and a T-shirt. Great. Very glamorous. Not.* There was a long pause whilst she presumed the receptionist was asking him what he wanted. *Oh great. Not at all embarrassing then.*

"He says he is here to take you to dinner and the table is booked in our restaurant to dine in half an hour. He says he will wait in the lounge while you ready yourself."

Presumptuous or what?! "Oh…okay…please tell Mr DeLuca I will be down as soon as I can… Oh and tell him I apologise for keeping him waiting." She waited whilst the receptionist relayed the information.

"He says…ahem…you are worth the wait, Ms. Johnston-Hart." Even though Vitale was not in the room, Felicity's cheeks heated at hearing his words.

"Thank you. Bye." She hung up and dashed to her wardrobe. Rifling through, she located the little black dress that she had brought for evenings out. Not that she actually anticipated needing to wear it at all. She showered quickly being careful not to wet her hair. Once out and dried she applied a little make-up and combed through her hair. After she slipped into her dress and black stilettos, she surveyed her reflection in the full-length mirror. The dress was her favourite, sleeveless and fitted with a slash neck. The little teardrop opening gave just a hint of cleavage, very elegant and not revealing. The fitted style accentuated her ample curves. Once she had grabbed her purse she made her way down to the hotel lobby. She glanced around and spotted him.

Her breath caught in her throat.

He was standing with his back to her. Very tall and broad shouldered, black hair neatly trimmed into the back of his neck. He wore stone coloured pants that fitted his form very well and a chocolate brown suit jacket. Suddenly, as if he sensed her presence, he turned to her. Under the jacket he wore a button down shirt in pale blue. He looked like he had walked here direct from an ad for some high-end aftershave lotion, all casual and sultry. And that megawatt smile…Oh boy was she in trouble.

He walked toward her, his handsome, panties-melting smile staying in place. When he reached her, he bent to kiss both cheeks.

"Bella… Sei un gioello." She recognised the phrase he had used last time. "You really are exquisite, Felicity." The way he spoke her name with the rich hint of an Italian accent sent shivers down her spine. She smiled as she felt the heat rise in her cheeks again and butterflies tap-danced around her tummy.

Pure. Unadulterated. Lust.

She gazed up at him. "Vitale. How lovely to see you. What brings you here? We didn't arrange anything."

"I know. My apologies again. I saw your work colleague…Lia? I saw her at the bar again and asked her for your number. She refused to divulge the information but told me you where staying here, and if I wanted to see you I had to go through the hotel. She must think a lot of you. She is protective, *si?*"

Felicity smiled. She would have to thank Lia on Monday. "It appears so. So what did you want to see me about?" She fiddled with her hair.

"I simply wanted to see you. No other reason than that. I couldn't stop thinking about you. It seems you have made an impersonation on me." He smiled.

Felicity couldn't help but giggle. "I think you mean I made an *impression* on you."

He rolled his eyes and his tanned cheeks coloured ever so slightly. "Oh my. Yes, I think perhaps you are correct. I get a little wrong sometimes with my words."

She smoothed her hand down his lapel immediately regretting the intimate gesture. "Not at all. You speak English very well, Vitale."

"Ah, you are too kind, *bella*. I think we should go. Our table... I hope it is okay that I choose the restaurant here?" He held out his arm to escort her to the dining room. She took it and walked beside him.

The panelled dining room was delightful in its rich, luxurious decor. Crystal chandeliers hung from the ceiling and refracted shards of light around the intimate space. Classical music played in the background, and there was a low mumble of conversation. They were seated at a table for two and a smartly dressed waiter brought over a wine menu, handing it to Vitale.

"Would you like to select a wine, Felicity?" He offered her the menu as her name danced off his tongue in the same beat as her skipping heart.

"No, no, you choose, that's fine." She smiled and shivered at the way he said her name again. He perused the menu and waved the waiter over.

"Could we please have a bottle of the Gosset Brut?" He handed the list back to the waiter.

"Brut? Are we celebrating?" She clasped her hands on her lap.

"I think we should celebrate your beauty and the fact that you allowed me to take you out this evening." He leaned his hands on the table, stretched out toward her. It was almost an invitation.

She felt her cheeks heat again. "Oh really, Vitale, you do flatter me."

He waved his hand dismissively. "Not at all. I simply speak the truth."

Over dinner they chatted mainly about Felicity's job and then briefly about Vitale's business. He didn't give much away about what he did other than he had studied medicine at university but had chosen not to become a doctor. She thought it was a shame and could imagine the female patients feigning illness in order to be seen by him.

Dinner was wonderful, three courses of the most delicious food and delightful company. Vitale insisted on paying the bill and left a generous tip. He walked her to the elevator bank.

"Thank you, cara mia, for a most wonderful evening. It has been an absolute pleasure." He lifted her hand and kissed it softly.

"W-would you like to…come up for…a night cap?" *Stupidstupidstupid woman.* She wanted to take back the words, but it was too late. His eyes lit up and she began back-pedalling, "Obviously I know you're a busy man and probably have things to do—"

"No, not at all. I made sure this evening was free just for you. I would very much like to come up for a night cap." *Dammit.*

"Okay…lovely." No. It really wasn't. It was a colossal mistake.

She unlocked her suite door and walked inside holding the door open for him. He glanced around. "Nice place you have here." He turned to her with a grin on his face.

"Why thank you. I think so, too." She returned his grin. "I'll get us a drink…brandy?"

Vitale nodded, silently watching her. She went to the oak bureau where the hospitality items were kept and located the small bottle of amber liquid. As she stood there pouring their drinks he walked up behind her and slid one arm around her waist. He pulled her hair to one side and kissed her neck softly.

Shivers traversed her spine and she felt annoyed at her body's betrayal. "Oh…when I offered a night cap… I'm afraid I meant *just* a night cap, Vitale." She clenched her eyes closed.

He turned her around in his arms so that she faced him. "Please forgive me, bella. I cannot help it. You drive me crazy with your accent and your beautiful eyes." He stroked her cheek and gazed at her. "Please, Felicity…let me kiss you just once, per favore." He bowed his head toward her and paused briefly before covering her mouth with his. His lips were soft but demanding. His skin moved smoothly over hers, and he groaned as he slid his hands into her hair. She couldn't deny the kiss was rather delicious, but it felt wrong. She felt guilty.

Before she could protest, he slipped his hands to her back and began to slowly slide the zip of her dress down, down, down. He caressed her bare back with gentle fingertips making her gasp. Her traitorous body reacting once again against her will.

"Il tuo corpo è bello…bella… Voglio fare l'amore con te," he mumbled huskily as he kissed her. Caught up in the moment and probably on account of his Italian mutterings, she began to help him remove his jacket. He pulled it off and threw it over on to the chaise. He slid her dress off her shoulders and gasped when he was presented with her black lace underwear. "Sei bellissima," he whispered.

He crushed his mouth into hers again and held her with one arm at the small of her back whilst he unbuttoned his shirt with the other. He released her momentarily to slip his trousers off. She clenched her eyes closed again. Scooping her up in his arms, he carried her over to the bed and laid her down hovering over her, his arousal evident through his black fitted boxers. "Si…si…bellissima."

Nervously, she looked up at him. "I'm so sorry but I have no clue what you're saying to me, Vitale, even though it sounds so beautiful."

"I am telling you that you are beautiful, and I want nothing more than to make love to you now." He slowly bent to kiss her again but she froze. "Felicity…what is wrong? Are you alright?" He lay down beside her and stroked her cheek. Her eyes began to sting with unshed tears and she bit her lip.

"Vitale…I'm so sorry. I can't do this. I can't sleep with you."

"But, cara mia, what is wrong? Did I upset you? I know you said no to begin with, but…but I did not mean for you to feel pressured…you seemed to enjoy—" He looked genuinely concerned, which made it worse.

A tear escaped. She pulled herself to a sitting position. "No, you did nothing wrong. You've been lovely. You're a very attractive man and I'm pretty sure I'm completely loopy…but—"

A look of confusion took over his handsome features. "Loopy? I do not know…what is this loopy, cara?"

"Crazy, Vitale. It means crazy. And I must be because I'm here in New York, single, and alone, and a sexy, intelligent, Italian hunk of a man is trying to seduce me and here I am crying like an idiot."

"Bella, why is it that you cry? Can I help? Are you unwell?" *God why does he have to be so effing nice?*

She let out an exasperated sigh. "Vitale, I can't sleep with you because I'm hopelessly in love with my ex-husband. My ex-husband, who doesn't even want me. There I admitted it to a complete stranger. A complete stranger who desires me and wants to have sex with me!" She laughed derisively. "I am totally mental! I must be." She threw her arms up and looked over at Vitale, who sat there looking sexy and unkempt in boxers and his open shirt with his sculpted hairy chest on show. *Goodness, he really is delicious.*

"He is your ex, yet you still love him?" Vitale continued to look bemused and there was no wonder.

"Yes. I left him years ago. I thought I wanted a different life, but I was wrong. And now...he doesn't want me anymore. It serves me right."

"Bella. Have you spoken to this...this...ex?"

"Jim...his name is Jim, and no...I haven't spoken to him because I'm a coward, and he would trample all over my heart, which is exactly what I deserve after how I treated him. I *do* need to get over him. I *do*. But I'm just not ready yet... I'm so sorry for wasting your time. Really I am." She looked into to his eyes and saw compassion.

"Well, I think he must be the loopy one." He smiled and tucked a strand of her hair behind her ear. "You are a beautiful woman, Felicity. And I want you very badly. But I see your heart belongs to another. I would be more than happy to help you get over your ex...but as you say this is not what you desire right now, and so I will step aside." He lifted her hand and kissed it.

"Vitale...you are so very sweet. And so gracious. I feel terrible and incredibly stupid." She suddenly felt very self-conscious about her semi-naked body. Somehow understanding her discomfort without her uttering a word, he dragged the comforter from the end of the bed and wrapped it around her.

"I will leave now. But if you would like to get out for a little sightseeing or to have coffee...lunch perhaps...you have my card. Please do not hesitate to call me...and if you should suddenly change your mind, I am happy to help you with your…how you say…exorcising the ex." He smiled that sexy, wonderful, perfect smile and her heart sank. She wondered if she was passing up a potentially wonderful relationship with an extremely attractive and pleasant man. But she really wasn't the type of person who could just sleep with someone for pure gratification. At that moment in time, she sincerely wished she was.

Vitale dressed himself and Felicity pulled on her robe. He kissed her softly on the cheek. He smelled so good and she wanted to pull him back to the bed and take advantage of his offer to help exorcise Jim. But she knew that as soon as things got hot and heavy the reality of her heart would spring to the forefront of her mind once again. And so she said goodbye and thanked him for a wonderful meal and apologised again.

Chapter 23

March 2012 – Three Years and One Month After the Break-up

Felicity's cell phone rang in the early hours of Sunday morning. Startled, she clambered out of bed and fumbled for her phone.

She finally spoke, out of breath. "Hello?"

"Felicity…There's been a break in…at the gallery." Lia's voice was filled with distress. "They're gone. The forgeries have been taken."

Felicity sat bolt upright. "What?! When?" Panic washed over her. "I-I…what about the other pieces?"

"That's the weird thing… Nothing else was taken. I can't call the police, Felicity. If I call the police and they find out that only forgeries were taken they will wonder why we didn't report them. We can't report them now. We'd been in so much shit… I don't know what to do. I'm so scared."

Felicity was shaking and her heart was beating so loudly she could hear the pounding in her ears. "Lia, are you okay? Are you safe?"

"Y-yes. I'm fine. Just a little shaken. We'll need to get someone in to change the locks."

"Hang on…why were *you* contacted about this and not *me*?" Felicity asked, puzzled.

"I guess Franco forgot to update the database with the security firm. It's no biggy. Don't worry. I'm fine. Just a little upset."

"Where are you? I'll come and get you." Felicity rushed the words out.

"No, no don't do that. I'm home now. The doors are temporarily secured and the security firm has been instructed to guard the premises. It'll be fine."

Felicity sighed. "Okay, well if you're sure. I'll be in early and I'll try to deal with this. We'll come up with something... I promise, Lia"

"The thing that's scaring me the most is that whoever was in charge of the forgery racket knows that *we know* something... Why else would they break in now to take the pieces? What if they come after *us*?" Lia sounded terrified.

"No...no...I think that now they have the paintings they have exactly what they want. Maybe it's over, Lia. I really hope it is."

"Me too, Felicity, me too. I'll see you soon."

Sleep evaded Felicity for the rest of the night as she tossed and turned wondering what the hell to do next. Eventually, giving in to her wakefulness, she showered and dressed quickly, leaving the hotel without eating. She arrived at the gallery early to find Lia already inside assessing the damage.

She rushed over and flung her arms around Felicity's neck, sobbing. "Oh, Felicity, I'm so scared."

"Hey, shhh. It's okay. I'm sure it'll be fine now. I think it's over. Like I said last night, they have what they want. They didn't take any of the other pieces."

Lia was shaking uncontrollably. "But what if they come after us?"

Felicity placed her hands firmly on Lia's shoulders. "Lia, you need to calm down. I *will* figure this out. Why would they bother coming after us? It's not like we really know anything. I'm going to the UK next week to meet a new artist, and I'll think all of this through. When I return, we're going to report this whole thing, first to Franco and then to the police. We'll do it together and back each other up. I just need to think it through." She bit her lip. "And maybe if we leave it awhile the criminals will think we're going to do nothing. If they are watching us, they will see things going on as normal. That way they won't know to expect the police. I need to put everything down in writing and get the facts straight so that you and I are not implicated at all. We need to be kept out of this whole thing, or it could ruin both of our careers."

Lia chewed on a fingernail. "Do you think that will work? If we wait I mean?"

Felicity nodded. "I hope so. I think…I think so."

Lia closed her eyes for a moment. "Okay. Have you booked your flight for the UK and everything? Hotels and a car?"

"Not yet. I need you to do that for me whilst I start compiling a report. Franco knows about the trip. but he doesn't know the reasons behind it as yet."

"Okay. I'll get on it right away. Will you be flying business class or first class?"

"Oh…I'll just fly regular economy. It'll be fine." Felicity turned toward her office.

"Economy? Ewww. How come?"

"No reason. Just go ahead and book. I'll be fine in economy." She went into her office and closed the door behind her.

Being here, surrounded by all this wonderful art used to thrill Felicity. The buzz of finding a new and unknown talent used to drive her. But hearing Julian talk about the new talent *he* had discovered and how this woman painted with such passion had made her long to paint again. All this talk of forgeries, break-ins, and criminal activity on her doorstep tarnished everything.

Being so far away from everything she loved and knew was difficult, and she had felt like a fish out of water ever since arriving in New York. It was such an amazing city and this had been the opportunity of a lifetime, but all she could think about was Jim and going home. She wanted to be with him. He had loved her once. Maybe if she returned to the UK she could at least go to visit him and try to make him see that she had changed?

There must have been something deep within him, some part of him that still wanted her. She just hoped that it wasn't only a physical pull that still remained for him. She wanted his heart to still desire her, too. The sex they had experienced together had always been great. The trust to share their desires and fantasies was something she had cherished until she had been convinced that sex and love weren't enough. But now she knew that career, money, and power weren't all they were made out to be either. Especially if there was no one to go home to at the end of the day.

She had decided, however, that whatever happened now, returning to the UK was the best plan. This was not the type of business you could be a part of if your heart wasn't in it. And her heart was, sadly, no longer in it. Her heart had only one place it wanted to be and that was with Jim.

Chapter 24

April 2012 - Three Years and Two Months After the Break-up

Felicity sat in the airport lounge clutching the little case that held her tickets and passport. She felt sick to the stomach just as she did every single time she flew. Ridiculous considering the very nature of her job. *International Art Dealer – pah! Laughable.* This time was worse, however, as she knew that she had to speak to Franco whilst in the UK and inform him of the fraudulent goings on in the New York gallery. She hadn't made Lia privy to this snippet of information, as she didn't want to cause her any further worry. But Felicity now had enough evidence to point the finger at former gallery Manager, Chester Withers.

Her palms were sweating, and her heart was presumably choreographing a new version of *Riverdance* in her chest judging by its erratic beat. She glanced around at the eclectic mix of people surrounding her: Business people in suits conversing seriously on cell phones; parents and young children playing eye spy games to try and fend off the boredom of waiting; couples saying their heart felt goodbyes.

Her heart skipped a beat as she thought about Jim. She was going to be in Glasgow for the exhibition, so she was going to make time to travel up and see him again or at least to ask him to meet her. There were so many things she needed to say that couldn't be said over the phone. Apologies needed to be made in person. She realised now that *he* was who she wanted. Despite their last encounter. She had to fight for him, prove to him that she had changed. And if it was too late, which she suspected it was, well…at least he would know the truth and she would have the opportunity for closure knowing that she had done everything she possibly could.

This was going to be her second to last trip back to the UK if things went as she planned. New York was not for her. She had once thought it offered her exactly the life she craved. But hearing about this fantastic new mysterious female artist had made her yearn for her brushes and canvas. She missed her friends. For goodness sake, she *even* missed her mum.

"Room for a little one?" A familiar voice broke her from her reverie. Looking up she smiled into the stunning face of Lia Cole.

"What are you doing here?!" Felicity jumped up and pulled her colleague into a death-grip hug.

"I should be asking you the same. I went by your hotel to check up on you, and they said you had already checked out. Why are you here so damned early?"

"Nerves, I guess. I always do this. I'm always scared that I'll realise I've forgotten something and have to go back. So…if I get here early, I have plenty of time." Felicity's face heated at the admission.

Lia laughed. "Hmmm, that's some twisted logic you got there, missy."

Felicity shrugged. "Yes, it is, but it works for me. So why *are* you checking up on me?"

"Well, you sounded kinda worked up about the flight and about seeing Jim, so I thought I'd come keep you company for couple hours while you waited. Give you a little moral support." Lia smiled sweetly. "I was kinda thinking that you'd be in your hotel room, but seeing as you're here…so am I." She held out her hands in a *ta daaaa* gesture.

"Oh, that's so lovely. Thank you so much. I could use a friend to keep my mind occupied. I do so hate flying. Come and sit." Felicity moved over to the sofa again.

"Tell you what. Why don't I go and get you something to drink? Calm your nerves a little?"

"Oh, I don't know. It's a little early and I know it's maybe a little too much information, but I tend to get sick before a flight. So it wouldn't work anyway."

"Sure it would. And you won't get sick because *I'm* here to take your mind off of things."

Flick pondered on the thought of alcohol on her already churning stomach. "I really don't think—"

"Don't forget you have to clear security yet, and then you'll be sitting around for a while or looking around the boutiques before you board. Anything you drink now will relax you for a little while but will have gotten out of your system way before that."

Felicity scrunched her nose, "Ahhh, I just don't feel—"

"Look, trust me, I'm a New Yorker." Lia tipped her head to the side and framed her face with her fingers playfully.

"Oh, okay. Just one then, I suppose."

Lia clapped her hands theatrically and headed for the bar.

Felicity sat and nervously stared up at the screen displaying flights and departure times. Flight nine forty-two was going to depart right on time. She had been sitting here for what had felt like a decade when in actual fact it had only been an hour or so. She had foregone her first class ticket and the sumptuous lounge that went with it out of guilt—a decision she now regretted—knowing she would be flying back here only to tie up loose ends before handing in her resignation and flying home again permanently.

Permanently. Her heart skipped once again.

"There you go. Jack and coke. With ice and a twist, seeing as we're celebrating."

Felicity took the glass from Lia and took a large gulp. "What are we celebrating?" Felicity knew the answer.

Lia rolled her bright green eyes. "Your future with your ex of course! Even though I think you're totally crazy."

Hearing those words made Felicity's stomach do somersaults as the butterflies took flight again. She took another large gulp and shivered as the bitter alcohol hit her throat. "I know…I just… I love him. I always have. So many things have gone wrong for us. But I need to at least try to get him back."

Lia's bottom lip protruded in a mock sulk. "There are so many hot guys in New York who would just adore you and your British accent. New York guys are the best. You just haven't given them a chance. Take that Vitale guy." She fanned herself. "He was so hot. Although I don't suppose he could be classed as a New Yorker…but anyways, I wouldn't have turned him down!"

"Yes, but that would just be lust and I want—"

Lia interrupted rolling her eyes again. "Love, yada, yada…love…blah blah. I get it." She smiled and leaning over she squeezed Felicity's hand. "Don't worry. It will all be over soon."

Felicity huffed and scrunched her nose. "Thanks for *that* vote of confidence." She gulped her drink again. A flush of nervous energy rolled over her and her stomach lurched. "Oh God, I think I'm going to be sick, Lia."

"You know what I mean…and oh em gee, you're such a *baby*!" Lia laughed. "Look, you go and…do whatever you need to do in the restroom. You can leave your stuff with me. Try to hold onto your breakfast though, okay? It's not good to fly on an empty stomach."

"I'm not sure that's going to happen." Felicity stood and her stomach rolled again.

Without another word, she ran to the nearest bathroom, her hand covering her mouth. Luckily, the ladies room was empty. She made it into a cubicle and hurled. *Alcohol plus nerves = a very bad combination.* Sweating and panting, she sat back onto the hard, tiled floor. Her head pounded. This was one of the most severe flight panics yet, hardly surprising under the circumstances. *I really should take a fear of flying course.* The cubicle began spinning. This was one severe panic attack. Lurching forward, she vomited again as her head swam.

~~~~~

April 2012 – Three Years and Two Months After the Break-up

"This place looks absolutely amazing, Jules. I can't thank you enough." Jim hugged his friend and ally. The exhibition, *Through the Glass*, was due to open in two night's time. Felicity would land at Heathrow later today and then get a connecting flight up to Edinburgh where she would stay overnight. From there she would pick up the hire car that had been arranged for her and drive to Glasgow.

Jim couldn't hide his excitement. There was also a little trepidation. What if his plan didn't work? He had hurt her deeply when he last saw her. Then there had been the letter from her father urging him on. She had to still want him. She *had to.*

"Jim, I'm honoured to have helped you, mate. I really hope this works. You two are just meant to be together." Julian squeezed Jim's shoulder.

Jim held out his hand. "Oh god, look Jules. I'm shaking. I'm so fucking nervous. Her flight will be boarding about now. She'll be here in a day! What the fuck will I do if she slaps me and walks away for good?" His voice wavered as he almost pleaded with Julian to tell him it would all work out.

Julian turned to face his friend and placed a hand firmly on each shoulder. "Look, mate, you are taking a risk, admittedly. But *think* about it. Her dad says she has never stopped loving you. And who knows a woman better than her dad, eh?"

Jim pulled in a long, deep, steadying breath. "Aye...aye...she *has* to be happy. That's all I want. And look at this place. She *has* to love this." He gestured around the room at Felicity's artwork as it hung there in all its beautiful splendour.

"Now, Jim. I want you to go back to the hotel. Take a long soak in the tub, chill out for a bit. Maybe even sleep because by the look of you, you haven't done much of that over the past couple of months since this whole plan was borne. You know Jasper is safe with your neighbour, so you've only to concentrate on picking up your suit from the hotel reception and awaiting the arrival of your gorgeous, talented girl. And Jim?"

"Aye?" Jim focused on Julian's words like his life depended on it. Because at this moment in time it really did.

"Trim your fucking beard, man! You look like the wild man of fucking Borneo!" Julian's face lit up with humour.

Flight nine four two was scheduled to land at four tomorrow morning, UK time. Jim checked his watch: Five thirty. So it would be twelve thirty there. *Right...shower, food, beard, and bed. Not necessarily in that order...well...apart from bed.*

The next morning, Jim awoke and checked his watch again: nine fifteen. *Great! She should be on her way north by now.* He did a little happy dance on the way to his rather luxurious en-suite bathroom in the fancy hotel that Julian had insisted on. "Mate, you can't have make-up sex in a dump." He had informed Jim. *Quite right*. Felicity deserved better.

Staring at his reflection, he sniggered as Jules' words came back to him. His beard had really gotten long and fuzzy. He would've looked at home as the fourth member of ZZ Top. And it was only fair seeing as Julian had shaved his off to look the part. It was the least Jim could do. He set about trimming it back into a goatee. Pleased with the result he switched on the shower, and when steam filled the room, he stepped in, allowing his muscles to relax as the water encased him in a cocoon of warmth.

He played over in his mind what he would say to Flick when she stepped through the doors of the exhibition. Would she like what he had called it? *Through the Glass* had been the obvious, choice considering the subject matter and the circumstances through which it came about. It reminded him of how she saw the world. She saw beauty in everything. She observed each vista she beheld as if it were already a framed masterpiece. He had always admired her ability to take a view through the glass on a train or car journey and turn into something transcendent. There was something poetic and fitting about the name.

Naming the artist Flick MacDuff was the next sticking point. The reasons for the choice were threefold. One, it wasn't her name and never had been, and so if word had been somehow leaked, she would *hopefully* see is at a striking coincidence. Two, it had a certain ring to it…like it always had to Jim, and three…he *wanted* the name to be his future. *Their* future.

Once out of the shower, Jim couldn't help but smile at his reflection. His eyes looked brighter already. He felt that familiar nervous energy course through his veins at the thought of seeing her and seeing her reaction to *her* exhibition. His heart flipped. The grin on the face of his reflection made him laugh.

He pointed at the mirror. "You, mate, are a complete fucking nutcase!" He shook his head and wrapped a towel around his waist. Drying his shaggy hair with another towel, he made his way through to the bedroom. He picked up his phone to check the time…again. He noticed that in the space of the twenty or so minutes he had been in the shower he'd had three missed calls all from Julian. He had forgotten he'd set it to silent the night before to ensure he got a good night's sleep. Couldn't see Flick with baggy, tired eyes, now could he? Sensing the urgency behind the need to ring him three times in quick succession, Jim's heart sank. *Oh great, I bet the caterer has bloody let us down. I knew he sounded flaky.* He huffed and dialled Julian, preparing himself for the news.

Julian answered after only one ring. "Jim? Oh God, Jim. Have you seen? Oh God, please tell me it's not true." His words came over the line in a blurred rush. A cold shiver settled over Jim at the distress in his voice.

"Julian, slow down. What the fuck is wrong?" Jim's heart rate speeded up. Images of vandals breaking into the gallery and trashing the exhibition flew through his mind like a terrible amateur movie.

The sound of Julian's deep intake of breath vibrated through the phone, then a sniff followed by muffled noises. "Jim…please just turn on the news. Channel one."

"Oh shit…that sounds ominous…okay. I'll call you back." Jim's stomach rolled. He just knew that the gallery had burned down or been flooded or struck by lightning…*shit*. Reluctantly, he flicked the on button of the TV.

"...reports coming in claim that the pilot made a distress call stating that two engines had failed but unfortunately that contact was lost briefly after. Rescue teams were dispatched immediately but when the first of these arrived flight nine four two from New York had already broken up. It's reported that...at this time there are no survivors..."

Jim sat, open mouthed, staring at the images floating across the screen in front of him as he felt the colour drain from his face. A shiver travelled the length of his spine. Then numbness set in.

Chapter 25

Jim sat in the drawing room of Felicity's family home, holding Penelope's hand. It was the day of the exhibition opening. He just couldn't face it. Not with Flick gone. And anyway, Penelope needed him. Ironic really, since he was the last person she'd needed for the last fourteen years. He had come to her as soon as the news had sunk in. The older woman's pallor was that of a corpse. Usually well made-up, Penelope sat, pale and shaking beside him as she sobbed. It was all too much to bear.

He couldn't even be bothered to wipe his own tears away. He simply let them fall. The numbness had given way to anger, which had given way to a deep sadness and guilt. *If only I hadn't set this whole thing up. If only I had just left her to her new life.* But what was the point of *if only*?

Felicity was gone.

No survivors. That was the news that neither he, nor Penelope, nor Felicity's friends wanted to hear but it was what they got anyway. The beautiful, talented, passionate girl had gone, forever.

And forever was a hell of a long time.

"I'll…I'll make more tea." Penelope stood in a zombie-like stupor and looked at her hands for a second as if she had forgotten her reason for standing. Confusion played on her features.

Jim stood and placed his hands on her shoulders. "Penny, let me…please." He squeezed lightly to bring her back to Earth. She had clearly drifted off momentarily, maybe to a world where Flick still existed. As if his small act of kindness had pierced her heart, she let out an anguished cry and collapsed into him.

"Oh, James, I'm so sorry. I'm so, so sorry." Her tears soaked through the fabric of his shirt as he held onto her to stop her from falling.

"Hey…shhh. It's okay. Don't apologise. You've nothing to apologise for." He stroked the distraught woman's hair.

"No, you're wrong. You are *wrong*, James." She raised her voice angrily shouting through her tears. "I *caused* this. This is *my* fault. *All* of this. Edgar was right." Her body convulsed and she clutched onto his shirt.

"No…no, Penny…no, you're not to blame. *I* am. I should've just let her get on with her life. She didn't need me confusing matters. She didn't need her paintings on display and me trying to put some pathetic surprise together to win her back."

The woman straightened up and looked directly into his eyes. "Jim, listen to me. If I had just let her be…let you *both* be…let her *really* love you…she would never have gone. She would still be here with us…with *you*." She visibly shook as she spoke. Her voice had taken on a calm and collected tone.

She called me Jim. He cupped her cheek. "Oh, Penny. What's the use, eh? We can't change things if we beat ourselves up. We have to forget blame. Please, can we do that?"

She placed her hand over his. "I don't deserve your kindness, Jim."

"Of course, you do. All you ever wanted was the best for Felicity. I can understand that. Because it's all I ever wanted, too."

Penelope lowered her gaze. "I told her you weren't good enough for her."

Jim tilted her chin to meet her eyes again. "Aye, and you were right." He smiled. "She deserved so much more than me. But I loved her, Penny. I loved her with all my heart."

"I know you did, Jim. I know. And I only wish that I could have accepted that your love was more important to her than you being a high flying, big shot executive. Love is what matters. Support, love, and happiness far outweigh the material things in life. You always felt that way. You were right, and I was wrong…especially about you, Jim. I know that now. But *now* is too late." The tears began to fall again, and Penelope's pained sobs made Jim's heart ache.

"You're wrong. It's not too late. You and me…we need each other now. I want to show you Felicity's true passion. I want you to come to Glasgow and see her work. Will you do that, Penny?" Jim squeezed her shoulders and she nodded.

~~~~~

The journey north had been a long, emotionally draining one. Jim had booked them two rooms at one of the best hotels in Glasgow. He was desperate to make this as easy on Penelope as possible. On arrival at the hotel, he called Julian about the exhibition opening.

"Oh, Jim, mate, it was astounding. The press loved the work. There was such a buzz in the gallery that I had to keep going out of the room, I was so emotional." His voice cracked as he spoke. "She would have been so happy, Jim. I hope you know that."

For a moment Jim couldn't reply. The words became caught. Anguish and pain constricted his throat. Finally he was able to overcome it. "Thanks, Jules. Thanks for everything. I…I…wish she was here to see it." Tears needled the backs of his eyes and his chest ached. Penelope had placed a hand on his arm, which had pushed him over the edge. "Sorry, mate, I've got to go." He hung up and clung to her. She did her best to soothe him as the raw emotion erupted from his soul like a volcano. His tears spilled like molten lava, burning a trail down his unshaven face.

After what felt like an eternity of letting him cry, Penelope placed hands on either cheek and looked into his eyes. "James... Listen to me... *Jim*, look at me." His bloodshot eyes met with hers. "I am *so* proud of you. To have loved my Felicity...*our* Felicity so much and to have done all this... I want you to know how proud that makes me. Do you hear me?" Her words were his undoing once again.

~~~~~

When they arrived at the gallery, Julian was outside the room in which *Through the Glass* was being shown. There with another round of press, answering their questions about the mystery artist, the identity of whom had been kept a secret until Jim and Penelope had seen the exhibition and were ready to face the emotional onslaught of being thrust into the public eye, which would no doubt happen given the circumstances.

Julian broke away from the group and came over to where they stood. He looked tired and drawn. He hugged both of them hard in turn. "Are you ready to go in? I've kept the room clear today until you've been."

Jim looked at Penelope and held out his hand to her "Let's go, eh?" He squeezed her hand in reassurance. She nodded, clearly nervous and glassy-eyed. They both took deep breaths as they followed Julian to the large wooden double doors. He pushed them open and stepped aside with a sad smile.

Jim's breath caught in his throat at the sight that met him. The antique wood panelled walls were adorned with Felicity's beautiful paintings. He'd known they were magnificent but didn't expect them to look as spectacular in this setting as they did. His hand came to cover his mouth as he tried to stifle an anguished sob. He looked over to Penelope who stood open mouthed, tears tracing glistening lines down her make-up covered cheeks.

Slowly Jim walked over to the beginning of the exhibition. The painting was of the view from a coastal road they had driven along on a weekend away to Devon. The sea rolled toward the sand, and the white horses skipped along with it toward the shore. The tall grasses that edged the cliff-top almost looked to be swaying in an imaginary breeze as a pair of gulls hovered overhead.

Next was a mountainous scene painted from a memory of Jim and Flick's honeymoon. The journey had been one they had made on one of the only overcast days. They had driven away from the coast toward the mountains, but the sun had broken through the clouds casting an ethereal glow to their surroundings. It was magical. She had captured the light perfectly. He was only truly seeing this now that it was hung in a gallery, like it should have been long ago.

Piece after piece, Jim and Penelope stared at the paintings created by the woman they both loved so dearly. Sadness that she could not see this most wonderful achievement hung in the air between them as they shared glances filled with pride but tinged with melancholy. Hours were spent simply gazing and absorbing what surrounded them.

The final piece, the painting she had finished so quickly whilst she was with him in Scotland, almost brought him to his knees. Julian appeared and grasped his shoulders, willing him to stay upright as he stared into the image of that special place that had stuck in her mind for all those years without revealing it's true meaning to her until he had taken her there. He covered his mouth again as another pained sob erupted from within. He glanced at Julian whose eyes had also given way to saltwater.

Images of Flick in her paint spattered clothing and grinning from ear to ear as she revealed her latest work plagued Jim's mind. How he had kissed her and told her she was the most wonderfully talented and sexy woman he had ever encountered; how she had blushed at his words and nuzzled his neck to hide her embarrassment at the compliments he bestowed upon her. His whole being ached to hold her again. Penelope came to stand before him and wiped his tears away with her thumbs. Tears he hadn't realised were still falling.

On the return to their hotel, neither had the energy to eat. They parted with an embrace and went to their separate rooms. Jim collapsed, fully clothed onto the bed, emotionally exhausted. He drifted into a sleep filled with dreams of Flick. *His* Flick.

~~~~~

The following day, Penelope had insisted on taking the train back to Hampshire, and Jim had only argued for a few minutes before realising her resolve was strong. He had a life to get back to. Didn't he? A derisive snort escaped his body. *That* life was supposed to be filled with him and Felicity together from this point. Well, he had *hoped* it would be; he had almost felt sure it would. But now...all he was left with were his memories.

Julian had assigned himself to dealing with the press and had become a temporary fixture at the gallery, hell bent on doing all he could to assure that *Through the Glass* was a success. He didn't have to try hard. Flick's true identity was going to be released once Penelope and Jim had been able to hold a memorial service, but that couldn't be done until the enquiries into the plane crash were concluded. No one knew how long that would take, and so for now, Jim headed back to his Highland home.

After the long drive and retrieving Jasper from his neighbour, he opened the front door to his little cottage and closed it behind him. The house he had loved since moving in now felt cold and lifeless. With a heavy heart, he walked into the lounge. He had been hoping and expecting to come back here with Flick. Even if it had been a temporary thing until they decided their next step. He was going to bring her in, build a roaring fire, and lay her out in front of it. He was going to worship her body like he should have the last time, never letting her go again. But instead he stood in his lounge without her.

Even though she had only been here with him for a brief time after Christmas, it had felt right, although he couldn't admit it at the time. Every inch of the place echoed with memories of her. She belonged here. He had realised this too late. If only he hadn't been so harsh. If only he hadn't misread the signs, she would be here with him now. She would never have left. She would never have gone to New York and she would never have boarded that damned flight.

Leaning against the wall and sliding down with a thump to the floor, he pulled Jasper into him. "She's left me again, Jasper. But this time it's for good. She's gone, Jasper…she's gone." He nuzzled the dog's fur and began to grieve all over again.

~~~~~

May 2012

The following days were spent in a numb haze. Jim had to make great efforts to carry out the simplest of tasks. His brother had arrived two days after his return from Glasgow after Tara's parents had insisted on paying for a flight. Tara had stayed home. Euan did his best to look after his older brother, but the fact was Jim had no interest in looking after himself.

"Jim, you're going to have to eat, bro. I made you some soup. After you've eaten this you need to take a shower. You stink, you know." Euan nudged Jim's shoulder as he sat beside him holding out the tray of food.

Jim took the tray and rested it on his knees. "Gee thanks, bro. I'm so glad you came," he replied sarcastically and smiled, but the smile only curled at his lips, not making it as far as his eyes.

"You're welcome. So…food…shower…bed, yes?" Euan patted his brother's shoulder.

"Aye. Okay," Jim acquiesced.

Euan began to walk toward the kitchen but stopped and turned to faced Jim. "Oh and another thing…"

"What now?" Jim looked up into his brother's concerned gaze.

"Please stop playing that music over and over, okay? I know they're pieces that remind you of her. But it's not healthy, bro. Listen to something else, eh?" Jim had played Pearl Jam's *Black* and Debussy's *Clair De Lune* pretty much on a loop whenever he was cocooned in his room. The lilting melodies and the memories of Flick that they evoked were like a security blanket.

"I'll listen to what I fucking like. It's ma house." Jim's tone remained steady but he narrowed his eyes at his brother.

"Aye, I know that. It's just… Well for starters it's doing my fucking head in and I used to love them both…but…you can't bring her back by playing them over and over. You know?" Euan's eyes were filled with sadness as Jim looked up at him through his matted hair.

Anger rose within him and he stood, throwing the tray to the floor. "Don't you think I fucking know that?!" he shouted. He was shaking and his fists clenched. "Don't you think I know that *nothing* I do will ever change this fucking awful pain I'm stuck with?" His voice cracked at he pointed to his chest. "It's a physical, excruciating fucking pain. I lost her once before, Euan. I can't deal with losing her again. It's too fucking much! It's not fair!" An anguished sob erupted from his throat and he dropped to his knees.

In two strides, Euan crossed the room and grabbed Jim into a strong embrace. "I know…I know…forget I said anything. I'm sorry, Jim…I am… I'm so, so sorry."

~~~~~

Jim was awoken from a dream by a strange noise. He sat bolt upright and checked the time. Four o'clock. He realised the strange noise was the house phone. *Who the hell rings at four o'clock in the morning?* An awful thought ran though his mind. *Oh shit, something's happened to Penelope.*

The ringing stopped as Jim dived out of bed and bolted downstairs. He flicked the light switch on in the lounge. Euan stood there holding the phone, shaking his head. Jim's stomach lurched and his heart pounded against his ribcage.

Euan covered the receiver and looked to Jim. His eyes once again filled with concern. "It's Penelope. Jim, she's rambling and I can't get a word in. I think she's had some sort of breakdown. She's not making any sense." He held out the receiver to Jim.

Jim grabbed the receiver. "Penny? It's Jim. What is it? What's wrong?" His breathing was erratic both from running down the stairs and from nervous energy and panic.

"Nothing's wrong, Jim! It wasn't true! None of it was true!" Penny's voice sounded manic, and Jim filled with fear. Her words were coming out in a rush. *Was* she having a breakdown? He had to remain strong.

"Okay, Penny, slow down. I think you need to take some calming breaths and explain what's wrong."

"Jim, you're not listening to me! She wasn't on the plane!" Penny virtually screamed down the line.

Jim's legs weakened. He heard a buzzing noise loud in his ears and felt the blood drain from cheeks. He slumped to his knees as Euan stood beside him.

"Jim, you alright, bro? Jim?"

Chapter 26

May 2012 – Three Years and Three Months After the Break-up

Jim sat in the passenger seat as Euan drove him to the airport. This morning's conversation played over and over in his mind. His heart rate had still not settled, and he just about pulled holes in his jeans where his nails dug into the denim covering his legs.

"Jim, are you there, Jim? You've gone quiet." Penny's voice had been filled with concern. "Jim, are you alright, dear?"

Jim had rubbed his hand over his face and snapped himself back to reality. Anger brewed up inside him. "Is this some kind of sick joke, Penny? Is someone trying to play us here? Because this sounds like someone has made a prank call to you." *How could people be so cruel at a time like this? To this poor woman who had lost her daughter?*

"No, Jim. It's real. I had a call from a Detective Rand with the NYPD. They discovered a collapsed female in the ladies lavatories at JFK. She had no I.D. on her and she was unconscious." Jim listened intently to every word, trying to decipher whether this was really happening. "She was taken to hospital where they had a terrible job of trying to find her identity. She had no luggage, and the search at the airport did nothing to resolve that matter."

"But…but she *died* in a plane crash, Penny. I don't understand. There were no survivors, remember?" Jim's voice was shaky and beads of sweat trailed cool paths down his overheated skin.

"No, that's the thing. They checked all the flights and the only person *not* checked in on any flight was a Felicity

Johnston-Hart. She fits the description they gave me, Jim."
Penny's voice was croaky and faltering as she spoke. "She
was apparently drugged, Jim… Someone tried to *kill* her.
She's in a coma." Penelope sobbed down the line.

The words stabbed Jim in the heart and physical pain
speared him. His stomach lurched. "Someone tried to *kill*
her? Why?"

"That's what they're trying to figure out, Jim. It was
deliberate. She wasn't a random target that's for sure. It
appears all of her belongings were removed when the
culprit left the airport."

Jim rubbed his hand over his head as the words sunk in.
"Fuck…oh God, I'm sorry for swearing, Penny."

He heard a faint laugh down the line. "Oh, Jim, don't
worry. I think I even swore a little myself at the news. You
need to get on a flight over there. My passport has expired,
and I have to get one as soon as possible so I'll meet you
over there. I've booked you into the Hilton. Please get
there as soon as possible. Your flight is booked and you
need to be at the airport by ten."

~~~~~

"Earth to Jim?" Euan broke Jim from his thoughts.
"Are you okay, bro?"

Jim cleared his throat and looked at his brother. "No,
I'm seriously *not* okay. What if it's not her? What if it *is* her,
and she dies? I can't stand this, Euan. It's tearing me apart.
I think *I'm* teetering on the edge of a fucking breakdown
here."

"I think it's unlikely they would drag you all the way out
there if they weren't sure, eh?" Euan smiled. "I'm guessing
that your going to identify her is just a matter of
clarification. Dotting the *i's* and crossing the *t's* kind of
stuff."

"Aye…maybe… I'm terrified though. Why the hell would anyone want to *kill* her? I just don't get it."

"Me neither, mate. Me neither. But thank fuck they didn't succeed, eh? Right?" Euan gave his brother's leg a firm pat.

"Aye…not yet anyway." Jim's eyes stung from all the crying and lack of sleep he had endured since the terrible news about Flick's death had come through…and now he was just downright confused.

~~~~~

After landing in New York's bustling JFK airport, Jim made his way through to the taxi rank outside. He didn't even bother to go to his hotel. He simply directed the driver to the Saint Cloud Hospital where the *Jane Doe* was lying in a bed awaiting official identification. The staff had been made aware of Jim's impending arrival, and as soon as he walked through the doors to the intensive care unit, he was ushered into a side room by the consultant in charge of her care, along with a man in a suit.

"Welcome, Mr MacDuff, please take a seat." Jim sat on a sofa situated along the wall. The two men remained standing. "I'm Doctor Felix Guzman and this is Detective Niall Rand. We've been dealing with the case of the woman we believe to be Felicity Johnston-Hart. Now, we wanted to go over a few things prior to taking you to see her. What lies ahead may be quite distressing for you, and we feel you should know the full extent of her condition."

Jim listened intently but just wished they would get on with it so he could go to her. "Yes…yes of course…whatever's needed." He nodded.

"Okay, so here's what we know so far… The woman was found in the ladies restroom at JFK on the day of the flight nine forty-two crash but after the flight had departed. She was covered in vomit and was unconscious. There was no I.D. on her person and no baggage was found in the waiting area. She was brought here by ambulance and was admitted in order that Dr. Guzman and his staff could carry out tests."

"Hmmm, it was a bizarre one, Mr. MacDuff. Large quantities of a very strong prescription drug were found in her blood stream. It's a drug that cannot be easily obtained. It comes in liquid form and it's almost without taste apart from a slight bitterness. However, it could be easily disguised. It's a powerful drug and is usually used to treat psychosis. Now, it appears that she may have been given the drug in an alcoholic beverage. The amounts that were found in her blood stream were enough to seriously harm her, but considering she had vomited a lot, possibly thanks to her body's desire to expel the overdose, we feel that the original amount *was* intended to kill."

Jim huffed the air out of his lungs like he had been winded. He shook violently and brought his hands to his face.

"Mr. MacDuff, are you alright? I know this is a lot to take in. Can I get you a drink of water?" Dr. Guzman asked

"Thank you…yes," Jim croaked. Dr. Guzman left the room.

"Mr. MacDuff—"

"Call me Jim, please."

"Okay, Jim…once we have ascertained the young woman's identity and if it does prove to be Ms. Johnston-Hart, we will need to ask you some questions, okay?"

"Yeah…whatever it takes. How…however I can help," was all Jim could manage to stutter.

Dr. Guzman returned and handed a cup of water to Jim. "Now, once you're ready, we'll go. But I have to warn you that the young woman is attached to a number of pieces of medical equipment to help sustain her. Please don't be alarmed. She is in the best hands here and we're doing our best to make sure she's comfortable."

Jim finished the cup of water in one gulp and stood, "I'm ready."

They walked along a long corridor flanked on either side by numerous rooms housing some seriously ill-looking patients. Shivers traversed Jim's aching spine. The doctor and detective came to a halt outside a room with a large window. Through the glass, Jim could see the body of someone lying on a bed, surrounded by large pieces of equipment just like he'd been warned. Wires protruded from the body. *Oh God, surely that's not her?* His blood ran cold and he placed his palms on the window.

"Okay, Mr. MacDuff, you can go on in. We're right here with you." Dr. Guzman held open the door.

Jim nodded. "Please…call me Jim," was his autopilot response.

Hesitantly, he walked into the room. An intermittent bleeping noise was audible, and situated by the bed was a large cylinder, which contained something resembling a concertina folded paper bag, expanding and contracting, hissing as it moved.

As if noting his concern the doctor spoke. "This apparatus is a ventilator. It's helping her to breathe at the moment, but don't worry, she is being kept in this state whilst we assess any damage caused by the overdose of the drug she was subjected to." Jim simply nodded again.

He approached the bed and inhaled sharply, almost stumbling backward at the terrifying vision before him. He ran his hands through his hair and rested them atop his head, struggling to take things in. A wave of nausea hit combined with dizziness. Someone placed a hand on his back to steady him.

"Do I take it you can confirm the identity of this young woman?" Detective Rand enquired.

Jim's voice was almost a whisper as he replied. "It's her. It's my Flick."

Chapter 27

Dr. Guzman pulled a chair over and beckoned Jim to sit beside the bed. "We'll leave you alone for a while, Jim. Please call if you need anything."

Jim spun around. "Wait! Can I…can I touch her? I'm afraid to but…I want to…just to hold her hand." He looked pleadingly at the doctor.

"Of course you can, Jim." Dr. Guzman patted his shoulder. The doctor and the detective left the room.

Felicity had been lying here for over a week, his poor, beautiful girl, no one knowing who she was. The thought yanked his heart into his throat and made his eyes sting. He took her hand in his and felt relieved that it was warm. Her face was pale and drawn, and her closed eyes were sunken and rimmed with dark circles, the lids had a distinct purple hue. A tube was strapped to her skin, which led to the ventilator, and at its end point distorted her once full and beautiful mouth. Her usually perfectly styled hair laid dully spread across the pillow.

At least her hand is warm. That has to be a good sign, right? Jim tried his best to eradicate the fear that was creeping over him. The feeling of dread lay heavy in his stomach. He stifled the sob trying to escape his body as a nurse walked into the room.

"Hi, Jim. I'm Norah," the kindly looking woman said as she smiled over at him. "I'm one of the nurses taking care of Felicity. If you need anything just holler. Oh…and talk to her. She may hear you." She patted his shoulder and then proceeded to mark things off on the chart she held.

When Norah left the room, he looked back to Felicity. She looked so frail and helpless lying there. He squeezed her hand. Clearing his throat, he began, "F-Felicity...it's...it's Jim. I don't know if what the nurse said is true but...I'm here. I came as soon as I heard. They *will* find who did this to you. I'll make sure of it." Tears stung his eyes and he blinked them away. Gritting his teeth he went on. "I can't believe someone would *do* this to you. I just can't."

He drew in a long shaky breath, "I have so many regrets, Flick. That last time I saw you... I should have been honest but...I was a coward. I was too afraid to tell you I still love you. I treated you so badly and I'll never forgive myself for that." He rested his head on their joined hands for a moment to compose himself. "That's the truth, Flick. I still love you. Always have, always will. I know I may have messed this up, but as soon as you're better I'll tell you again. If you don't want me, I'll understand. But at least you'll know. I don't deserve you though. I never have. Your mum was right. The funny thing is...and if you were awake you'd laugh...she's decided she likes me. Can you believe that? It's only taken fourteen years, a plane crash, and an attempted murder, but hey..." He smiled, wishing he could look into her sparkling eyes once again.

He squeezed her hand gently. "I want you to come home. I want to take you to Scotland and look after you...forever, Flick, if you'll have me. I want to set your easel up and watch you paint. I want to cook for you and go for walks with you. I want to snuggle up with you and watch sappy movies and to feel you next to me in *our* bed. To wake up with you and bring you breakfast. To take you for long walks up to the viewpoint...*our* viewpoint. I just want to have the chance to be with you again." His lip trembled and saltwater escaped his eyes once more. "You should see the gallery, Flick. Your paintings are amazing. They look stunning hung there in Glasgow. *Everyone* loves them." He glanced at her face to check for response but there was none. "Julian has worked so hard. He's a great guy. He said seeing as you discovered him he wanted to discover you right back. He'll be so happy you're okay... You *will* be okay, Flick. Any time you want to open your eyes will be fine...there's no rush... I'll wait for you. I'll always wait for you."

After a while Norah returned. "Jim? Detective Rand would like to speak with you. And we feel it's best if you get some sleep and come back tomorrow, okay?"

Jim shook his head. "No...no I can't leave her... What if she wakes up and needs me?"

Norah smiled reassuringly. "If she wakes, we'll call you. Please don't worry, honey. The test results are due in very soon. Once they are and if he feels it appropriate, Doctor Guzman will begin to bring her around."

Jim was too tired to fight. He followed Norah to the room where Detective Rand was waiting. Detective Rand shook his hand and offered him a seat.

The detective sat, too. "Okay, Jim. Is there anything at all that springs to mind that you can tell us that may lead us to who tried to kill Ms. Johnston-Hart? Anything at all. No matter how small or insignificant it may seem. For example, do you know of anyone who may have held a grudge? Or anyone you know who may have been on the medication that was found in her system?"

"I'm sorry... I know nothing at all. We were divorced and didn't really keep in touch. Our last meeting was when she told me she'd been offered a job here. She wasn't on any medication herself that I know of, so I have no clue."

"Okay, that's kind of what we figured, but we have to ask, you understand?"

"Sure, sure. Have you got any leads at all? I mean, is she still in danger from someone waiting for her once they know she's alive?"

"Well, apart from the obvious possibilities of organ damage, we presume that currently the perp presumes she's dead. Hopefully it'll stay that way until we catch up with them. We're interviewing people at her work place right about now. There's a guard posted on the door from the time I leave, so please don't worry. No further harm will come to her while she is here, and we'll ensure that none comes to her once she's well enough to leave. It's my intention to solve this case before she's discharged and leaves for home. In my opinion, this was an amateurish murder attempt. I think we'll close in very soon on the culprit."

"Thanks…thanks so much, Detective." Jim vigorously shook the man's hand.

~~~~~

A yellow cab transported a rather dazed Jim MacDuff back to his hotel. Penny had thought of everything, bless her.

Jim called her once he was in his room. "It's her, Penny."

The scream that came over the line was joy-filled but piercing, forcing Jim to pull the handset away from his ear. He couldn't help but smile. Once she had calmed down, he filled her in with the details he had been given.

Her joy was short lived. "Oh, Jim, who would do such a thing to our darling Felicity?" She sobbed. "She didn't have any enemies that I know of."

"I have absolutely no idea, Penny. But they *will* figure it out. They're already covering every possible angle. I spoke with Detective Rand again today, and he seems to be determined to get it sewn up quickly. We have to have confidence in them. They know what they're doing."

"Oh, Jim, dear... I do hope so... I just want her home now."

"Me too, Penny...me too."

The call ended late in the evening, and Jim decided to shower and order room service. He stood under the large showerhead as the soothing hot water cascaded down his back, relaxing his tense and aching muscles and washing his worries temporarily down the drain. He vowed to himself that he would be back at the hospital first thing in the morning. His mind whirred with the events of the past two days, and he clambered to make sense of the knowledge that someone had tried to kill his ex-wife. *Nothing* made sense. After he had half eaten his dinner, he gave in to the need for sleep.

Chapter 28
May 2012

Jim arrived at the hospital at eight the following morning but wasn't allowed to go straight in to see Flick. She was being taken off the ventilator, and the next couple of hours were crucial, he was informed. He paced around the family room with a pounding heart, chewing on his nails, awaiting news.

Eventually running out of nervous energy, he slumped into a chair and clasped his hands together. "God…I know that I've never been a church person…and I know I've never really prayed before…and…and I know I swear…rather a lot…probably too much…but…if you are watching over my Flick…please, please bring her through this. *Please.* I can't be without her again. I just can't…please. I'll try harder…I promise. I'll do everything in my power to make her so very happy." He rubbed his hands over his face and continued to wait for news.

At eleven o'clock the door opened and Doctor Guzman walked in. He held out his hand. "Good to see you again, Jim. I hope you managed to get some sleep."

"I think my body just gave up, to be honest. I fought it though." Jim's voice was weak as he spoke.

"Well, I'm pleased to be able to let you know that we've removed the ventilator, and Felicity is managing to breathe unaided."

The news winded Jim, and although relieved, he leaned forward and rested his elbows on his knees and his head in his hands as tears of relief welled in his eyes. "Thank you, God," he breathed.

"We also have the test results. As you're here as her next of kin and we've been given permission by her mother to discuss her condition with you, we're able to share those results with you. Is that okay?" the doctor asked, placing a hand on Jim's shoulder.

When Jim nodded the doctor sat in a chair opposite.

"Okay, now, it's not great news but it's not as bad as it could have been," the doctor began. "Felicity has suffered slight liver damage, but the liver is probably one of the most robust organs with the ability to repair itself to a certain degree, and so we are hopeful that this won't be permanent…although there are sadly no guarantees. Her kidneys are functioning normally. Heart is good and strong. The only thing is…" The doctor paused.

Jim lifted his head. "The only thing is what?" Dread washed over him and he feared the worst.

"Well, at this stage it's hard to say if there is any brain damage caused by what was to all intents and purposes an overdose of a mind altering drug. We've done all the tests we can while she is unconscious, but…well we won't know the full extent of any damage until she is fully conscious. We have to be prepared for what may happen if and when she wakes up, Jim."

"*If* and when? Well which is it?" Jim could hear the desperation as it vibrated through his own voice. He sat upright and faced the dark haired, olive skinned man opposite him.

"We…don't know at the moment. We just need to wait for her body to repair and for her to gain consciousness. We *are* hopeful, Jim. But please try and understand that we can't say for sure at this stage of her recovery."

This was *not* welcome news. Penny was arriving tomorrow and hearing this would almost kill her. But all they could do was wait. Jim was allowed to Felicity's bedside once again. He sat in the same place as the day before. Seeing her now, without the ventilator tube was strange. She was still pale, and her eyes still had that same purple hue. But she was breathing.

He squeezed her hand and stroked his thumb over her knuckles. "Felicity, it's Jim. I'm here again. No getting rid of me, eh?" He leaned and kissed her hand. There was bruising visible where an intravenous line had been removed. He hadn't noticed it yesterday. But then again, she had been surrounded by all sorts of machines yesterday. "I...I...spoke to your mum again. She's on her way. I'll bring her to see you tomorrow." He was desperate for a response but none came.

"Flick, come on. Wake up, eh? Show them what you're made of... You can fight this thing. I *know* you can. And...I *miss* you...so, so much." Emotions constricted his throat and words came out as a strangled whisper. "I've missed you ever since you left Scotland. In fact, I've missed you ever since you left me three years ago, Flick. I want to see you smile again. You have the best smile... The first time I saw it I think my insides melted... You certainly made your mark on me."

Norah came in and checked Flick's vitals. "How are you today, Jim? Did you sleep?" she asked whilst she filled in numbers on the chart again.

"I did, thanks. I'm okay... I'll be better when Flick wakes up." He didn't shift his gaze from his sleeping beauty.

"Well, we're all hoping for the same thing, Jim. Just hang in there, honey." The older lady smiled kindly and then left the room.

~~~~~

After a restless night, filled with dreams of Felicity, Jim met Penny at JFK the following morning. She hugged him so tight he felt like he was going to pass out. They made their way to the hospital by cab as soon as they had dropped Penny's bags at the hotel and she had freshened up. She squeezed Jim's hand throughout the whole cab journey. Jim was still astounded by the change in their relationship.

On arrival at the hospital, Jim opened Felicity's room door and Penny stepped inside. She gasped and rushed to her daughter's bedside. "Oh, no…no, no, no." She turned to Jim with a pained expression, and he hugged her to him as she sobbed, her hands covering her mouth. He let her cry until her tears subsided, and then he pulled a chair next to the bed and helped her to sit. Her legs had apparently weakened through the shock of seeing her only child lying unconscious.

Once she was calmer and he felt better about leaving, he touched Penny's shoulder. "Look, Penny, I'll leave you to have some time alone with her, okay? There must be things you want to say."

She looked up at him with puffy, sad eyes. "Say? But…she's not awake, Jim."

"No, but the nurse said she may be able to hear you… Go ahead…I'll leave you to it." He smiled reassuringly and left the room. He walked to the family room and pushed the door open. Thankfully, it was vacant. He pulled out his phone and called Euan.

He answered the call after one ring. "Hey, bro, how's it going? Is everything okay?"

"Hi…it's not great. Flick's off the ventilator and breathing by herself. She looks so different though. She's pale…kind of grey. There's been no response from her. They say there could be brain damage, Euan."

He was silent for a moment at the other end of the line. "Aw hell, Jim, I don't know what to say bro. That's not good, eh? How soon will they know more?"

"When she wakes, I guess. It's all a waiting game. Penny's here now, so at least I'm not alone. We can support each other."

"Bless the poor woman. She must be devastated."

"Aye. She's a bit of a wreck…pretty much like me."

"Well, keep your chin up, eh? Stay positive. And make sure you both eat and rest. Don't worry about shit here. Jasper is great, and I'm a big hit with the local *ladies* so the business is doing fine."

Jim snorted. "Euan, the average age of the *ladies* around there is sixty-five, so I'd be careful about bragging there, mate." He couldn't help but smile and shake his head.

Euan chuckled down the line. "Look after yourself. Love you, bro."

"Aye, love you too you ugly swine." Jim hung up.

~~~~~

The next two weeks followed the same routine. Hospital, eat, shower, sleep, etc. Friday of the second week came around, and Penny was feeling unwell. She stayed in her room to get some rest, and Jim went to the hospital alone. He walked into Flick's room to find Norah going about her hourly checks.

"Hi, Norah. Any change?" His words were hopeful as always. But as always, Norah's words did nothing to fan the flames of his hope.

"Not yet, sweetie. But she's a tough cookie. We haven't given up and neither has she." She patted his shoulder as she did every other time and left him.

He clutched a piece of paper to his chest. It was a print out of an email that Julian had sent him. It showed the front page of The Glaswegian, the headline of which read, *Mystery Artist Takes Glasgow By Storm.* He intended to read it to Flick as he sat with her.

"Hey, gorgeous. You're looking brighter today." He spoke softly, leaning in close to kiss her forehead. "I think you have a bit more colour to your cheeks." He pulled up a chair and held her hand as he read the article to her. He watched for any response as he read but received none. "Anyway, it sounds like the exhibition is going down really well. People just love your work, Flick. I want to take you to see it soon, so you need to wake up…Flick? Wake up for me, eh? Please."

Nothing.

Feeling lost and drained, he leaned his head on the bed beside her hand and eventually dozed off.

He dreamed about Flick again. This time they were lying on a bed in a white room. She was stroking his hair as he looked lovingly into her eyes. He touched her cheek and covered her mouth with his own. He feathered her cheeks and eyes with kisses. "Please don't leave me again, sweetheart. I couldn't bear it," he whispered. She didn't speak. "I keep losing you. I don't want to keep losing you." She simply stared into his eyes and ran her hands through his hair over and over. "I love you," he told her again.

But no sooner had he said that than she started to drift away from him. Tears trailed down her beautiful face, and she held out her hands to reach for him. He grabbed for her and managed to pull her back. Her hands found his hair again and he leaned in to kiss her. "Don't go…please don't go, Flick…don't go." But she began to drift away again. He tried to call after her but his throat constricted trapping the words before they could be spoken.

His eyes sprang open. His breath was huffing in and out in short, sharp spurts. It took a moment for him to realise he was still beside her in the hospital, lying with his face turned away from her. He could still feel her hand stroking his hair as if it had been real...*wait a second...that is real*. He sat bolt upright and turned toward her face.

"Oh my God!" He jumped to his feet and leaned over her. "Flick, it's me, Jim!" His voice was urgent and panicked. He stroked her cheek waiting for a response. Her eyes fluttered open weakly.

Shakily, she reached her hand to his cheek. "Jim...please take me home."

His eyes stung with the tears that threatened to overspill. Okay, she knew who he was, but did she know what had happened? Did she know where she was? Did she know what she was saying?

He took a deep calming breath. "And where's home, Flick?"

"Wherever you are, Jim."

Chapter 29

Jim paced around the family room as he nervously chewed at the skin around his nails. Why had they rushed him out? It was a good thing that she had gained consciousness. This wasn't one of those scenarios where she suddenly wakes up to say goodbye and then dies, was it? *Fuck! No it can't be like that. It just can't.*

Penny burst into the room. "Jim! They won't let me see her! What's going on?" The anguish in her eyes tugged at his heart.

He pulled her into him. "I don't know, Penny. She woke up, and then when I called for the doctor they ushered me out and asked me to wait in here. It's driving me mad." They hugged, clinging onto to each other as they waited.

After half an hour, Doctor Guzman finally came into the family room. He asked them to sit. Jim didn't like that. It made him think the worst.

Dr. Guzman smiled warmly. "Jim, you look terrified."

"I *am* terrified. Please…what's going on?"

"Okay, well she has regained full consciousness, which is marvellous. We have done the necessary tests, and we are very pleased to see that cognitive function appears to be unharmed. Felicity's just speaking with Detective Rand and telling him what she remembers of the events leading up to her being discovered in the rest room. She's a little upset as you can imagine, now that she's aware of the implications of being in here. But all in all, she's very fortunate to have escaped permanent damage. Now I know it's tempting to go in there all guns blazing…talking to her, asking questions, etc. But I feel it would be best if you let her be for today."

Jim stood, holding his hands up. "Whoa…no way, mate. I'm not leaving her. Never again am I leaving her."

The doctor placed a firm hand on Jim's shoulder. "Jim, believe me, I understand fully how hard it must be to hear this, but she's been though quite a traumatic ordeal both physically and now emotionally, and from hereon in, it may be a bumpy ride as she's learning about what's happened to her. She needs time to process it all and to maybe let things sink in. She has a lot to come to terms with here."

Jim exhaled what felt like all of the air from his lungs as he sat down again. "Please, Doctor Guzman. Please, you don't understand. I *have* to talk to her, even if it's just for a few minutes. And her mum will want that, too. We won't overcrowd her. I can promise you that. We'll even go in separately if that's better but *please*." He pleaded and prayed that the doctor would understand.

Doctor Guzman pursed his lips and for a moment it seemed like he was sticking to his guns. "Fine. Five minutes each and then you go and come back tomorrow. That's my final say on the matter."

"Thank you, Doctor Guzman. Thank you." Penny was wringing her handkerchief.

"Aye, thanks for that." Jim nodded. "I can't tell you how much I appreciate your help, doctor."

Back in the room, Felicity was slightly more elevated in her bed. Her face brightened as she saw Jim enter. He rushed to her bedside and leaned in to stroke her hair back and kiss her forehead.

"Hi, gorgeous. How're you feeling?" He caressed her face lovingly.

"Jim...you came all the way to America for me?" Her lip trembled and a tear escaped the corner of her eye. He caught it with his thumb.

"Of course I did. I couldn't stay away. I...I couldn't believe that you were alive when I was told. When that plane crash happened...I thought....that you were gone...that I'd lost you. I had to come and see for myself that you were still here." He stroked her cheeks happy to be touching her again.

"Thank you for coming, Jim." More tears were set free. "It means such a lot to me that you came."

"Hey, hey...shhh. It's okay. You're okay. You're going to be fine. You're safe now. I won't let anything happen to you again. No one will get to you again. I promise." He pulled her head into his chest as he smoothed her hair down and kissed the top of her head as she clung to his arms. "There are so many things we need to talk about, Felicity. So many things I need to explain."

Norah knocked on the door. "Jim, it's time to go so that Penelope can come in and see her daughter." She left again.

He looked down into Flick's eyes. "We'll talk tomorrow, okay? Your Mum has been so worried."

"Wait, what? The two of you are here t-together? And you're both still alive?" She smiled.

"Oh you'd be surprised what can happen whilst you're in a coma for a couple of weeks." He kissed her forehead. "I'll see you tomorrow. I lo—" He stopped before the words escaped. "I'll tell your mum to come in." He turned to leave the room feeling relieved.

~~~~~

Penelope squeezed Jim's hand as she passed him in the doorway. A sob escaped her as she reached Felicity's bedside.

"Hey, Mum, don't cry. I'm going to be fine. The doctor has said so. I'm so sorry for scaring you."

"Felicity, you're lying in hospital thousands of miles away from home after someone tried to kill you and you're apologising for scaring me? My darling silly, silly girl." She leaned forward and kissed Felicity's head. "Felicity, sweetheart, it's me who needs to apologise."

Her lip trembled again. "Mum...really...don't—"

"Felicity, please. I need to get some things off my chest and I only have five minutes. *Please.*" Penelope squeezed her hand. "They're saying you need rest, and I promised to be brief. So I'll just speak and I want you to listen." Felicity simply nodded. Penelope took a deep breath. "I have brought all of this on."

"Mum—"

"Felicity, please. If I'd just stopped being such a busybody you'd have had a long, happy marriage with that wonderful man out there, who adores every hair on your head by the way. You would have probably had children, and I would be a grandma. Your father would maybe have seen his grandchildren, too. This is *my* fault entirely. If not for me you'd never have been over here trying to be a high-flying executive in the art world.

"You'd have stayed doing what you loved and what you were so good at. You would still be painting, darling. But above all else you would be *happy*. Jim has been wonderful, Felicity. Despite my *disgusting* treatment of him, he has been so gracious, and I don't deserve that. He has been kind and warm. He has taught me what it means to really love someone. And that you don't need flashy cars and big houses or lots of money. He's been like a son to me over these past weeks when we thought we had lost you." She let out a sob and Felicity squeezed her arm, her own tears now falling freely.

"Sorry, love…I want you to realise that it was *me* who caused your divorce. I put so much pressure on you to be successful and to marry into wealth. I will understand if you want me out of your life. I had some misguided opinion of what life should entail. Which is stupid considering I adored your Father, and we *had* true love…hah…he must have really loved me because he put up with such a lot."

"Oh, Mum."

"I want you to know that you have my complete and utter blessing to be with Jim. You should have had it all along. You never really stopped loving him. And I have it on good authority that he feels the same. Once you're well, tell him how you feel. Promise me?"

Felicity sighed as she touched her mum's cheek. "I promise…and, Mum?"

Penny covered Felicity's hand with her own. "Yes dear?"

"Don't ever say anything about me not wanting you in my life, okay? All I ever wanted was for you to be proud of me."

Penelope sobbed. "Oh Felicity…darling…I've *always* been proud of you, so very proud."

Norah opened the door and peeped her head in. "Mrs. Johnston-Hart? I'm sorry but it's time to go."

"Okay, thank you, Norah dear…and please call me Penny." Norah smiled, nodded and left the room.

Felicity smiled. "Penny, eh?" She raised her eyebrows. "That's what Jim and Dad always called you."

Penny looked thoughtful for a moment. "Yes…I like the sound of it." She kissed her daughter and left the room.

~~~~~

The following morning when Jim and Penny arrived at the hospital, there was a buzz of activity outside Flick's room. Detective Rand spotted them and came rushing over.

"Jim, Penny, would you come with me please?"

"Why? What's happened? Is she okay?" Jim's heart rate had increased, and Penny's face had paled.

"Sorry, yes Felicity is fine. We have news and need to update you on what's happened."

The three of them walked into the family room and closed the door. They sat, and Jim and Penny waited expectantly.

"Okay, we have arrested a young woman by the name of…" He glanced down at his notepad. "Lia Cole. She gave herself up late last night. She was in quite a state. It appears she was the one who added the drug to Felicity's drink."

"But why? Who the hell *is* she? Did she know Felicity?" Jim frowned at the detective, trying to understand.

"She was Felicity's personal assistant at the New York gallery. It appears there was some art forgery going on at the gallery, and Felicity uncovered it."

"Shit…art forgery? But…but…to try to *kill* her? Isn't that a bit extreme?"

"It certainly is. But there was a lot of money at stake…millions… Apparently, the former gallery Manager, Chester Withers, was in a relationship with Miss Cole. He had gotten her involved. She insists that she didn't want to do it and that she thought a lot of Ms Johnston-Hart, but her life was threatened if she didn't cooperate. I guess it was a difficult situation for her…if what she says is true…but she should've come to the police before taking such drastic action. Obviously, a warrant is out for Withers' arrest, and we'll find out if what she says is true. It appears he may have fled, but my team are good at what they do, and I have no doubt they'll find him. Miss Cole insists that the drugs were those belonging to Withers. He had a nervous break-down on account of all the stress of what he'd gotten himself into but had also been having other problems."

With widened eyes, Jim exhaled noisily and ran his hands through his hair, resting them on his head. This was a real blow.

Penny sat, open mouthed at the news. "But…what if Felicity is still in danger?" she asked, her hands shaking in her lap.

"Mrs. Johnston-Hart, I can assure you we have posted a guard on Felicity's door, and we are investigating every single lead provided by Miss Cole. To say she was distraught is an understatement. She knows she will do time for this, yet she's determined to squeal on those involved, which is very helpful indeed. We've interviewed Felicity and have all the details from her that she can remember."

"Is Felicity implicated in all of this? You know with the art forgeries?" Jim wasn't sure he wanted to hear the answer.

"No. We have no reason to suspect her involvement. She was trying to compile evidence about the forgeries and was going to inform the gallery's partner, Mr Nilsson, while she was in the UK. What she says is corroborated by Miss Cole. Felicity just needs to get well and go home."

Both Penny and Jim sighed with relief.

"I'll update you again once we have more."

"Great, thanks. Can we go see Felicity now?"

Detective Rand nodded and gestured toward the door. Penny and Jim hurriedly made their way to Felicity's room.

She was sitting up, still pale but looking much improved. A smile spread across her face when her visitors walked past the burly looking guard on the door.

"Hey, Felicity you're looking great." Jim's grin felt a mile wide on his face. He wanted to rush over and kiss her but held back and allowed Penny to step forward. Felicity, however, didn't move her gaze from Jim's. Penny looked from her daughter to Jim and kissed her daughter's head.

"Darling, I'm going to go and get a coffee. I sense that there are things that you two need to discuss." She patted Felicity's arm and turned to Jim. "Hear her out, Jim dear," she whispered.

He pulled up the chair up to Felicity's side and sat. His hands itched to hold hers, but now that she was fully conscious he felt awkward and had no clue what the limits were. As if she read his mind, she reached for his hand.

"Jim...I need to... I want to...erm..." Her eyes dropped to her lap. "I think we need to talk."

"Felicity...I know all about the art forgeries. Don't worry. They're on the case. It'll be fine. You're not implicated and no one will get to you. I won't let them."

"Jim, that's not what I meant. I think we should talk about...about *us*." She squeezed his hand. "There are things I need to say to you."

Jim sat up straight, suddenly realising he was about to find out where the limits were and whether or not there was a future for them. "Yes...yes, I suppose you're right."

"I know this involves dragging up the past, but I want to apologise, Jim. I put you through a lot of awful stuff because I thought I was lacking in my life. It turns out I was only lacking in *myself*. It was nothing *you* did." She took a deep breath. "You were wonderful and supportive and stood by whilst I tried to achieve this amazing career that I was *so sure* I wanted. I lost you because I was trying to aspire to a lifestyle that my mother, at the time, convinced me was right, and I was stupid enough to listen. She admits it now. It doesn't excuse my behaviour, I know."

Her words came out in a rush, and her chest moved up and down quickly. "Jim…the truth is…I…I never stopped loving you. I just *convinced* myself that I didn't, but…seeing you in January was *so hard.* And then we made love, and I thought that maybe you felt the same." She lowered her gaze, and Jim saw the tears that glistened in her eyes. "I realise now that you are over me *and* our relationship and that you care deeply for me as a friend, otherwise you wouldn't have come all this way. And I'm so grateful for that," her voice trembled. "And I *will* learn to get over the rest. Having you as a friend is so much better than not having you in my life at all. You *were* my best friend, Jim, and I miss that." A sob escaped the confines of her throat. "I miss that so much. But I needed to say sorry and to tell you…I love you…that I'm still *in love* with you. I just…needed to say it and… I thought you should know." More tears escaped the corners of her eyes. She pulled her hand away from Jim and wiped them away. Her lip quivered.

His heart ached to see her like this and his own eyes stung. "I know Felicity. I've known since you left Scotland. That manuscript your dad sent me…there was a letter. Ed told me everything."

She nodded but avoided eye contact. "Oh…I see. Well, now you've heard it from the horse's mouth, eh?" She smiled and laughed once but sadness clouded her eyes. "I'm still glad I said it. I think it was important that you heard it from me. And…well, now I can try to move on." Her voice wavered as she spoke.

Jim grasped her hand again. "Flick...what if I don't *want* you to move on?" He rubbed his thumb back and forth over her knuckles.

She smiled wider. "You called me Flick."

"Aye, I did." It was Jim's turn to take a deep breath. "Flick...I've never stopped loving you either. I let you go because...I thought that I didn't make you happy. That was all I ever wanted...for you to be happy. So I figured I loved you enough to let you go." He leaned toward her and cupped her cheek with his free hand.

Her mouth fell open at his words. She was silent and her brow furrowed as she seemed to be allowing the news to sink in. "Oh, Jim...what did I do?"

"Hey, stop that. It's over...forgotten." He waved his hand dismissively and then returned it to her cheek. "It's what we do from now that matters."

She nodded slowly. "So...what *should* we do?" Her tears were relentless now, and she covered his hand with hers, leaning into his touch.

"Flick, I don't know if you remember but you said...when you woke from your coma...that you wanted me to take you home... My home is Scotland... I don't know whether that changes things."

Another sob escaped her throat. "Oh, Jim...you want to take me home to Scotland?"

"Sweetheart...there's nothing I would like more. Is...is that what you want, too?" He blinked as his tears finally overflowed and he swallowed hard. She couldn't speak. She simply nodded.

He stood and bent toward her. Tilting her chin up, he kissed her gently. Her hands snaked up around his neck, and she deepened the kiss. "I love you so much, Jim."

He wiped away the tears from her cheeks. "I love you too...no more tears, eh?"

Chapter 30
June 2012

The cab pulled up outside the restaurant where Jim had secured a table in a quiet area at the back. Glasgow city centre on a Saturday night wasn't known for its serenity or composure, and Flick was still panicky in crowded places. Since her release from hospital a week ago and the flight back to Scotland, she had recovered well and was only now on minimal medication. They had spent the first few days down in Hampshire with Penny and had travelled home on the insistence of Jim who had a surprise to share.

Investigations into the attempted murder of Flick had resulted in Lia Cole and Chester Withers being arrested, awaiting trial for this and several counts of forgery. The surprising thing, and the thing that had hurt Felicity more than anything, was that Vitale DeLuca had been arrested for illegally supplying the drug that had almost killed her. He, too, had been involved in the forgeries and had known both Lia and Chester. Initially, he was supposed to coerce Felicity by way of his masculine charms into becoming involved in order to implicate her, blackmail her, or keep her quiet about the whole thing. Flick turning him away had clearly scuppered their plans, and she felt glad that she hadn't fallen for his apparent sensuality. He had seemed so sincere when they almost spent the night together, and she had thought he genuinely liked her. Discovering it had all been a ruse to acquire her coercion made her feel ashamed and *incredibly* foolish.

It was now the middle of June, and Julian had been in touch again to ask her to view the exhibition of the artist he had discovered. She had explained that she had resigned from her job, and had no interest in this anymore. But had eventually agreed to go and look as a last favour to Nilsson-Perkins—who had been roped into things following an explanation from Julian.

Jim and Flick met Julian at the restaurant with hugs and handshakes. "Wow, you really look amazing, Felicity, considering what you've been through." Julian held her at arm's length.

"That's sweet, thanks Jules. I feel much better. I just want to get this evening over with and get home to Shieldaig with Jim." She gazed lovingly up at him standing beside her with his arm tight around her waist.

They chatted over dinner about Julian's latest work and enjoyed a wonderful meal together, and even though she had been a little reluctant to go to the exhibition as the time drew closer, she felt the excitement building. They climbed into the waiting cab that took them to the gallery. Julian had arranged to show Felicity the exhibition when the gallery was closed so that she would feel safer.

They walked through the large wooden doors and followed Julian to the exhibition hall. "So do I get to know the artist's name yet?" she asked.

"You will soon enough, don't worry. The exhibition is called *Through the Glass*. That will suffice for now." He stopped at the double doors. "Now I want you to close your eyes."

"Julian, I'm not five. This is about *art*, remember?"

"Oh shut up moaning, woman, and humour me." Jules laughed.

With an eye roll and a sigh, she did as he requested and allowed him to lead her through the doors and into the stunning wood panelled room that she was already familiar with. It was a room in which she had viewed exhibitions in years past. Jim hung back and watched her walk in. Julian walked her to the beginning of the exhibition.

With his hands on her shoulders he whispered, "Okay...open your eyes." He released her and she heard him step away.

Felicity fluttered her eyes open as instructed and gazed up at the first painting. Waves of confusion and recognition washed over her simultaneously. She spotted the stand, which showed the exhibition title and the artists name 'Flick MacDuff'. She gasped and her hands shot to her face. She looked over to Julian who stood with one arm across his middle and the other resting on it, his finger on his lips, watching her reaction. He grinned widely. Her eyes shot back to the painting.

Slowly, she walked toward the next piece, took her time viewing it, and then moved on. Scenes she had encountered on countless journeys with Jim, with friends, and with her parents all hung before her. Scenes she had looked at through the glass and had recreated first in pencil and then in paints. What an unexpected situation to find herself in.

The colours, the brush strokes...all her own. Every mark remembered. Every memory so special. She walked on until she had viewed all but the last painting. Standing before this final piece overwhelmed her, and a sob escaped as she looked into the scene that had plagued her memory for years until she was taken there by Jim. Only then had the memory of looking back through Jim's family holiday snaps as they finished university come flooding back into her mind. The place was somewhere she had thought she had imagined. She had so desperately wanted it to be real, and discovering that it *was* had filled her heart with such joy.

She couldn't quite take it all in.

As she walked around again, a wide smile spread across her face. *Through the Glass...this is me...this is what* I *see through the glass...I understand now. All this time, I've been living a life that wasn't mine. The high-flying career, the status symbols...it all means nothing. It's like I've been watching* myself *through the glass. But I need to step back into* my *life...this life...the life I was meant to have. With Jim.*

She glanced over to where he stood. He was leaning against the wall with his arms folded across his chest, observing like he always used to. But this time it was different. *This* time the smile on his face was genuine and full of adoration. *This* time she could see who she was through his eyes and it all fell into place.

Finally Felicity turned and looked at Julian. Her face streaked with mascara. "How? Why?" was all she could manage to say.

"Felicity...you're such a talented artist. This is what you deserve. Your own exhibition." He held his arms out to gesture toward her paintings. "What do you think?" Julian looked worried now.

"It's...it's *wonderful*, Jules. Thank you...thank you so much." She rushed toward him and flung her arms around him, burying her head into his shoulder.

"Um...Felicity...I think your gratitude is aimed in the wrong direction, honey. It was Jim who did all of this."

~~~~~

Slowly, she turned to look at Jim, who now stood with his hands in his pockets watching as the realisation hit his beautiful Felicity. Myriad emotions coursed through his body and his eyes stung with the familiar feeling of unshed tears.

"You? You did this? For me?" Her voice was almost a whisper as she slowly walked toward him.

He cleared his throat. "After you left to go back to London and I read that letter, I realised I needed to do something to get you to remember how much you love painting and maybe that way you would come back to me." A little saltwater escaped and he wiped at his eyes.

"Oh Jim. I wanted you to come after me…desperately."

"Aye and I would have if Euan and Tara hadn't turned up just as I'd arranged to do that very thing. Then I heard that you'd left for New York. I asked Jules for his help and he's being far too bloody modest if you ask me. I couldn't have done this without him. I just had the idea… *He* made it happen."

She made her way to stand in front of Jim and looked up into his eyes. She smoothed her hands up over the lapels of his suit jacket, and he pulled her into him as his heart pounded in his chest.

His lip trembled as he looked down at her. "*This* is who you are. *This* is who I love." He leaned to kiss her. Brushing his lips softly over hers, he felt her melt into him.

"I get it now… I understand…and you're right…I love you so much, Jim… Thank you for reminding me."

He stroked her face and ran his thumb over her lower lip. "Flick?"

"Yes, Jim?"

"Please, can I take you home now?"

~~~~~

December 2012

Being back at the cottage for the last few months had been wonderful. Flick had forgotten how much she had loved it there for those few short days at the beginning of the year. They settled into life back together with ease, but this time things were so much better. It felt like it did in the early days when they had first met. The long walks together with Jasper were so special, and she had been painting such a lot. She told Jim how much she loved him as often as possible as if she was making up for lost time, and whenever she did, the look in his eyes made her heart skip and swell.

Christmas morning arrived and Flick was rather giddy. She had been working on a little painting for Jim in secret, and she was eager for him to unwrap it.

"Jim...wake up sweetie... I think Santa Claus has been," she whispered, sliding her hand down his naked back. He murmured and rolled over, wrapping his arms around her.

"Mmmm... Merry Christmas, gorgeous. I love you," he said huskily in his delicious, deep morning voice. His Scottish accent sent shivers travelling the length of her spine, and she decided maybe the gifts could wait a while. She slid her hand delicately down his smooth skin and grasped his prominent, morning arousal. He groaned his approval, and while caressing him, she moved to straddle his waist. Once she had guided him inside, she gazed down and began to move, keeping her eyes firmly locked on his. She smoothed her hands over his toned chest, and her fingertips traced his defined abs as she moved, revelling in the fullness of having him inside her body again. She would never get enough of this feeling.

He caressed her waist and moved up to cup her breasts lovingly, toying with the buds that peaked as she arched into his touch, needing more and more of him.

Rocking her hips back and forth she watched Jim's eyes darken with lust as he moved his hands down to grip her hips. With one hand, he pulled her down so that he could take her mouth. His hand cradled her head as her tongue explored and tasted the man she craved with every fibre of her being.

She had so much lost time to make up for.

She could feel the warm glow building in her belly and that Jim's movements had become more urgent. When she pulled herself upright again, he slipped his hand down between their bodies and massaged her sensitive place pushing her higher and sending tingles through every nerve ending in her body. It was the most amazing sensation. She threw her head back as they climbed together, up towards the stars, calling each other's name in the heat of their passion, and covering one another in warm kisses. This was the way love should be. This was *real*. And it felt so good to be in his arms again.

Once their breathing had calmed, she pulled on his T-shirt and went downstairs to light the fire that he had built in readiness before bed on Christmas Eve. She made fresh coffee, and he arrived in the kitchen behind her, sliding his arms around her waist and nuzzling her neck.

"Mmmm, you smell delicious. Have I told you I love you this morning?" he mumbled into her hair.

She covered his arms with her own. "You have…but I never tire of hearing it."

~~~~~

After eating croissants and drinking their coffee in the kitchen whilst Jasper looked on, apparently waiting for their leftovers, they went and sat beside the Christmas tree in all its pine-fragranced freshness. Flick handed him a small parcel. He ripped the paper off, being careful not to damage the contents.

When he took out the canvas, he gasped. "This is the view of the valley that you painted while you were here when the snow hit."

"It is. I wanted you to have this, seeing as the original is on display now. It's somewhere that means so much to both of us, and although we can walk up and visit there whenever we like, it felt like the right thing to paint for you."

"Flick, it's so beautiful, thank you so much. It means such a lot to me too… I just love it." He kissed her deeply. He looked a little overwhelmed and cleared his throat. "Erm… here's your gift… Merry Christmas, gorgeous."

Flick eagerly tore the paper off, not taking as much care as Jim had. He laughed as he watched her. Taking out and looking over the contents, she began to sob quietly, her body shaking and tears flowing freely. She looked up into his eyes where she saw her own tears mirrored in his eyes.

Looking down again, she read the cover of the book. "*Reaching Everest, a Biography of George Leigh Mallory* by Edgar Johnston-Hart." She curled her lips up into a huge grin. "Oh, Jim…it's wonderful. I'm so proud of you. Of both of you." She flung her arms around him and kissed him once again.

~~~~~

They prepared their Christmas lunch together and enjoyed a slow dance in the lounge to Bing Crosby's *White Christmas*. After sitting on the old tapestry couch snuggled up together, Felicity lifted her head from Jim's chest. "C'mon, let's go for a walk up to the view point."

"Awww, Flick I'm comfy and cosy right here with you," Jim whined, nuzzling her neck. Jasper had clearly heard the word *walk*, and his ears had pricked up. His tail had begun wagging frantically in a rhythm all of its own.

"Too late, Jasper's ready, too. C'mon...please?" She pouted and fluttered her eyelids at him, and he finally gave in to her feminine whiles.

After wrapping up warm, they trudged along in the biting air of the chilly December afternoon up to the view point depicted in Felicity's painting and the old photo from Jim's childhood. They stood and admired the view in silence, their arms wrapped around each other and Jasper sitting beside them.

As Flick glanced up at the sky, she gasped. "Jim, it's snowing!" The sparkling flakes cascaded from the sky and began to settle all around them, carpeting the bracken with a white blanket. The landscape was rapidly transforming into something of a winter dreamscape.

After they had watched the snowflakes flutter down for a while, Flick turned to Jim. "I was wondering...why did you put my name on the exhibition as Flick MacDuff?"

He chuckled. "Ah...It was mainly because we didn't want you to put two and two together if word got out about the exhibition...although looking back I think it was a bit daft really."

"It has a nice ring to it really, doesn't it?" She smiled out at the view.

"Aye, well I always thought it did." His smile was tinged with a little sadness

She pulled away from him and grasped his shoulders, turning him to face her. He looked a little confused.

Undeterred, she gulped in the cold air. "Jim, I know that we've had a rocky relationship and that I was stupid on more than one occasion. But...I want you to believe me when I say that it will never, *ever* happen again."

"I know, Flick, you don't need to—"

"Jim, please let me finish… I have something I need to ask you…but I'm a little scared of the answer. And I distinctly remember you saying that *you* were only going to ask once…so I figured…it must be my turn…" She rambled as confusion still clouded his eyes, a line appeared between his brows. Felicity continued regardless. "The name, Flick MacDuff…I'm hoping it's still up for grabs?"

"Flick…I don't understand…you want to change your name? But we can just change the name of the artist on the exhibition now that everyone—"

She rolled her eyes. *God, he can be so dense.* She stopped his words with her fingertips. "How about you stop talking and listen to me properly, eh?"

He clamped his mouth shut and nodded his acquiescence.

She fumbled in her coat pocket and dropped to one knee, warm salty tears now trailed a heated path down her chilled face. She held up the silver Celtic band toward him. "Jim…I want to be *her*…I want to be Flick MacDuff…please…will you marry me…again?"

He stared down at her with his mouth open, but didn't speak.

Oh shit…"I know it's sudden and I know that maybe it's too soon…but—"

He dropped to his knees before her and took her face in his hands. "Felicity?"

"Yes?"

"You took the words right out of my mouth…. The answer's yes."

They sealed their engagement on their knees in the deepening snow with a passionate kiss, surrounded by snowflakes falling like confetti—as if they knew.

This wasn't really a second chance at love. It was a first chance at being who they had always been deep down.

Having had the chance to step back and view their own lives, like observers looking through the glass, they knew that this was who they were.

Flick and Jim.

Together, this time, forever.

Epilogue

February 2013 — Three Years After the break-up — Eight Months After the Reconciliation

Jim stared across the table at Flick. She looked stunning, his fiancée. She was letting her hair grow and had stopped attacking it with the straightening irons. It looked golden in the amber glow of the roaring fire, the natural waves falling just past her shoulders.

He couldn't help but stare.

Valentine's Day hadn't exactly been filled with good memories for them. But this one was going to be different. Jim was determined about that. He arched his mouth up into a smile without realising it.

"What are you smiling about?" She tilted her head to one side and looked at him through long lashes.

"You," he replied simply.

"What about me?" She placed her knife and fork down and rested her chin on her hands.

"Just that…you're so beautiful, Flick. More beautiful right now than I've ever seen you look."

Although the lighting in the pub was low, Jim could see her cheeks colour slightly. "Oh Jim, that's so sweet." She reached across the table and squeezed his forearm.

"Aye, well it's the truth. I want this Valentine's Day to be special, Flick. I want the memory of this one to replace all the others. We've wasted so much time. All I want to do is take you home and make love to you all night." He reached for her hand and trailed circles around the back of her arm.

"That sounds like a wonderful way to spend the evening." She flicked her hair back exposing her long neck.

Jim loved to kiss her neck. It was a particularly erogenous zone of hers. She tilted her head so he had an amazing view from her bare shoulder where the top she wore had slipped down, all the way up to her pretty jaw line. A flush of colour rose from her chest up her neck to her cheeks. Definite signs of arousal.

His mouth went dry.

He cleared his throat and pulled at the collar of his shirt. "So…was your meal good?" He changed the subject before pouncing on her in public.

She giggled as if fully aware of what he was doing. "Mmm. It was delicious. The combination of spices was amazing… I'm so glad we have this place on our doorstep… Having said that…what I would really like would be to skip dessert and have that at home."

"I couldn't agree more, sweetheart. I'll go pay the bill."

He walked over to the bar where he briefly chatted with the owner. Once he had paid, he came back over to her. Gazing down at her, he caught himself staring again. *Wow…she really is stunning.* He had been filled with trepidation about giving things with Felicity another go, but up to now everything had been amazing.

Her attitude to life had completely changed. She was so enthusiastic about painting again. Her passion shone through when she stood at her easel. He could sit, pretending to read a book and secretly watch her for hours, her paint spattered face begging for him to kiss her. Every so often she would catch him and a smile would play on her lips. Sometimes she would just continue with her work but sometimes—the times he loved the most—she would walk over and remove her paint covered clothing seductively and straddle him where he sat. He'd never really fallen out of love with her, but giving in to what his heart really wanted had been difficult. And she was what his heart truly desired.

Would she walk out on him again? He honestly no longer thought she would. He trusted her again. And it felt good to be in that place.

Snapping himself from his thoughts, he stood beside her. "C'mon, lassie. I'm taking you home." He held out his hand, and she slipped hers into it, intertwining her fingers in his.

As she stood, she stopped smiling and leaned on the table. "Oooh. Went a bit dizzy." She smiled.

"You okay?" he couldn't hide his concern.

"Yeah, I'm fine. I think I just stood up too quickly. Head rush." She giggled.

"Well at least we can't blame the wine. You hardly touched yours."

"No, I didn't fancy it. And anyway, I wanted to keep a clear head for later." She raised her eyebrows at him, and he groaned, rolling his head back.

"Och, you're killing me. C'mon, lassie. I want you at home and naked…now!" He squeezed her bottom and helped her on with her jacket and scarf. They didn't have far to walk, but the bitter chill in the air demanded appropriate winter clothing.

As they walked on the icy pavement back to the cottage, she began taking deep breaths. He looked to her and again concern washed over him. "Are you sure you're okay?"

"Do you know what, Jim? I have an awful feeling that I'm coming down with something. I keep going dizzy."

"Oh, no. I hope the food hasn't disagreed with you, sweetheart. That's all we need, eh?" He rubbed her back.

"No, it wasn't the food at all. It was cooked to perfection as always… I…I think maybe I'm getting the flu or…something. My immune system isn't quite as it should be yet after the…well you know." He watched as she lifted her hand to her head. They walked as fast as they could in the icy conditions.

Bloody typical. The one Valentine's Day that we actually get to spend together properly, and my woman's starting to feel bloody ill. Damn that idiot for drugging her. I wish I could get my bloody hands on the bastard. He felt selfish at his thoughts then. He was worried about her.

When they arrived home, she rushed up to the bathroom. He heard unpleasant noises coming from up there. This wasn't ordinary flu. This was turning out to be something like stomach flu. He followed her up and sat on their bed, feeling helpless, running his hands through his hair in a bid to keep them occupied. The urge to ring for a doctor was overwhelming, but he had to try to stop panicking every time she sneezed, coughed, or threw up. She never did like him to be there if she got sick. He'd offer to hold her hair, but she would shout at him and tell him to get out. So this time he sat. Waiting. The sickness started again.

This is so bloody unfair. The poor wee girl. All I want to do is hold her, but I know she'll shout at me if I even attempt to go in. Oh shit…what if it's her liver? I'm going to have to ring the bloody hospital. I can't just sit here and bloody do nothing. No…I'll wait awhile… If things don't calm down, then I am ringing a doctor…and she can complain as much as she bloody likes about me being over bloody protective. Tough. I love her, and I won't sit by and watch her being ill. I can't stand it. Yet another bloody Valentine's Day ruined.

Jim's train of thought stopped and he began to laugh. *Shit, I think I must have spent too much bloody time with Charles.* He shook his head.

After pacing around the room awhile longer, he realised that everything had gone silent in the bathroom. She had been in there ages now. Had she fainted or something? Panic washed over him again, and he decided to go check on her. Just as he got to the bathroom door, he heard sobbing.

He tapped on the bathroom door. "Flick, you're really worrying me now, would you please open the door?" The sound of retching came loud again from within the bathroom. "Flick? Maybe I should call the doctor, eh?" He tapped again but the sobbing and sniffing continued. "Stomach flu can be serious, Flick. If that's what it is, you should really see someone. You could be dehydrated, and I'm really worried." He tried the door; she hadn't locked it. She looked up as he walked in. Her eyes were bloodshot, and she was so pale. He noticed she held something in her hand.

"What's that Flick?" Suddenly he realised what it was, looked back at the distraught expression on her face, and his heart broke. He shook his head. History was repeating itself right before his eyes. "No…no I don't think I can go through this again." He ran his hands through his hair, and he released a long breath.

Shakily, she stood and walked over to him. He had covered his face with his hands and tears were threatening to escape, but he was trying to hold them back. This would be it. This would be the end of them. She took his hands and pulled them down so she looked into his eyes.

Croakily she spoke. "Jim, I knew this morning but just presumed it was false, so I didn't say anything. Then I started feeling sickly at the pub and put it down to the flu or the spices in the chicken—"

"Just don't, okay? What does it matter? Your face tells me everything I need to know." He squeezed his jaw tight. "I remember that expression from the last time we thought we were in this position."

"Well tough, because I'm going to speak and you're going to bloody listen… I came home and as you could probably tell I got sick. It happened yesterday, too, whilst you were out at the shack. I didn't think anything of it after the overdose. I just presumed it was connected to that. But I've just worked out the dates and done another test." Tears welled in her eyes and cascaded down her already damp, pale face.

"Aye…well, I've already said I can't go through this again. You broke my heart last time when you didn't want this, and the look on your face tells me nothing has changed on that front. But I'm telling you, I can't go through it, Flick… All the heartbreak of knowing it's not what you want. I can't handle you feeling this way." His voice wavered and his throat tightened. "Not now. Not after everything that's happened. I've lost you over and over again and now this? This is just fucking cruel, Flick. Why can't things to go right, eh?" A sob escaped his throat. Her face was filled with unreadable emotions but none of them looked like the positive kind.

She clenched her teeth. "Jim, will you just bloody shut up for one second?!" she shouted at him. More tears came.

He was torn between asking her to leave and wrapping his arms around her. "Sorry. I'm guessing you have something you need to say then, eh? Some speech about how you're not ready and how it's too soon? How you've got *decisions* to make." He watched her expression change to one of hurt.

"Jim…I do have something to say. And I need you to listen, okay? Let go of the bitterness and just hear me out…please?" She placed her hands on his biceps.

He folded his arms across his chest and braced himself for what was coming. His heart pounded against his ribcage. "Go on then," was all he could force his quivering voice to say.

Confusion surged through him as he saw a smile appear on her face. Her hands moved to his cheeks.

"Jim…Happy Valentine's Day… You're going to be a daddy."

Meet the Author

© CraigPhotography Studio 2013

Lisa is a happily married Mum of one with two crazy dogs. She especially enjoys being creative; has worked as a singer and now writes full time. Lisa and her family recently relocated from Yorkshire, England to their beloved Scotland; a place of happy holidays and memories for them.

Writing has always been something Lisa has enjoyed, although in the past it has centered on poetry and song lyrics. Her stories have been building in her mind for a long while but until the relocation, she never had the time to put them down in black and white; working full time as a High School Science Learning Mentor and studying swallowed up any spare time she had. Making the move north of the border has given Lisa the opportunity to spread her wings and fulfill her dream. Writing is now a deep passion and she has enjoyed every minute of working towards being published.

https://www.facebook.com/#!/LisaJHobmanAuthor

http://glipho.com/livingscottishd

http://livingthescottishdream.wordpress.com/

https://twitter.com/LivingScottishD

Printed in Great Britain
by Amazon.co.uk, Ltd.,
Marston Gate.